ODIN'S VOICE

LINWOOD HIGH SCHOOL LIBRARY

ODIN'S VOICE

SUSAN PRICE

LINWOOD HIGH SCHOOL
LIBRARY

SIMON AND SCHUSTER

R06550
(F)

SIMON AND SCHUSTER

First published in Great Britain in 2005 by Simon & Schuster UK Ltd
A CBS COMPANY
This paperback edition first published in 2006.

Text copyright © 2005 Susan Price
Cover illustration by Larry Rostant © 2005
Title lettering by www.blacksheep-uk.com

www.susanprice.org.uk

This book is copyright under the Berne Convention.
No reproduction without permission.
All rights reserved.

The right of Susan Price to be identified as the author of this work has been
asserted by her in accordance with sections 77 and 78 of the Copyright,
Designs and Patents Act, 1988.

1 3 5 7 9 10 8 6 4 2

Simon & Schuster UK Ltd
Africa House
64-78 Kingsway
London WC2B 6AH

www.simonsays.co.uk

A CIP catalogue record for this book is available from the British Library

ISBN-13 9781416901457
ISBN-10 1 416 90145 0

This book is a work of fiction. Names, characters, places and incidents
are either a product of the author's imagination or are used fictitiously.
Any resemblance to actual people living or dead, events or locales
is entirely coincidental.

Printed and bound in Great Britain by
Cox & Wyman Ltd, Reading, Berks

The Gathering

Kylie kissed Apollo's cheek and squeezed his softness in her arms until he wriggled, giggling, and she said, 'Never let your weapons be more than five paces from your hand! So say I, and you must hear Me.' Her voice was both soft and hoarse. It purred, then caught and grated, scratching in her throat.

The blinds were drawn in Freewoman Atwood's conservatory, dimming the strong sunlight, tinting it orange. The people sat among the flowers and foliage in armchairs, on straight chairs, on stools, even on cushions on the floor. Kylie stood in the middle of them, twisting and swaying at the waist and looking, not at them, but at the child in her arms, smiling at him, blowing him kisses, crooning to him. She hardly seemed to listen to the words that her mouth chanted. Partly for that very reason the others gathered in the room listened intently to her every word, and watched her every movement.

'Never let your weapons be far from your hand! You think these words are not for you? You think yourselves safe and happy?'

The light, steel frames of the chairs creaked as people shifted, leaning forward. Kylie was not beautiful. Though thin, she was stocky in build, with short legs and arms, and her dress was cheap, sack-like and a faded navy blue. Its graceless drab marked it as the sort of dress an owner bought for a bonder. She lifted the child above her head, looking up at him, laughing as he laughed down at her.

'I speak these words for one among you more than most! Beware! Be aware! Never let your weapons be more than five paces from your hands!'

Several of her listeners felt a stab of recognition, knowing themselves to be the special one for whom the words were meant. A woman sitting beneath the plumbago's swags of sky-blue flowers feared for her job, and could think of several eager to see her gone. The man near the tall cactus had rowed, yet again, with his partner, and was pricked to a dread of loss, loneliness, trouble. A young woman by the small pond was in growing debt, but had told no one and done nothing except fret. And there were others, with fears less distinct.

'Can you . . .?' Freewoman Atwood began. 'Lord, can you not tell us who the message is for?'

Kylie hugged the child close to her and turned, slowly, to look at them all. Her face – not beautiful, not even pretty – was striking in its oddity: the skin pale, yet the hair, brows and lashes very dark, far darker than in most pale-skinned people. The broadness of her face across the cheekbones made it seem childishly round, and the vague, hazel-green eyes were Asiatic. She let her gaze wander, letting it move from face to face as slowly and vaguely as if she stared at distant clouds – though, in fact, she was acutely aware of every person there: of their expressions, their stance, their movements. She had been since her arrival. The gathering held its breath, waiting for her to speak.

When her gaze had moved round the room, she stilled and stared at nothing, silent. They waited. Through long seconds of chair creaks and stifled coughs, they waited. The child, bored, squirmed in Kylie's arms and whined. She hugged him closer, soothing him, and stared still. Even when the pause seemed overlong and painful to her, she let it go on. Let them stew. Make them wait.

The gathering felt their hair prickle and caught their breath. They could feel the presence in the room now: a great, bearish, but invisible, body, filling the space between them, looming at the right shoulder of each of them, making their skins tingle with awareness. They waited for the little, ignorant bonder to speak: this girl with no education, no training, and yet – she had brought God Odin among them.

Kylie spoke, in a low, throaty voice. They heard every word. 'I keep My silence,' she said – Odin said.

A thrill went through them, and they looked at each other. A bonder would seek to please, to give them what they wanted, not deny them. Kylie's mouth was the mouth of a small, cheap bonder girl, but the voice and the words were those of the greatest, wisest and most masculine of Gods. Strange He should choose her as His mouthpiece, but Odin was not to be fenced in by human understanding.

'It is woven,' said Odin, His voice a little rasping. 'It is not to be unpicked. You will know when the time comes. Keep your weapons close at hand, be of good courage, all will be well. And I leave you.'

Kylie threw back her head and left it tipped back on her

shoulders, her throat drawn tight, her eyes closed, her mouth gaping at the ceiling. Her audience didn't know how to react. They glanced at each other, and then continued to watch the unmoving girl.

It was easy for Kylie not to laugh: she had too much contempt for the people gathered in the room. They believed! Because she spoke a few of the words of Odin, known to them all, they believed that Odin was with them. They knew nothing of the God, except what they heard in the temple, and they seemed to think that He would come at any time – even to their little gathering. Kylie, who knew Odin far better, could only despise their ignorance, and their readiness to believe in whatever performance she chose to give. Odin – that shifty, deceitful God – would share her amusement and contempt.

It wasn't until the child in Kylie's arms laughed at her and patted her face that she lowered her head and smiled at him. They giggled and pressed their foreheads together. Kylie pirouetted away from her audience, ignoring them – or forgetting them. Either way, they were not used to being ignored or forgotten by bonders. But, of course, Kylie was an exceptional bonder, and they had to make an exception for her.

Freewoman Atwood rose and swooped to the front of her gathering, stooping, her hands clasped before her. 'Now I think we'd like some quiet time for personal meditation, wouldn't we?' She nodded at them and said, firmly, 'Yes.' She caught the dancing Kylie in her arms, to still her. She didn't mind touching the girl, though she could feel her warmth through her clothes and a slight dampness, too. But Freewoman Atwood was quite used to Kylie. 'Perhaps Apollo would like something to eat or drink? Perhaps you would yourself?'

Gently, she steered Kylie out of the conservatory and into the next room where a buffet was laid out. Certainly, her friends would like time to reflect on their experience, but it also gave her a chance to feed Kylie before they came through to eat. Of course Kylie was unusual, and gifted and charming – favoured by the God, even – but she was still a bonder. Some people felt at ease with bonders – she did herself – and you had to respect where the God chose to give His voice – but not everyone wanted to queue for their food with a bonder.

'Do put that child down, dear. I'm sure his legs will support him.' Kylie set the little boy on his feet. 'Freewoman Perry is certainly lucky in you, I must say.' There was no need to worry about young Freechild Perry when he was in Kylie's care. The girl doted on him. 'Would you like some orange juice, Apollo?'

The little boy looked up at her and put his fingers in his mouth while he considered. Was Freewoman Perry lucky in her son, though? thought Freewoman Atwood. There was something about the boy . . . He was four years old and, supposedly, bright. Well, anyway, Artemisia Perry told everyone how very bright he was. And yet he couldn't speak properly. This, of course, according to Artemisia Perry, was supposed to prove, in some strange way, how very, very bright he was. He was so bright, it seemed, he couldn't be expected to concentrate on minor things, like learning to talk. Freewoman Atwood had her doubts. Artemisia Perry had been so keen on a child, and naturally, no mere, unexceptional child would do.

Apollo was certainly pretty, in an odd, cherubic way, with large, silvery blue eyes, and wonderfully thick, flaxen hair, but perhaps Artemisia had been tempted to value looks over intelligence. Yes, there was definitely something about Apollo . . . Though impossible to say what. Perhaps he was just a little slow, and in a couple of years' time, would be perfectly normal. Freewoman Atwood poured a glass of orange juice and gave it to the child.

'Take a plate and help yourself, dear,' she said to Kylie. 'Have as much as you like.' She needed to let the girl know that she wouldn't be rebuked or punished for eating whatever she fancied.

She watched as Kylie helped herself to two of the bread rolls shaped like ravens – rather odd, misshapen ravens, but that was what they were supposed to be, in honour of Odin. She also added slices of beef and ham, with salad and pickle, some cheese and herring. She started eating, even as she was still scanning the table and loading her plate. The little boy, on the other hand, wasn't much interested in the food, apart from the cakes and biscuits, of which he had one in each hand. Not hungry. Freewoman Atwood wondered if Kylie's mistress fed her properly.

'You must be sure to thank Freewoman Perry, when you get back, for lending you to us today – especially after she said she couldn't spare you.'

Kylie looked at her from the corner of her eye, hearing the suspicion in the freewoman's tone. She chewed hard on a mouthful, so she could answer. 'I asked her, madam, as a favour, to let me come, and she said I could, if I got back on time. I mustn't be late.'

'No, we'll see you off in good time.' Freewoman Atwood doubted whether Kylie really did have permission to be there. She wouldn't have tolerated such disobedience in her own bonders, but Kylie's presence had made a success of her gathering, so she kept her suspicions to herself. 'Are you happy at Freewoman Perry's, dear?'

Again the girl gave her a quick look from the corner of her eye, hearing more in the question than a gracious attempt to set her at ease. 'Freewoman Perry is a good mistress, madam.'

'So you'd be unhappy if Freewoman Perry were to sell you?'

Another quick glance that seemed, to Freewoman Atwood, positively alarmed. 'Freewoman Perry is a good mistress, madam.'

'I'm sure she is, but—' Sounds of movement came from the garden room. The gathering was rising and coming in to eat.

'I must go, madam,' Kylie said. She had no more wish to mix with the free citizens of the gathering than most of them had to mix with her. She hated their attempts to talk naturally with her, while at the same time looking down on her as a bonder. Even worse were the contorted efforts to respect her as a superior, favoured by Odin, while simultaneously despising her as an ignorant girl who wasn't even free. 'I mustn't be late. Freechild Apollo, come here.'

'Can't you stay a little longer? I'm sure some people would like to talk to you.' Not eat with her, but talk with her, certainly.

'I mustn't be late, madam. I have to get Freechild Apollo home.'

'Oh well, if you must . . . Perhaps Freewoman Perry would lend you to us again?'

Kylie lifted Apollo into her arms, smiled vaguely and hurried from the room before the first of the gathering entered by the other doors.

Odin's Temple

Please, Odin, let me get away with this one last time, Kylie prayed, and I'll never go to another gathering ever again.

Not a prayer that Odin was likely to grant and, besides, she knew that she would go to the next gathering, and to every one after that.

Apollo dragged on her hand and grizzled. He was tired, and not happy about being taken away from Freewoman Atwood's cakes and biscuits. 'Never mind, sweetheart,' Kylie said, picking him up again and nuzzling his neck. 'Be home soon, and you can play with your toys.' Apollo had many expensive toys, and Kylie was proud of them, though she had had nothing to do with choosing or buying them. In her childhood, she had had to share the few battered old toys provided for the bonders' crèche. It made her eyes shine to see Apollo surrounded by his toys, and hardly able to decide which to pick up.

'Walk! Walk!' Apollo said, wriggling, so she put him down and held his hand, pointing out flowers and pussy cats and dogs as they went along, to keep him amused, and to teach him. Freewoman Perry was worried that he was slow to speak for his age. Kylie thought – not that anyone cared what she thought – that he only had to be given enough love and attention and time and everything would come out all right. Apollo didn't need doctors, still less did he need to be sent away to a special school. She prayed for him every night and morning, to all the Gods: to Thor, the protector; to the loving Frey and Freya; to motherly Frigga and, most of all, to Odin because with Him, she felt, she had most influence. Praying made her feel safely cupped in the Gods' hands, her and Apollo together.

Despite her faith, her heart squeezed small and cold with fear at the thought of Apollo being sent away. If he boarded at a special school, weeks, months would go past without her seeing him. The mere thought hurt as if her chest was being carved open and her heart scooped out. She didn't think she could bear the reality.

A thought that she usually tried to avoid forced itself on her: when he was seven, Apollo would be sent away to boarding school anyway. All boys were, Freewoman Perry said. There was no question about it. His education would begin, and Kylie did not like what he would be taught.

Apollo loved Kylie. He liked her company better than anyone's. You could tell by the way he smiled when he saw her, the way he asked for her when she wasn't there – to Freewoman Perry's annoyance. He was always happy to be picked up by her, and cuddled, whereas he was often cool with Freewoman Perry.

But all that would change at boarding school, as Freewoman Perry well knew. He would learn that he was free and rich, and that Kylie was a bonder and poor. He would learn that he owned her, and could sell her, and that she was far from the most valuable of his possessions. There were watches and necklaces more valuable than her. He would learn that boys who were attached to their bonder nannies were pathetic, were babies and losers. He would learn to despise her – and to despise himself for having loved her. Kylie couldn't bear it. She couldn't let it happen.

She would run away and take Apollo with her. She always thought of doing that, whenever she remembered about the boarding school.

A familiar – painfully familiar, boringly familiar – sequence of thoughts trudged through her head. She couldn't stop them, though she wanted to, because she knew they were futile.

In her pocket she had a phone, given to her by Freewoman Perry, so that, when she was out and about with Apollo, she could stay in touch, and pay for taxis and food, and entries into parks. They could get into a taxi, her and Apollo, go to some new part of the city – or even another town – and vanish!

Except that she couldn't for so many reasons. What would they do for food? The phone could be used only at certain shops. If it was used in any other way – to buy a plane ticket, or to rent a room, or to buy clothes – it would alert both Freewoman Perry and her bank. And anyway, every time she used it, it would signal where she was.

And that was without even thinking of the transmitters implanted in Kylie's buttock, which would tell searchers exactly where she was, at any time. Apollo had one, too, in his arm, so he could be found if he got lost or was kidnapped.

She realised, again, as so many, dreary times before, that

she couldn't run away. Instead, she would tamely go back to Freewoman Perry's house, and hand Apollo over to her, and go about her work until the next time she was allowed to look after him . . . Which might be never, if Freewoman Perry found out where she'd taken him today.

Let me get away with it this time, Odin, please, and I'll—

She drew back from repeating a promise to the God that she knew she couldn't keep.

Forgive me for saying, before, that I would never go to the gatherings again, Odin. I couldn't give them up. But let me get away with it this time, Odin, and I'll be more careful in the future, far more careful – I do promise that.

She thought about telling Apollo not to tell Big Mummy where they'd been, but that wouldn't work. He wasn't good at lying or keeping secrets.

Please, Odin, don't let her find out. Frigga, Mother, don't let me be parted from him. Do this for me and . . .

But she had nothing to offer. That was why she couldn't swear to stay away from the gatherings. They were all she had.

Without the gatherings, her life would be work and sleep. All day long spent doing Freewoman Perry's chores, all the dirtiest work: nothing for herself. And too little sleep.

There would be the occasional treat of looking after Apollo – but then, Apollo would be sent away to school, and would grow up and turn his back on her, despising her. And then she would have nothing but her routine of work. No one to love, ever, and no one, ever, to love her . . .

She had first gone to the temple of Odin because one of the few memories she had of her own mother was that she had worshipped Frey, Freya and Thor. She remembered her mother telling her strange, funny stories of Thor and giants. That had been while they'd lived in the bonders' crèche, before her mother had been sold.

Sometimes, Freewoman Perry would send her on errands – delivering cards to her friends, fetching groceries or collecting parcels from shops. And on these errands, Kylie often passed the temple of Odin. She knew that Odin had been one of her mother's Gods. Not a favourite one, not like Thor or Freya, because Odin was grim and frightening. But she didn't know where the temples of Thor or Freya were. So Odin would have to do.

She had as much right to enter the temple as someone free – it was one of the few rights she had. So she went into that great building, where fire glimmered against darkness, and sat on one of the benches of polished wood, among the tree-like columns, and looked at the statues. A woman saw her – a well-dressed woman, obviously free. Kylie thought she was going to be told to leave, but the woman smiled and asked, was this the first time she'd come to the temple? When Kylie said yes, the woman smiled again, and said she hoped they would see her there many times in the future.

Kylie did go many times after that. She felt that she'd been invited. There were little booths in the temple, with computers in them, where you could sit and listen to the stories of Odin, and watch films. She could never stay long, but would snatch a few minutes, going into the temple and finding a screen that had been left running by someone else – someone who had switched on in idle curiosity, but who didn't care about what they heard and had wandered off. Or she would hear part of a sermon preached from the platform. But as she listened, part of her brain was calculating how far she had yet to go to complete her errand, and how late she would be, and how far Freewoman Perry would believe yet another tale of long queues: 'They push me to the back, madam, because I'm only a bonder.' She would panic, and rush from the temple, while aching to stay. The stories, the music, the images of darkness and firelight stayed with her.

Had she been able to sit as long as she liked and listen in an orderly way, perhaps Kylie would have then walked away and forgotten them. But the disconnected fragments filled her mind, and before she slept and while she worked, she puzzled over them. She had to go back.

She started sneaking out of the house at night, letting herself in and out of the kitchen door. At last, she had time to watch the films all through. She saw Odin emerging from the darkness of the deep, deep past, with floating, turning skulls, and arrowheads and long, sleek ships lit by fire and announced by thrilling music. She heard the story of how He gave an eye to gain wisdom, and how, with His one sighted eye, He stared steadfastly at a future He knew to be doomed, and yet still resolved to fight.

Something in her resounded to that. Her own future was bleak, and here was a more courageous response than resignation or despair. Fight! Always fight, even though you know there's nothing ahead but defeat. Better fight to a standstill than give in.

Every night now, she returned in the early hours, gently opening the kitchen door and edging inside to creep through the dark house. The computers guarding the house recognised her fingerprints and retina patterns, and so the alarms stayed silent, and allowed her to fall into her bed for a few hours' sleep before she had to drag herself, leadenly, downstairs for another day's drudgery. The house cameras had filmed her, of course, even in the dark, but Freewoman Perry hardly ever looked at the films and, when she did, hadn't the patience to watch all of them.

Then came the night when Freewoman Perry's voice cracked out through the kitchen's darkness, making Kylie's heart jump and her whole body leap upwards.

'You little whore,' Freewoman Perry had said. 'Who is it you're sneaking out to see? What's his name? I'll make him rue the day. And as for you – I'm selling you. I won't have you turning your dirty tricks in my house.'

It had taken hours – hours of gabbling and weeping – to convince Freewoman Perry that she'd only ever gone to the temple of Odin. Freewoman Perry had laughed. She wouldn't believe it. What would the likes of Kylie want with a temple? And Odin? Odin was a rather downmarket God, to be sure, but not *that* downmarket. He was a God for soldiers, sportsmen, actors, that sort. Not for bonders.

It had ended with phone calls to the temple and confirmation that, yes, young Kylie had been visiting a lot lately. Freewoman Perry relented. After all, the girl did have a way with Apollo, and her replacement might not; and getting a new bonder and training her up would be such a nuisance. And, though sneaking out at night was bad, it was rather amusing that she'd only been going to a temple to listen to midnight sermons. So Freewoman Perry made a deal with

Kylie. Two nights a week she might go quite openly to the temple, provided her work wasn't neglected in any way. Honestly, the things you did to keep bonders happy.

'But why Odin?' she'd asked. 'Wouldn't you be happier with Aphrodite? Or Artemis? You're a girl.'

'If you please, Freewoman, why not Odin?'

Freewoman Perry had looked baffled. It was so obvious, she had never expected to have to put it into words. 'Well . . . You're a *girl* . . . And a bonder. Odin is such a . . . Well, not for you.'

'Odin always had women priests, Freewoman,' Kylie said. She had learned that from the films at the temple. 'They foretold the future. He spoke through them.'

Freewoman Perry had looked at her in amazement. 'Yes. Well. You're *not* a priestess. You're my bonder. Remember that, please.'

'Yes, Freewoman.' But Kylie didn't forget Freewoman Perry's scorn, or the fact that she had made her weep and beg for permission to go to the temple. She prayed for her all the time. 'Odin, Father of All, look on this world with Your sighted eye, and on the next world with Your blind eye, and lend me Your sight and help me *see*. Help me see how to get away from this life, and take Apollo with me, and settle Freewoman Perry's hash.'

He hadn't done that yet, but He was working for her, of that she was sure. Before she'd come to Odin – or He to her – she'd just been a skivvy, working most of her waking hours, and with no friends. But when she went to the temple, she was welcomed, more and more each time she went back. The people at the temple – though they were free and rich, many of them – learned her name and told her that they expected to see her there again. It was good to know that people were expecting her.

They asked her to speak at the gatherings where people stood and told everyone how Odin had come to them, or helped them. At first, Kylie had nothing to say, but their words ran round her head as she worked, or lay sleepless in her bed. And there came the time when they asked her to speak, and she opened her mouth and words came out.

She hadn't planned it, and hardly remembered what she said, but afterwards people had come up and thanked her, and said they'd never heard anyone speak so well. It had been inspiring, they said. She must speak again.

She didn't, for a long time, because she didn't know why people had liked what she'd said before, and she didn't think she could speak so well again. But then it came to her that Odin *wanted* her to speak, and she should, for Him. So she did, and people said she was remarkable. After that, they would greet her, when she arrived at the temple, by asking, 'Are you going to speak?' Soon after that, Odin started to speak through her. She just opened her mouth and let the words come. First, they would just be what she felt – about Apollo, or the temple, or Odin – but sometimes they would change, without her meaning them to, or knowing that they had, into Odin's own words. Then she would tell the people what they should do; give them advice. They said they felt honoured and humbled to have her, chosen by Odin, in their temple. She heard them pointing her out to newcomers, boasting about her.

Some people, naturally, didn't approve. They spoke up at

temple meetings, and said it wasn't appropriate to have a bonder – and a female bonder! – claiming to speak for Odin. It brought them into disrespect, they said, with other gatherings at other temples. They wanted Kylie to be forbidden to come to the temple – or, at least, forbidden to speak in Odin's name.

Kylie had been thrilled by the furious arguments that had followed. Who could doubt it was Odin they heard speaking through Kylie? Hadn't her predictions come true? How did anyone dare to tell Odin where He might and might not give His favour? Why should a girl not speak for Odin? Were they so ignorant as not to know about the völvas, the great witch priestesses of ancient times? Were they saying that Odin didn't like girls – were they denying his virility? Those who spoke against Kylie spoke against Odin, and they should humble themselves, beg His forgiveness, and try to learn what He was teaching them.

No one had ever defended Kylie like that before. Even better, it had ended with her detractors leaving the temple. They went to other temples, and continued to say she was a fraud, or ungodly, or both. But people from those *other* temples came along to hear her speak for Odin, and some left their own temple and joined hers.

People had never been proud to know her before. That was the favour of Odin. It made her want to learn all she could, to think more and more about Odin and His nature, to be a more perfect channel for Him.

Freewoman Perry said it took her mind off her work. Freewoman Perry said she didn't like her taking Apollo to 'that place'. Freewoman Perry said she wanted her to stop going to the temple. It was ridiculous, she said, for a bonder girl to fancy herself inspired by a God, any God – even by such a coarse, vulgar God as Odin! Just ridiculous! And people were beginning to gossip. Friends and neighbours had asked her about her God-speaking bonder girl. It was embarrassing. Kylie had to forget this nonsense, and there was an end of it.

But Kylie couldn't. And so she had to creep into the house again without Freewoman Perry noticing she was late, without Freewoman Perry guessing where she had been.

Freewoman Perry was waiting for her in the kitchen, sitting at the table. When Kylie came in, leading Apollo by the hand, Freewoman Perry looked at her with a face set hard. 'Take Apollo to his room, and then come back here,' she said.

Kylie knew she was in trouble. Even Apollo knew. As she led him down the hall to the stairs, he said, 'Big Mummy anger. What you do?'

'It's all right,' Kylie said. She settled him in his room, with some favourite books and toys, and then went slowly back down to the kitchen.

Freewoman Perry remained on her chair at the table, and let Kylie stand in the middle of the floor for some time. Then she said, 'I know where you've been. You were seen going into the house. And I just called Freewoman Atwood and confirmed it. And I also know that you lied to Freewoman Atwood and said that you had my permission to go to her gathering. And you took my son with you!' She made herself calm again. 'An explanation, please.'

Kylie knew that she had no explanation that her mistress would accept. She could only say that she was sorry, and beg and plead – but there was a hardening within her. She was not at all sorry, and would not say that she was. Why should she always whine, and plead and say sorry? Even though she laughed about it later? She revolted at forever twisting her feelings out of place, and pretending to feel what she did not.

'Well?' Freewoman Perry said. 'I am waiting. Your explanation, please.'

'I had to go,' Kylie said.

'Oh? Why, if I might ask?'

'Odin wished it. What He wants is more important than anything.'

Freewoman Perry sat quite still, absorbing this and thinking it over, growing more white-faced and furious by the second. 'You insolent—! How dare you? A bonder – *my* bonder. How dare you think yourself—?' She was so angry, she couldn't find the words.

'I dare because Odin is with me,' Kylie said. She wasn't calm. She felt exhilarated, excited and happy. She felt relieved, as if she'd stood up straight after stooping for hours. She felt gleeful, mischievous, *alive*.

Freewoman Perry rose abruptly from her seat, slapping her hand down on the table. 'Enough! I've had all I can take of your insolence and lies and slyness and – oh, you're just a nasty girl! A bad influence on Apollo. I'm selling you. Tomorrow.'

'You can't,' Kylie said, alarmed, speaking what she felt, without thinking.

Freewoman Perry had been walking towards the door. She stopped. 'What?'

'You can't sell me.'

'I assure you, I can – and I will.'

'Apollo,' Kylie said.

Freewoman Perry pretended she didn't understand. 'What has Apollo to do with it?'

'I have to stay with Apollo.'

'I am not arguing with you. I am going to phone the agency and tell them to take you back.'

Kylie jumped the space between them and seized Freewoman Perry by the arm. 'I won't let you!'

Freewoman Perry, alarmed – remembering news stories of people who had been killed by their bonders – tried to push her away, but Kylie would not let go. 'He's *mine* – not yours – *mine!*'

Freewoman Perry pulled Kylie's fingers away from her arm and shoved her hard. Kylie crashed into the table. 'You—' she began, and then thought better of squabbling with a bonder. In quick strides, she left the kitchen, slamming the door behind her.

Kylie gathered herself up and ran after her, wrenching open the door and slamming it back against the wall, shouting, 'No, Freewoman Perry, don't, please – I'm sorry! I'm sorry! I'll never do anything again. Please don't, please don't!' All her feelings of glee and freedom were gone, replaced by an intense sense of her own foolishness, and painful distress. Catching up with her mistress, she grabbed her arm again. 'No, no, don't, please – I'll kill you, I'll kill you!'

Freewoman Perry, now frightened, fended her off, shoving her away again. Running for the front door, the woman ran out into the street, crying, 'Assault! Assault! It's my bonder – help!'

A Gift for Odin

Odin was the treacherous God. He knew that knowledge is power. So highly did He value learning and understanding that He paid the price asked for a single drink from the well that springs at the roots of the World Tree, and grants all that Tree's wisdom. The price was His right eye, and He thought it a fair price.

With His sighted eye, Odin looks on this world. With His blind eye, He looks into the darkness of the next.

From the chaos of the Giants – first builders of the world – Odin stole mead, the drunkenness of trance, ecstasy and poetry, and He spilled it over the Earth, so men could share His sight, His wisdom, His rage.

In the old, old days, long, long ago, He called kings and warriors to Him by promising them victory in battle. He promised poets inspiration and fame, if they dedicated themselves to Him and served Him, accepting His gifts, and accepting His price.

Always He – the treacherous God – betrayed them. Always. Perhaps He gave them their victory, or let them see their goal within reach – then took their life, or sent His servants – the valkyries – to maim them. He let poets live beyond their gift to see their fame mocked.

Those who dedicated themselves to Odin and accepted His gifts, had first to embrace His treachery; to learn to love uncertainty and chance and change; to take what He gave wholeheartedly, with joy; and to accept as willingly, the pain and grief and loss that, inevitably, followed – to accept the pain of the gouged out eye.

Kylie had learned the stories about Odin from the films she'd watched in the temple. They had taught her that the stories were more than stories: that they had many meanings and lessons hidden in them if you thought about them. It had been her pleasure, while she worked, to run through the stories in her head and unravel their layers for herself. Often, she felt that Odin was speaking to her, teaching her, because the ideas she had were so unexpected and unlike her own thoughts.

She had begun to think that there was nothing else she needed to learn. After all, didn't Odin speak through her, and didn't people – free people, rich people – listen respectfully?

She had thought that, since Odin favoured her, He would treat her more kindly than others.

Now she knew differently. She learned that knowing that her God was treachery, and *feeling* that treachery, was as different as thinking about being burned and putting her hand into fire so the skin shrivelled and the flesh melted. She learned that being high in Odin's favour could mean more suffering, and greater, not less. And the question asked of her was: will you still pay My price? Or shall we break our bargain now? Will you still be My voice? Or will you choose silence?

Freewoman Perry had been so frightened by Kylie's

attack that she'd called Security, and this big man had turned up, twice Kylie's weight. Freewoman Perry told him she wanted Kylie removed at once; that she was too afraid of her to have her in the house a moment longer. The security man sighed and asked, did she want to press charges?

Kylie, standing by, her hands at her face, held her breath. Tears trickled through her fingers. She was very afraid of being jailed.

But no, Freewoman Perry didn't want to press charges – she made it sound a very vulgar thing to do. She simply wanted the girl taken back to her agency. She couldn't be in the house with her while she waited for the agency to come and pick her up. The girl was too dangerous.

The security man looked at Kylie, as if to assess the danger in her. To her surprise, he winked at her – on the side of his face away from Freewoman Perry, so she couldn't see. Then he offered to stay in the house while Freewoman Perry called the agency.

Freewoman Perry agreed to that. 'Fetch your things,' she said to Kylie, when they were back inside. Kylie began to sob again, and to plead: let her stay, please let her stay, she was sorry, she would be good . . . She was ashamed even as she listened to herself. Did this snivelling sound like a voice of Odin? But it had worked before.

Not this time. 'I've had enough,' Freewoman Perry said. 'Get your things.'

That didn't take long. Kylie had her basic kit: a change of clothes, soap, a toothbrush, things like that – and her ancestors. She could put them in her pocket. They were nothing but four trinkets, threaded on a thin, transparent string. The first – tied on with a single knot either side of it – was a shiny, blue bead. That was her great-grandmother, whom she had never met or seen, and whose name she didn't know. The second, tied on with a double knot, was a small, tarnished locket, in the shape of a heart. That was her grandmother, whom she had also never met and whose name she also didn't know. The locket opened, and inside was a tiny holograph of a smiling woman with dustily fair hair.

The third object on the string, tied with three knots, was a little devotional medal, showing Freya with the sun behind her, and animals at her feet. That was from Kylie's mother, of whom she had only the vaguest memories, since she had been sold on when Kylie was five, while Kylie had been left behind in the agency's crèche. She couldn't remember what her mother looked like: her memories were more of a sensation of warmth, of being held and murmured to. She knew that, in the agency, her mother had been known as 'Brittie', but that was the sort of name people gave to bonders. Whoever her mother had been, and whatever she had looked like, she had left a reminder of herself on the ancestor string. Her faith must have been important to her, Kylie thought: that was why she'd left her the medal. It was a message to the child she'd left behind: I want you to worship Freya too. Well, I do, Kylie thought; but Odin is my guide.

It had been a nurse at the agency who had explained the importance of the ancestor string to the children in her care – they all had something similar. The nurse had explained the knots, but Kylie had brooded for herself on what the trinkets meant. The heart – was that 'I love you'? Was the photo of her grandmother, or had she just found the locket somewhere and used it as a token? If that was so, wouldn't she have taken the photo out? And the blue bead: what did that mean? Blue was the colour of Frey and Freya's cloaks – did that mean that her first ancestress had worshipped them too? That it was a family tradition?

Kylie had added to the string herself, tying on a little thing she had been given: a small, sharp arrowhead made of stone. She knew the message she meant it to carry: be strong, be fierce, defend yourself. But now her child would never have the string. If she left it behind, she knew Freewoman Perry would throw it away, as rubbish, and she couldn't bear to think of her mother and grandmothers being thrown away.

So here she stood, outside the front door – Freewoman Perry wouldn't have her in the house – clutching her kitbag, too miserable to respond to the chat of the security man, until the car from the agency came to pick her up. Freewoman Perry came out then, to feed the necessary information into the car's computer, and Kylie got into the back seat, which locked on her, and off the car went, guided by its computer. It carried her right into the garage of the agency, where someone came down to collect her. They identified her, by her iris print, and by running the scanner over her buttock, where the ID was implanted – and they processed her, made her shower, and allotted her a bed in a dormitory. She had no sense of homecoming – this was no home – but only a sense of failure, and of misery.

If this was how Odin repaid devotion and service – with this pain and loss, this humiliation – why should she serve Him? His price was too high. She would never speak for Odin again. She would never speak again.

When others greeted her, she looked at them, or nodded, but did not speak. She accepted orders in silence; did her work in silence. If others wished to talk, she might listen – though often she didn't hear them, her mind elsewhere – but she would say nothing. It was no affectation. It felt as if a great weight lay on her breast and on her tongue, and to find breath or speech against that weight was too much effort. At most, if it was demanded that she speak, she sighed out a yes or no.

All the time, day and night, whether trooping from her dormitory to wash in the shower rooms, or lining up for meals, or sitting listlessly in the recreation room while some shopping channel twittered on the TV, mocking those who couldn't buy, there was a fierce point of pain at her centre, at her heart. Apollo, it said, Apollo, Apollo. Even when she was not thinking about him and missing him, the pain was there, and she was aware that she had lost him. If she hadn't been so proud, if she hadn't answered Freewoman Perry back, if she'd sobbed and begged and abased herself at the outset, she wouldn't have been sold. She would still be with Apollo.

She'd thought more of herself and of Odin, not of Apollo – and this was what her selfishness and pride had brought about. She could not speak. When other bonders tried to talk, to be friendly, she shook her head. She could not heave her troubles up into her mouth. She could not speak.

Odin bided His time. He had the patience of millennia. The routine of the agency rolled on, day by day: breakfast at six, and work in the kitchens or laundry, or at endless dusting, polishing and floor cleaning. Kylie had no preference. It was all numbing drudgery. There were a couple of breaks in the routine, when she was assessed, to discover her IQ and skills, so her CV could be updated. It was decided not to give her any further training: her assessors thought her rather stupid, and unlikely to learn.

Her dullness, and silence, made it difficult to resell her bond. Potential buyers viewed her, either in person or by web cam, and were repelled by her dullard face, her apathy and silence. She was sent for a medical, but nothing seemed physically wrong.

'Still here?' one of the old women in the kitchen said to her one day. 'Sweetheart, they'll be selling you for cat's meat next.'

Without Odin, Kylie realised, she was nothing, and had nothing.

The only thing worth having that had ever been hers, had been Apollo, and he was gone, for ever.

For ever. The word went ringing on and on. For ever and ever. She would never see him again. Never, never.

He would not even remember her, because he was only small. Freewoman Perry would not teach him to remember her. He would be sent away to school, and taught that he was better than dirty, stupid bonders. He would never have to ask why, or how. It would be an unquestioned fact that he knew, as he knew stone was hard and water wet.

He would never know that there had once been a bonder who cuddled him and washed him and loved him – loved him as herself, and more than herself. She would remember him, and ache, but there would be no answering ache in him. He would have forgotten her entirely, as if she had never been.

Odin's treachery. But acceptance of the God's gifts always brought betrayal and pain – as painful as His own purchase of wisdom.

She could suffer and gain nothing. Or she could accept Odin's price and at least buy a little wisdom with it. Either she could be silent, for ever, or she could be Odin's voice. For sure, she had no words of her own worth speaking.

She said, 'Odin, take anything from me, take everything. Take my eyes, my tongue, my life. I accepted Your gift, and every gift looks for a return. Now I must pay Your price.'

But still, when someone spoke to her – even if they only wanted 'Hello' or 'Morning!' in reply – she couldn't find the strength to speak. She still rose to her work in the morning: stolid, enduring. For however long she must, she would endure. Odin hung on the Tree, a sacrifice to Himself, and was pierced through by His spear, to buy more wisdom – the knowledge of the runes. But even that agony ended at last, after nine long days. As that had ended, so would her time. Everything ended, at last, if she could only endure.

When she was called again to the manager's office, she put aside the sharp blades she was cleaning from the food processor, and set off through the long, dull corridors. She went slowly, indifferently, and stood outside the manager's door for some minutes before remembering that she had to knock.

The manager called her in and, after a pause while she gathered her strength for the effort, she opened the door and shuffled inside. She stood, looking down at the dark blue carpet, waiting. She wasn't curious about why she had been sent for. She didn't care.

'Kylie, is it?' the manager said, and then apparently

29

checked her identity, possibly against the database on her computer, because she said, 'Yes, Kylie.'

'That's Kylie, all right,' said another, warmer and familiar voice. 'That's our Kylie!'

Kylie thought about raising her head to see who the speaker was. She wondered if it would be worth the effort. No. If it was needful for her to know, she would be told.

'Kylie!' said the voice – it was a woman's voice. 'Aren't you going to say "hello"?'

Kylie tried, but succeeded only in half raising her head before lowering it again. Her lips opened slightly, but made no sound.

'Freewoman Atwood is thinking of buying your bond,' the manager said.

Freewoman Atwood? Kylie was almost interested.

'Can I be clear?' said Freewoman Atwood's voice. 'I don't want merely to buy her bond. I want to buy her outright, fully, in total. I want to buy out the agency.'

That made Kylie raise her head. Freewoman Atwood, looking as neat and composed as ever in her plain, old-fashioned dress and clumpy shoes, was sitting on a chair in front of the manager's desk, her bag in her lap. Her composure hid her shock at the change in Kylie. The girl's attentive, intelligent face had become dull and apathetic; her strong, capable body was slack and hunched.

'Oh,' said the manager. 'That's not – well, not usual. I don't know about that.'

'Whatever do you mean, you don't know about that?'

'People don't usually – I mean, I don't know if it's policy – I don't know if it's allowed.'

Listening to the manager stutter, Kylie felt the first trick-lings of amusement, returning like a spring after drought.

'There must be an account, somewhere, of everything she's cost you. There must be a way of calculating her price,' said Freewoman Atwood. She settled herself more comfort-ably. This might take a long time; but she had plenty of time. 'Tell me the price and, if I can meet it, I shall pay it, and she will belong to me, not the agency. It's very simple.'

'But – I don't know . . . Her price in full – I don't know.'

'Dear me,' Freewoman Atwood said. 'What a bothera-tion. Is there somewhere in this place where I can buy a coffee?'

'What?' the manager snapped, confused by the sudden change of subject.

'I was just thinking that while you consult your com-puter – I daresay you will have to spend ages on your computer, talking to people up and down the world – Kylie and I could go and sit somewhere, and have a coffee and chat, and leave you in peace to get on with it.'

Kylie admired the way Freewoman Atwood managed things: always polite and mild, but never doubting that her wishes would be met. Peeping sidelong at the manager, Kylie saw her shocked, baffled expression. Freewoman Atwood seemed respectable and obviously had money – but she wanted to drink coffee and chat with a *bonder*. An eccentric.

'There is the little waiting room outside. It's not very comfortable, but you could – I'll ask someone to bring you some coffee. Perhaps – er – Kylie, I think you should go back to your work for now.'

Kylie nodded, and made to withdraw, but Freewoman

Atwood said, 'Oh, by no means. I want to talk to her. And, as I shall own her soon – oh, add the time our chat takes to your price, if you must, if you really are so desperately grasping.'

The manager laughed nervously. 'Oh, I don't think—'

'Very good,' said Freewoman Atwood, as she rose and gestured to Kylie to leave the office through the door that clients entered. 'We shall be waiting when you're through.'

Kylie was nervous about going through the door: it wasn't for bonders. But Freewoman Atwood required her to go through it, so what could she do? On the other side was a large, attractive room, with clean, bright paintwork, and new, comfortable furnishings. Small screens were built into the arms of the chairs, so people could read or e-mail while they waited. There wasn't another room in the place like it. Bonders didn't need attractive rooms, or screens.

'Sit down, dear,' Freewoman Atwood said, but Kylie didn't dare. When Freewoman Atwood had chosen a chair, seated herself comfortably and looked up, Kylie was still standing. 'No, no, this won't do. Come and sit here.' Kylie obeyed, perching on the very edge of the seat. 'I daresay you're wondering what I'm doing here?'

'Buying a bonder, Freewoman.'

'No, that's where you're wrong. I'm setting one free!'

Kylie looked at her. Freewoman Atwood was gleeful.

'Do you remember that last message you gave us? About keeping your weapons near your hand? Well, do you know, the most amazing thing – Hermes O'Toole was taking a walk – when was it? – about two days after the gathering – and two men attacked him! It was all about some woman.

But he'd been thinking of the message and what it might mean, and he says he was half ready for them. He fought them off! Isn't that wonderful?'

'Yes, Freewoman,' Kylie said. She felt barely interested. Instead, she was wondering what was going to happen to her when Freewoman Atwood went home. She supposed she would be punished for having gone into the clients' waiting room. Privileges, such as watching TV, would be withdrawn. She didn't care.

'We had a meeting at the temple. We decided that we couldn't lose you, just because your mistress had a fit of pique – oh, yes, we found out all about that. Silly woman. We decided there was only one thing to do – buy you!'

Kylie merely sat, listening. She saw no reason to get excited about being bought.

'So we prayed and asked Odin if it was His will – it would have been much easier with you there, dear! But it was extraordinary!' The Freewoman leaned forward, trying to engage Kylie's interest. 'We talked, and all of us felt so strongly that this was something He wanted us to do. And we needed you back among us. So we agreed. But we soon saw that buying your bond would be no good, so we looked into the possibility of buying you outright – and we think we can do it! It's going to be in my name, but everyone is contributing!'

Freewoman Atwood paused, and seemed to want a response, so Kylie said, 'Thank you, Freewoman.' She didn't quite understand how she was to be bonder to everyone at the temple. Perhaps they intended her to spend a short time working for each of them in turn? Or was she to be a servant at the temple: sweeping, polishing, looking after the sacrificial animals? She thought she would quite like that, being in the temple all the time.

'And when we've bought you,' said Freewoman Atwood, 'what we mean to do is, give you your manumission!'

Kylie looked at her blankly.

'Your freedom! We mean to give you your freedom! And you'll be our priestess, we hope, and lead us. There'll be a room for you, and a small income. Will you like that?'

Kylie lowered her head again, stunned into quietness. She felt nothing, thought nothing. And then, without her will, her head rose and her mouth opened. She said, 'Give me to Odin.'

'What?'

'Buy me and give me to Odin. I don't want to be free. I want to belong to Odin.'

'But—' Freewoman Atwood struggled to see the difference between being owned by no one, and owned by a God.

'Give me to Odin.'

'I shall have to ask—'

'Give me to Odin.'

Before Freewoman Atwood could speak, the door opened and the manager looked in. 'Ah – Freewoman Atwood. If I could see you a moment.'

Freewoman Atwood rose. 'Stay here, dear. I don't think this will take long.'

A Message for Affroditey

'Hey,' Berowne said, as a bonder fixed the wreath of shining corn, vine leaves and berries in her hair, 'like my sister, right? She and her partner, they're, like, breeding – and, get this, they're not designing. Can you *believe*?'

'Eeuw!' Affie said. 'It'll be ugly! It'll be stupid! Like a bonder!'

'Yeah,' Berowne said. 'My mother's spitting blood, and my father, he's like, you're *unforgivably selfish*. We all hate *him* anyway. He works.'

'Works?' Affie said.

'Yeah. Works. Actually works. Can you believe?'

'Explain! How?'

'I mean, *works*. Like, does things for *pay*.'

'What things?' Affie said.

Neppie sighed heavily. He was having his fingernails painted a deep purple, almost black, with gold spots and stripes. He said, 'Everybody works. My father works, your father works—'

'He does not!' Berowne said. 'He advises.'

'Work!'

'It is not!'

Affie thought she would end the quarrel. 'How can they

not design? I couldn't. An undesigned child . . .' She shuddered.

'Matter of fact,' Neppie said, 'not *every* undesigned baby is ugly or stupid. Face it, not all bonders are, now are they? Not all bonders are even *born* bonders, are they?'

He was always irritating like that, Affie thought, but really, really intelligent. Of course, he'd been designed. 'Sure, one or two might be clever or pretty,' Affie said. 'By accident. You might get a clever turnip or a pretty pig, *by accident.*' Berowne giggled, and Affie was pleased. 'But mostly, bonders are—'

'Stupid,' Berowne said.

'And ugly,' Affie finished.

Neppie opened his mouth again, but Berowne got in first. 'It's just the *truth*, Neps, whatever you say.'

'You've got to face up to reality in this world,' Affie said.

'Oh, right, so look at this . . .' Neppie said. He touched his fingertips to the studs in his belt, a little clumsily because he was using his left hand: the nails on his right still being wet. The bonder at his feet sat back on her low stool and waited until he should give her his hand again.

Neppie was looking at his palm. 'Got it. Look. See?' The bracelet around his wrist had picked up the signal from his belt, and was projecting a hologram of a girl to hover just above the hollow of his hand. She looked like a bonder, with mundanely dark hair cropped short, and she was screwing up her face in a most unflattering way.

Berowne and Affie looked. 'So?' Affie said. 'Who's that?'

'Is she brain damaged?' Berowne asked. 'Pulling faces like that?'

'Hang on,' Neppie said. 'That isn't the best pic.' He touched the studs at his belt again. Another photo appeared, showing the same girl, but with longer hair, though it was still the same dull, natural black. Her face was round and yet thin, and her eyes Japanese, though she wasn't. 'That,' Neppie said importantly, 'is Odinstoy.'

There was a pause while they all studied the photo. 'Are we impressed?' Affie said. 'Don't ask!'

'Is she really a bonder,' Berowne asked, 'or is she trying to make some point by going about looking like that?'

'Don't say you haven't heard of her?' Neppie said. 'Wake up! *Odinstoy?*'

Both the girls felt a stab of guilt at the idea that there was something they hadn't heard of yet, but Berowne said, 'Oh, Gods! Not another of your preachers!'

Affie was glad that Berowne had shown her the way to put Neppie in his place. 'You and your preachers, Neppie! So boring!'

Neppie took his fingers from his belt and the photo vanished. 'She's not a preacher. She's a God-speaker. Don't you even know *that?*' He held out his hand to the bonder, who resumed painting his nails.

'I don't know a single thing about bonder styles,' Berowne said. 'Please accept my grovelling apology. I'm not interested in looking stupid and ugly.'

Affie giggled, delighted at the way Neppie wriggled irritably in his chair. Then she felt sorry. Neppie was very bright, after all, and interesting, and rich.

'So, tell me about this – Odin – Odins—?'

'Odinstoy,' Neppie said. 'She's – well, really incredible.

Unbelievable, really. And *she's* a bonder – she was born a bonder, anyway. So it's just not true that bonders are always ugly and stupid.'

'Well, we know *that*,' Berowne said. 'There're lots of bonders who're singers and models and painters and things, but—'

'A nano ago, you said they were all stupid and ugly!'

'They're still *bonders*, aren't they?'

'Your nails are done, Freechild,' the bonder said to Neppie. 'Can I do anything else for you?'

'No, go away,' Neppie said.

'Your whatshername is ugly,' Berowne said. 'And she looked stupid. Screwing her face up like that. As if she wasn't ugly enough.'

'She is not ugly!' Neppie said.

Berowne looked at Affie, inviting her to join in the tease. 'She doesn't make the best of herself,' Affie said.

'You two,' Neppie said, 'all you can see is nail polish and design. Styling. You're entirely blind to *soul*!'

'Oh, no – soul?' Berowne said. 'Who does soul any more?!'

'Odinstoy has soul,' Neppie said. 'She's intense, she feels things that we don't. She can talk to the dead.'

'Who wants to talk to the dead?' Berowne asked. 'What do they know?'

'You're so proud of being free,' Neppie said, 'but you don't see that it's your very refinement that cuts you off from the sort of – *life intensity* that Odinstoy has.'

He's so intelligent, Affie thought. Imagine being able to say things like that just any time, without a script.

'Oh, that is such garbage,' Berowne said.

'She may not be conventionally pretty,' Neppie said, 'but she has something beyond that. There are pretty girls everywhere, but Odinstoy is *beautiful*.'

'She's funny looking,' Affie said, not wanting to fall out with him, but driven to truthfulness.

'She's earthy,' Neppie said. 'She's real. Why can't you silly little girls see that?'

'You poser,' Berowne said. 'You're only fifteen. What do you know?'

'You're only fourteen,' Neppie said. 'What do *you* know? And you're such a hypocrite. You're all for design, but I bet you worship Demeter. At the right time, of course, when everybody else does.'

'Who's Demeter?' Berowne asked.

'Oh, Gods! – don't you know *anything*?'

'It's so *boring* when you fight,' Affie said, but she couldn't resist showing Neppie that she knew more than Berowne. 'Demeter's one of those fertility Goddesses – all corn in the hair and babies round her skirts.' The touch of scorn was meant to keep her friendly with Berowne; and then she changed the subject. 'Do you think I should have my hair redone?' She could see herself in the mirror: a lovely, big-eyed girl with skin the colour of dark toffee, and thick, waving, light brown hair that fluoresced because of her jellyfish genes. Or was it squid genes? Whichever. As her mood changed, or her temperature did, her hair sparkled with glowing cloud patterns of blue, pink or green. 'I'm glad *I* was designed.' Her parents, like any good, responsible parents, had gone to a designer and had their genes read, to choose the best possible baby they could have. And then they'd had the genes tweaked a little here and there, to improve even on the best. That had been before they'd fallen out, but she was still grateful to them, for that, at least.

'Are you telling me that you don't think I'm beautiful?' she asked Neppie, leaning towards him.

'Of course you're beautiful, but in such an ordinary way.'

'Oh, thank you!'

'Your parents had you made like every other girl – tall and slim and oval-faced, big-eyed and full-lipped and all that. In a few years, people will be able to date you by your looks.'

'Neppie only likes funny little squashed up faces with piggy little eyes,' Berowne said.

'Odinstoy is unique,' Neppie said. 'There's nobody else like her.'

'There are hundreds of trashy poor people and bonders *just* like her,' Berowne said. 'Ugly and stupid.'

'Neppie – do you want to sex?' Affie asked. It was all right for Berowne to squabble with him – her marriage was signed and sealed. Affie's was off again – her father had told her so a few weeks before. 'Don't worry about it,' he'd said. 'It'll all sort itself out.' She'd never met the boy in question, so she wasn't even a little bit heartbroken, but it was so embarrassing, being the only girl whose future wasn't in place. Affie thought it was up to her to do something to make things happen. Neppie was fantastic husband material – rich, and so intelligent.

Neppie was surprised, but smiled. 'You're still ordinary – but let's see if you can persuade me.'

'Oh, that'll be difficult! Let's ask for the Aphrodite room – I love that one.'

'The Aphrodite room for Affroditey – yeah!'

'Have you finished?' Affie asked the bonder working on her nails. 'Oh, leave it, leave it, I'll come back later.' Affie and Neppie both jumped up from their chairs. 'Have fun!' Berowne called after them.

Pookie uncoiled herself from the spot where she'd been lying at Affie's feet, and stretched each leg in turn, almost bending her backbone in half. Her beauty – she was a miniature, silver cheetah with smoky blue markings – distracted the bonder working on Berowne's manicure. Berowne rapped her on the head.

Pookie, her stretch finished, bounded after Neppie and Affie, caught them, passed them, and reached reception first.

In reception, Affie and Neppie's personal bonders were waiting, sitting in a row on hard, straight-backed chairs against the wall. They all stood as Affie and Neppie came in. Affie's bonder looked even more worried than usual. 'Oh, Freechild Affie—'

'Don't bother me,' Affie said, a flush of pink clouds running through her hair. 'Try not to be such a pest. I'm busy.'

'But, Freechild Affie—'

'Go away! Go and sit down and wait. Whatever it is, you can tell me later.'

'Any messages?' Neppie asked his bonder. The man shook his head.

Affie's bonder sat down with the others, looking unhappy, but then, she always did look unhappy. Worrying was her hobby. Affie thought it only fair to give her plenty of worrying to do. 'Do you think I should get a new bonder?' she asked Neppie, so her bonder could hear. 'I've had this one for years. She's almost worn out. It's about time I got rid of her.'

Neppie gave a faint, polite smile, and said to the receptionist, 'Is the Aphrodite room free?'

'You want to hire a consent parlour?' the woman asked.

'Yes,' Affie said, smiling at Neppie to share the joke of the woman's stupidity. '*Is* the Aphrodite free?'

'I'll just check . . .' The woman tapped computer keys and looked at her monitor. 'Yes. Now, if you can just look through these forms for me, and sign them . . .'

She pushed a small screen towards them. Neppie went first, hardly bothering to read the form, just scribbling in his age with the electronic pen, and ticking the boxes for 'No disease' and 'I consent' before signing at the bottom.

Affie had a little more to do, since she had to tick the box that said she had been advised on contraceptives before she signed.

'The Aphrodite room is straight down the corridor, to your left,' the receptionist said.

As they turned to leave the desk, Affie's bonder stood up again, but Affie said, 'Don't start! Sit!' The bonder sank onto her chair.

Pookie would have followed Affie, but was shooed away, and the door leading to the Aphrodite room shut in her face.

Pookie yowled and trotted to and fro with light, springing steps, her high shoulders and hips heaving up and down. When her mistress didn't reappear, she threw herself down at the feet of Affie's bonder.

The bonders sat in silence while the receptionist ignored

them completely, her eyes passing over them blankly when she had to look in their direction. She might not be much, but she was unbonded at least.

'Never mind,' Neppie's bonder said, eventually, in a quiet undertone. 'You're only doing what she told you. It's not your fault.'

'I'll get the blame, though,' Affie's bonder said. 'You heard her. I'm almost worn out and should be replaced.'

'*She* told you to shut up and not bother her,' Neppie's bonder said. 'What were you supposed to do?'

Berowne's bonder glanced at them, with a mild interest, but stayed quiet.

'I was supposed to tell her immediately,' Affie's bonder said. 'Tell her and bring her home.'

'You tried,' Neppie's bonder said. 'It's not your fault if she told you to shut up. What were you supposed to do?'

'I should have insisted,' Affie's bonder said.

Berowne's bonder said, 'You're too soft.'

'They might sell me on!' Affie's bonder said, and her hands clenched on the material of her dress, crushing and twisting it.

'What if they do?' Neppie's bonder asked. 'You might get a better place.'

'At my age? It's all right for you, you're still young. Nobody's going to take me on now. I was hoping that this place would see me out.'

Berowne's bonder gave a short cough of laughter.

Affie's bonder leaned forward to look at her. 'Go on, laugh! I don't see you getting any younger. What are you going to do when Beroonie doesn't need you any more?'

'Beh-ron-ay,' Berowne's bonder said. 'Her name's Beh-ron-ay. And I shall buy myself out. I've been saving.'

'Hah!' Affie's bonder said. 'Yes, I know you will. Yes, very likely, that.' Berowne's bonder said nothing. 'I shan't hold my breath until I see you holding your own bond, no.' Berowne's bonder still said nothing, and the conversation lapsed, although Affie's bonder occasionally said something like, 'That'll be the day' or 'I'll believe *that* when I see it.' Once, Neppie's bonder said, 'Don't worry about it,' and the receptionist said, 'No smoking!' when Affie's bonder lit up a cigarette, and glowered until the bonder stubbed it out and put it away. Apart from that, they sat in silence until the door of the Aphrodite room reopened, and Neppie and Affie came out together, rosy and smiling. Pookie stirred and sat up, yawned, and scratched her flank.

'Tell her now,' Neppie's bonder said, as all three of them stood up, and then spoke himself: 'Forgive me, Freechild Affroditey, but Freda has something to tell you.'

'Oh, what *is* it, Freda?' Affie said. She stooped to pet Pookie, who had strolled indolently over to her.

'I'm sorry, Freechild Affie, but I did try to tell you – they want you to come home straight away.'

'Why?'

'I can't – I can't really tell you, Free—'

'Don't stupify. You have to tell me.'

'I was told – I was asked – it's difficult, Freechild.'

'No. It's not.' Affie spoke very loudly and clearly. 'It's very simple. Even for you. Just tell me, now, what's going on.'

'Forgive me, Freechild,' Neppie's bonder said. 'It's a discreet matter.'

'Oh! So she's told you!' Affie said. 'How dare you? How dare you talk about my business to other bonders, you stupid old clapped-out mare? I'm going to sell you on, I am!'

'Forgive me, Freechild,' Neppie's bonder began, but Neppie said, 'Ing. Shut up and keep out of it.'

'Now,' Affie said, legs astride and hands on hips. 'What is all this about?'

Freda stooped, clasping and wringing her hands. 'I can't tell you, Freechild, I was told not to tell you—'

'And I'm telling you that you have to tell me.'

'Please, Freechild, listen to me, please, I don't think—'

'No, you don't think. You're not supposed to think. You're supposed to do as you're told.'

'Please, Freechild—'

Affie threw herself down into one of the big padded chairs meant for clients. Pookie jumped into her lap and curled up. 'I'm not going anywhere until you tell me why I have to go home.'

Ing whispered, 'Tell her,' and Berowne's bonder smiled faintly.

Freda said, 'Oh, Freechild – I didn't want to tell you – don't blame me – but, oh Freechild, your father's killed himself.'

Affie's hair turned blue.

Minerva's News

'What?' Affie said. 'Of course he hasn't.' She pushed Pookie off her lap. The little cheetah landed on its feet, flicked its tail and yowled. 'Don't stupefy.'

'But that's what they told me, Freechild, that's what the message said.' The bonder, flustered, lightly touched her ear, where she'd heard the message, transmitted through her tooth receiver. 'Free Affie should come home urgently, it said, because her father's killed himself.'

'My father is perfectly fine,' Affie said. 'I spoke to him – like, *days* ago, that's all. He's fine, flawlessly fine!'

'Maybe you should go home, Affie,' Neppie said.

'But we were to shop!'

'Yes, but—' Neppie spread his hands. 'I'll go with you.' To the receptionist, he said, 'A cab.'

Putting her hands on her hips, Affie said, 'It's a mistake.' The little sparks and flurries of colour in her hair were changing through indigo and green to orange and red. '*She* got the message mixed – didn't you, stupid? Admit it.'

'You've got to go,' Neppie said.

'When we get there,' Affie said, glaring at Freda, 'and my father's like, "What's all this fuss?" I shall be like, "Sell Freda straight away! That's why I've homed early – because I want to sell Freda – to the dog-food factory!"'

'I'm sorry, Freechild Affie,' Freda said. 'I'm sorry, I'm sorry . . .'

The cab cruised through the streets, with Pookie sitting elegantly upright, looking through a window. Affie lifted her hand, turning it so she could see the small screen on the inner side of her gold bracelet. With the tip of one nail, she tapped the screen, choosing the phone function, then the numbers, and then her home number. A moment later, she heard the phone ringing, through the transmitter in her ear-ring.

'Hello?' It was a strange voice.

'Who is this?' Affie said, her voice shaking very slightly, and the colour in her hair cooling.

'This is the Millington house,' said the voice.

'I know that! Who are you?'

'I'm a police officer, Freewoman.'

In a fright, Affie tapped 'End call', and the phone went dead. 'The police are at my house.'

'Cool,' Neppie said. 'We'll soon be there.'

The cab turned into Affie's street. There were people standing on the pavement outside her house; people with cameras. Neppie spoke to the cab's computer: 'Command. Don't stop. Take us to the back of the house. The back of the house. End command.' The cab faltered slightly, unbalancing Pookie and making her jump to the floor, then picked up speed and kept moving. To Affie, Neppie said, '*Something's* happened, if the press are here.'

'My stepmother's partying,' Affie said. 'She always is. She'll have tipped them off. Or whatever. You'll see.'

The cab circled the block and crawled along a narrow service street. 'Would you believe?' Neppie said. Outside the rear entrance of Affie's house, standing beside the bins, were more photographers. 'Command. Keep going. End command. Affie, you should phone again.'

'No! Stop! Stop, stop, stop! Command! Stop! Let me out! End command.'

The cab swerved to the kerb, and stopped. Affie jumped from the car, followed by Pookie, and hurried back up the street with the cheetah bounding along beside her. Freda stumbled after. 'Pay the thing,' Neppie said, and left Ing fumbling for his mobile.

The photographers were taking shots of Affie as she came near, and crowded even closer as she scooped up Pookie, to save the cat from their great feet. 'Got anything to say?' they asked her and shouted, 'Affroditey! Over here! Over here!' as she shoved her way through them. Pookie snarled at them and lashed her tail.

Neppie came up, and they turned on him. 'Who're you? Heard the news? Have anything to say?'

He clamped his mouth shut and shouldered through them, into the small yard that smelled of damp cardboard and fermenting rubbish. The reporters followed them, still yelling, right up to the kitchen door, where Affie and Freda were being questioned by a policeman. After a few words, he let them through, but stopped Neppie. 'Sorry, no admission.'

'I'm a friend, I've come with—'

'Family only,' the policeman said. 'Ongoing investigation.' And the policeman stepped back into the house, shutting the door almost on Neppie's nose.

Inside, Affie looked about at the steel work surfaces, the stoves, the microwaves and sink. At the people, too: the servants and bonders who were staring in that silent, guilty way that meant they'd been talking about Affie when she'd arrived.

Affie kept hold of Pookie, not wanting to put her down in this place. 'Where do we go?' Affie said. She hadn't been down here for ages. Why would she?

Freda led the way through the kitchen, past the staring people, to a door at the far end which opened into a dim, narrow service corridor with walls of bare breeze blocks. A flight of stairs rose into the main house above.

Affie set Pookie down, and the little cheetah sprang up the stairs, silver fur gleaming in the dim light. Affie ran after her. Freda, left behind, panted, 'Go – go to your – room, Free, and I – I'll find out—'

Affie had a momentary flash of what it would be like, sitting in her room, waiting and waiting. 'No!' She shoved open the door at the top of the stairs, letting Pookie through, and emerged into the wide, sunny entrance hall with its glass stairs, and flowers and mirrors.

There was a policeman standing in the sunlight like a dark blotch. Pookie skirted warily round him, and the policeman eyed her with distrust. She might be small, but she was still a cheetah. He held out an arm, indicating the drawing room. 'In there, please, Freechild.'

Affie put her hands on her hips. 'This is *my* house!'

'Yes, Freechild. In there, please, Freechild.'

'You don't tell me where to go in my own house!'

'Please understand, Freechild. We're investigating the scene here. It can't be contaminated. So if you'd please go and wait in that room there.'

'I want to see my father,' Affie said. 'Where is he?'

'Please, Freechild,' the policeman said again. 'Please go and wait in there.'

Affie looked at him, wonderingly. Why was he so stupid? 'Don't you know who I am? I'm *free*! You can't order *me* about!'

The policeman sighed. 'We're not ordering you about, Freechild. We're asking you to co-operate with us in our investigation of this scene.'

'Why? What's happened?'

'I think you'd better go in there, Freechild. Your – mother? – is in there. She'll explain.'

'*She's* not my *mother*!' Affie's hair took on a scarlet shimmer. 'Where's my father? I was told something had happened to my father.'

'Please, Freechild. Go in there and talk to – Freewoman Millington.'

'This is outrageous,' Affie said. But she didn't really want to insist on searching the house for her father because a dread was settling heavily in her belly, and her hair was cooling to indigo. She was afraid of what she might find. It was better to pretend that she was forced to wait in the drawing room. '*You* will be reported,' she said to the policeman, and flounced towards the door he indicated.

She had opened the door, and Pookie had skittered through, when Freda wailed, 'Free Affie! What shall I do?'

'What do I care? – oh, come on!'

Thankfully, Freda scuttled after her mistress into the drawing room: a large, bright room, all in cream and gold. Minerva Millington had chosen the colours and furnishings. She had insisted on a fireplace: it was in the centre of the room, a gleaming bronze bowl with an 'eternal flame' burning in it. The long couches and the drapes at the windows were 'Grecian'. The room was, Minerva said, 'tasteful, yet cosy'. Affie called it 'dreary, dreary, dreary', but no one asked her opinion.

Minerva sat in a small armchair beside the fire's bronze bowl, glowering at Pookie, who was sniffing at one of the couches, ready to yell if the cheetah started clawing. Minerva was very beautiful, and had invested a lot of money to make sure she stayed that way. Her face was an adult's – she was thirty-five at *least* – but her skin was a child's: unlined, unblemished, apparently poreless. The curls framing her lovely face were so blond they were white, and her deep tan was entirely natural and never faded, but hadn't harmed her skin at all because it owed nothing to the sun – indeed, it protected her from the sun.

She looked round as Affie and Freda entered, stared at them a moment, then jumped to her feet, throwing up her arms, yelling, 'Look what your useless father's done now!' She turned on Freda. 'Get out, get out! And take that *thing* with you!' The bonder grabbed up Pookie and fled.

Affie was left facing Minerva. She wanted to be angry, but was too taken aback. Pink lights shifted, glittering, through her hair.

'What a useless shit he was!' Minerva said. 'What did he ever do right in his whole useless life?'

'You married him!' Affie's hair fluoresced with crimson clouds. 'How useless does that make *you*?'

'If I'd known you were sticking around, I never would have done! He said you'd be living with your cow of a mother! Bloody useless shit of a liar!'

Tears of rage filled Affie's eyes. 'I stayed to spite you, you poisonous old stem-celled witch.'

'He shot himself! And you know why? Because he'd made another mess! Because he was in the shit! So the shit shot himself! And left *me* to deal with it all!'

'Good!' Affie shouted. The crimson lights in her hair threw a soft glow on her face and shoulders.

Minerva paused and studied Affie, her own face sweet and rosy. 'Good, is it? I hope you enjoy it, *darling*. Because you don't know the half of it!'

'If it upsets you, that's enough for me!'

Minerva grinned with rage. 'Then I wish you joy. We're bankrupt. Broken. Finished. Are you happy, Affroditey, dear?'

Affie drew back her head as if she'd been struck. The cloud waves in her hair cooled to orange, but then she clenched her fists and the light reddened again. She was unwilling to show any dismay to Minerva. 'One blessing – I'll be rid of you! *You* won't stay around if there's no money!'

'You'll be rid of so much unnecessary baggage,' Minerva said. 'All those clothes and shoes and make-up. You can develop your spiritual side. And make new friends – because your old ones will soon disappear!'

'*My* friends aren't like that! *Yours* might be!'

'No more dreary school,' Minerva said. 'No more draggy beauty parlours and cab rides. No more little . . .'

Affie, realising that she didn't have to listen to this, turned and slammed out of the room. Freda was waiting in the hall, seated on a straight chair placed near the door, with Pookie crouched at her feet. She stood, and Affie ran to her to be hugged, sending Pookie bounding into a corner. 'Freda, is it true, is it? My father isn't really dead, is he?'

Freda, hugging Affie, looked over her shoulder at the flowers on the hall table, beneath the mirror. The policeman gave her a sympathetic grimace. Freda was trying hard to think of something soothing she could say, both to be kind and to spare herself Affie's tantrums. But, in the circumstances, any lie or half lie she told would rebound. 'I'm sorry,' she said, 'I'm sorry, but it's true, he's dead. I've been talking to the officer and—'

'But he might get better?' Affie said, lifting her head.

'No, sweetheart. I'm sorry. He isn't hurt, he's *dead*.'

Affie looked blank.

'I don't want to upset you, darling –' No, because Affie, upset, could make her life a misery. '– but he shot himself in the head, so—'

'But they'll take him to hospital! He'll be all right – he'll get better.'

Freda still looked at the policeman, who shook his head. 'No, darling. It's too late. He is dead. It's certain. And he left a note.'

'A note?'

The policeman said, 'A suicide note, Freechild Millington.'

Affie let go of Freda, walked over to one of the hall chairs, and sat down. She stared at the sunlit wall and thought, quite clearly: my father is dead.

Everything that meant came in on her, all at once.

Her father had been so unhappy that shooting himself in the head had seemed better than living another minute.

He hadn't cared enough for her to want to see her again, even once.

She would never, ever see him any more.

She started to cry, but the thoughts continued to cram into her head. What was going to happen to her? How could she go on living? Who was going to look after her?

It was as if the thoughts had weight, and they weighed her head down, and grew so heavy that they overbalanced her and toppled her from the chair, onto the hard stone tiles of the hall. She wailed.

'Where's the doctor?' Freda shouted at the policeman. 'Fetch a doctor.'

Collateral

The doctor's sedative left Affie in a leaden daze, dully staring at the fact that her father was dead, her life ruined.

A night of restless half sleep and short dozes followed, from which she woke with heart shocks, shivering, feeling dread. Three nights seemed to drag past before morning, and even then, light came too soon. The sedative wore off, but still she felt dull. She lay on her bed, hugging Pookie, while her thoughts ground round and round.

Her father was dead. What could she do now? Who would look after her? Where would she be safe? The future seemed an impassable wall, blocking her way. It did not seem possible to do anything except stand, staring at it. Her brain would not, *could not*, suggest a single thing she might do.

'Go to school,' Freda said. 'Meet your friends. Take your mind off things.'

Affie shook her head. Her hair, unwashed, was lank and a little greasy, and only the faintest of blue light pulsed through it. She could not face school: the noise, the questions, the curiosity. 'The funeral,' she said. There must be one, she supposed. It had to be arranged.

'Don't you worry about any of that,' Freda said. 'Your stepmother's arranging it all.'

'Of course,' Affie said bitterly. Of course Minerva would muscle in and take over. 'I want to see the note.'

'No, my love, you don't want to do that! Why upset yourself? Anyway, it's with the police.'

'Is it *really* true, Freda? Really?'

Freda tried to speak, but gulped instead, choked by her own fears. She would be sold, she knew, along with the house and everything in it – but who would want to buy her? Only someone who couldn't afford a younger, livelier, more personable bonder – and being cheap didn't inspire kindness. When she thought of her future, she felt her chest tighten and her breath come hard.

'Don't you worry, my love,' she managed to say, in a thin, unconvincing voice. 'I'm sure it'll all be all right in the end.' For you, her thoughts added. Not for me.

Minerva came to visit one day, or two days – or perhaps it was three days or four – after Affie's father shot himself. Affie had simply been sitting in her room, stroking Pookie, when Pookie would stay with her; playing music her father had liked; and crying, without keeping note of time. When ravenous, she'd eaten whatever was to hand – usually something Freda had brought on a tray – and had fallen asleep when she couldn't stay awake any longer. Now, Minerva rapped on the door of her sitting room and came in, calling her name before knocking on the door of the bedroom.

'Go away!' Affie shouted.

Minerva came in. Pookie jumped from the bed and hid underneath it, growling.

'Pookie's such a good judge of character,' Affie said –

though, in fact, the cheetah was a nervous creature, and would have hidden from almost anyone.

Minerva said nothing. She wasn't as groomed as usual. Her white-blond hair was not freshly washed or styled, and her face, wearing nothing but its tattooed lipstick and eyeliner, even looked a little tired. Young, but tired. 'Affroditey, I have to talk to you.'

'I don't want to talk to *you*. Get out of my room.'

'Can we be less childish for a moment, please, and talk seriously?'

Affie had been lying on her bed. She sat up. '*You* are calling *me* childish?'

'I said some horrible, unreasonable things, I know. I apologise. I was upset. I'd just been told that my husband had shot himself.'

'Yes, I understand,' Affie said. 'You'd lost your free ride. Poor you.'

Minerva sat down, unasked, in the chair beside the dressing table. While Affie glared, she slowly crossed her legs and made herself comfortable. 'Affroditey. We have never got on. Perhaps that was my fault as much – or more – than yours. But now we are facing a very difficult and complicated situation, and I need you to be sensible and adult.'

'Why should I do anything to help you?' Affie asked.

Minerva gave a small smile. 'To make things easier for yourself?'

Affie considered, and then said warily, 'What do you want?'

Minerva took a deep breath and leaned forward, clasping her hands around her upper knee. 'I've been talking a lot with solicitors and accountants over the last few days.'

Affie choked back a comment about Minerva's deep and sincere concern for her father's money.

'I'm afraid I have to tell you that we are going to lose everything. Every last teaspoon and earring.'

'We can live on credit,' Affie said eagerly, the idea suddenly occurring to her. 'Lots of people do – they have cars and holidays and horses and everything, and they're in mountains of debt.' She'd heard someone use that phrase once: one of her friends' fathers had said, proudly, that he had 'mountains of debt'. 'They just keep borrowing more. Nobody minds.'

Minerva was tired. She sat still, listening patiently. When Affie finished, she sighed and said, 'But we've no collateral.' Seeing Affie's blank face, she added, 'We don't *own* anything – nothing that we could offer as security. That's what I've been talking about with all these people . . .' She leaned on the dressing table and put her hand to her brow. 'It all belongs to the banks and – oh, others . . . Now everything's collapsed, they're claiming it. Everything. Every single thing. That's what I want to tell you. Affie . . .' Her voice trailed off. She leaned more heavily on the hand that supported her head. It was almost as if she'd fallen asleep.

Affie waited. Pookie looked out warily from under the bed. Affie coughed. Still Minerva didn't move. 'What?'

Minerva raised her head. 'Oh, Affie . . . Your father borrowed money against you.'

Affie didn't follow that. Her mind came up against that blank wall again. Sitting on her bed, she stared across at her stepmother.

'He gave you as security for one of his loans. One of his

more desperate loans. He was borrowing and borrowing, trying to put things right. I'm afraid . . . that he didn't. He made things far worse. A gift of his.'

'But? How? How could he borrow money – against me? I'm not – you can't buy *me*.'

'Of course you can be bought!' Minerva snapped. 'We all can! Your Freda was bought for you, wasn't she?'

'But she's a bonder!'

'Yes,' Minerva agreed. 'And now, so are you. That's what I'm trying to tell you.'

In a whisper, Affie said, 'What?'

'You belong to the bank, Affroditey. They own you. They're going to retrieve the money they're owed. By selling you.'

Texting for Help

'They're going to sell me?' Affie repeated, in a whisper, as if by repeating the words she could make sense of them. They made even less sense. 'But they can't.'

'They can,' Minerva said. 'And will.'

'They *can't*.'

Exasperated, Minerva sighed. 'Why can't they?'

Because bankers didn't sell girls like her. Some of her friends' fathers were in banking. They were *nice*. As she, Affie, was nice. She went to a nice school and had nice friends and knew how to behave. She was *designed*. Not like bonders, who were ugly and stupid and rude, until they'd been trained, and dirty, secretly dirty – under their nails and between their toes, in their ears and mouths – dirty, dirty, dirty. *Not* like her.

Aloud, she said, 'Daddy would never sell *me*.'

'But he did. I've seen the papers, all drawn up and signed. Probably, he thought that it would never—'

'Did he bond you?' Affie asked.

'Ah. No.'

Affie sat still, staring at her. 'Daddy wouldn't sell me.' Her mind struggled, while her hair pulsed with waves of blue. Then orange light flickered over her head. '*You* sold me.'

'That's not so.'

'You hate me.'

'I won't pretend to like you, Affie, but when have you ever tried to like me?'

Affie darted from the bed, swinging slaps and punches at Minerva. Pookie, alarmed, shot from under the bed and careered around the room, leaping at the door, snarling. Minerva, trapped in the little chair, ducked her head and folded her arms over it. 'Stop it! Stop it, Affie!'

Affie silently, savagely, continued to hammer at her and pummel her, until Minerva was driven to try grabbing the girl's hands – though, with her head bowed, she was almost blind. With one hand seized, Affie kicked Minerva with her bare heels, and struck at her with her knees. The woman's cry of pain made her kick and punch twice as hard. She tangled her free hand in Minerva's hair and yanked, bringing almost a scream from the woman.

'I'll tear it all – tear it all out!' But Affie was panting. After a few more seconds and a few more good kicks and punches, she fell back, breathless, to the bed. Red waves flickered through her hair. Pookie was huddled in a corner by the door, growling.

Minerva remained huddled in the chair, waiting to be sure the attack was over. Cautiously, she sat up straight and looked at Affie, her face pained and frightened. Affie stared back, triumphant, defiant, and equally afraid. The colours in her hair cooled rapidly to blue.

Minerva jumped up from the chair, and Pookie darted to the opposite corner, where she crouched again, lashing her tail.

Minerva's legs shook under her. Her head and back were sore from blows. 'Well done,' she said, her voice trembling. 'If ever I was disposed to help you, I've changed my mind now.' And she left Affie's rooms as quickly as she could, on shaking legs, slamming the doors.

Affie sat on the bed, getting back her breath; and then she took the glass bottles from the dressing table and threw them into the mirror, smashing it and them. Pookie ran and cowered under the bed.

An overpowering reek of perfume filled the room. Affie threw bottles of foundation against the walls, staining them, and trod lipstick and eyeshadow into the carpet. She dragged the covers from the bed, and was trying, panting, to pull down the curtains when Freda came in.

'Free Affie!'

'If it's all going to be sold—' Affie, out of breath, had to sit down on the disarranged bed. 'Let them see if they can sell this!'

Freda came and sat beside her, and put her arms round her. 'Oh, Free. I'm so sorry for you.'

Affie looked at her. 'They can't sell me, really – can they, Freda? Not really.' She was still hoping that it was just some spiteful tale of Minerva's.

Freda simply looked at her, and that look hurt Affie, somewhere about the heart. It meant that yes, of course she could be sold, just as Freda could be sold.

'But I'm not like *you!*' Affie said.

Freda said nothing, and looked at the floor.

'I can't be sold!'

'It's not the end of the world, my love,' Freda said. 'You're young. In a few years, your stepmother might buy you free.'

'Her?' Affie said. 'Never! She sold me!'

'You might earn your own freedom. Lots of bonders do.'

'You never did,' Affie said.

'Well. No,' Freda said, guilty and ashamed. 'I was never clever.'

'And how am I going to earn anything? I don't work! Who's going to buy me?' A new terror gripped Affie's heart. What happened to bonders when nobody wanted to buy their bond? Where were they kept? What were they fed? Ideas of cold, dark dungeons, full of spiders and rats and worms, crowded her head. She'd only seen such creepy-crawlies in pictures, but Freda had taught her that they were slimy and horrible. The thought of being near the real thing horrified her.

'You've got lots of friends,' Freda said. 'Couldn't they help?'

Affie stared at her. A brilliant idea! And she hadn't thought of it. Freda, a bonder, had. It was a measure of how distressed she was that she hadn't been able to think of such an obvious idea. She stood. 'It's smelly in here. I'm going in the other room while you tidy up.' Pookie came from under the bed and trotted after her.

Affie threw herself down in a chair. Her mother! Of course. Her mother was very comfortably situated, and who was more likely to help? She could remember when her mother had still lived with them – she'd been very loving, and had always sent Freda to pick Affie up if she fell down. In fact, it had been her mother who had chosen and bought Freda for her.

She touched the little screen on her bracelet, calling up

her mother's number, because she couldn't remember it. She tapped 'Call' and the ringing began – to be quickly replaced by a recorded voice saying, 'Freewoman Lloyd is not available. Please leave a message.'

'Mummy,' Affie said, her voice shaking into sobs. 'It's me, Affie – something terrible's happened. Please ring me back.' And then she sent a text saying the same thing. And waited, expecting her phone to ring any minute.

Two hours later, Freda had cleared up the broken glass, vacuumed the floor, washed down the walls, remade the bed, and brushed as much of the crushed make-up from the carpet as was possible. She had opened the windows, to try and disperse the thick, sickly vapours of mixed scents. But when she went through to the other room, she found that Freewoman Lloyd hadn't rung back.

'I've phoned her five times,' Affie said. The waves of light in her hair were a deep indigo, and pulsed slowly. 'I've texted. I've *told* her what's happened. Why doesn't she phone back? Do you think something's happened to her, too?'

'No, no,' Freda said, without looking at Affie. 'I'm sure she'll ring you back as soon as she picks up your messages.'

Freda thought no such thing. She'd known Freewoman Lloyd when she'd been married to Affie's father. If you wanted *that* woman's attention, then you had to say, 'I have something lovely for you, I want to compliment you, I want to tell you the best of good news.' If you said to her, 'Something terrible has happened, someone has died, I need your help,' then you lost her entirely. She became deaf, developed a headache, remembered an appointment somewhere else. This was a woman who had plenty of money, but would hide bills in drawers, or wipe them from her in-box, and forget – or rather, refuse to remember – that she'd ever seen them. Or ever bought the billed item. Anything that made the slightest demand on her was 'too much, too much . . .' She would never, Freda guessed, phone her daughter back.

'Phone some of your friends while you're waiting for your mother to call back. I would.' It was a small chance, but better than counting on Freewoman Lloyd.

So Affie phoned Berowne and Neppie, and Artia, and Diana and Venus. It was strange, but she couldn't get an answer from any of them. All day, she sat in her room, with Pookie in her lap and the sickly stench of perfume seeping through from her bedroom, and she called, and left messages, and texted and checked her in-box, and nothing. Nothing.

Eventually, she concentrated on her mother and Neppie. One of them would answer, one of them would help her – Neppie, because: well, he was her boyfriend, wasn't he? They'd sexed. And he was kind. And her mother was her mother. One of them would answer. One of them would.

It was midnight, and still no one had taken her phone calls, or answered her texts. 'What's happened?' she said to Freda, who sat on a stool beside her chair. 'The system's not down, is it? One of these messages must have got through to *somebody*.'

Freda said nothing, just looked at her, sadly.

'Tomorrow,' Affie said. 'Somebody will get back to me tomorrow.' The lights in her hair were darkest blue.

Being Texted

'Freew'm Lloyd? Freewoman? There's another message.'

Freewoman Lloyd groaned. She was lying in her bed, the room darkened, an eye mask darkening the world even further. 'Deal with it, can't you? My head aches, I can't think straight.'

'Freew'm, it really isn't anything I can deal with. It's from your daughter. She's in—'

Freewoman Lloyd rolled onto her side, curling up. 'Oh, tell her I'll call back. Just leave me alone – can't you see I'm ill?'

'Freewoman,' said her bonded maid, 'your daughter is in trouble.'

'Isn't there any peace and quiet? Can't I be left alone for a moment?'

'Freewoman, your ex-husband has shot himself—'

'Call the doctor! I can't endure this pain any longer.'

'Freewoman, your daughter has been *sold*.'

'Oh, leave me alone. I don't want to see anyone until the doctor comes.'

'But, Freew'm, what—'

'Go away!'

'If you insist, Freew'm, if you insist,' said the bonder, retreating from the room. Once outside it, she whispered, 'You selfish, shrivelled up, useless, spineless old bitch!'

'Oh, Gods!' Berowne said, rolling back her eyes and letting her head fall back, as if about to faint with boredom. 'Affroditey Millington texting me *again*! Can you believe?'

'What face that girl has got!'

'She's sent me *millions*. Listen to this. "In terrible trouble – really, really need to talk." What about? What does she expect me to do?'

'Did you hear what happened?'

'Didn't her father hang himself?'

'Shot himself,' Berowne said. 'In the head. Blood and brains all *over* the walls.'

'Eeuw!'

'I can't unshoot him, can I?'

'I heard he was in trouble.'

'My father's like, "He was a big fool,"' said Berowne. '"Got himself into a mess and took the coward's way out." Daddy's like, "Stay clear. Don't get drawn in."'

'There's nothing you could do, anyway. What could you do? Realistically.'

'But *how long* does it take someone to get the message?' Berowne demanded. 'I answer none of her texts, not one, and she *still* sends!'

'How stupefied can you get?'

'I never honestly liked her that much,' Berowne said. 'Not honestly. Not really liked. Did you?'

'No. She was always a bit – well.'

'I know flawlessly what you mean. I always thought that too.'

'Why don't you block her?'

'Stupefied! I did! Her voice calls anyway.'

'Who's stupefied? Block her mails too!'

'You know,' Berowne said, taking up the tiny flat screen of phone, 'I shall.'

'You're too soft, Berowne.'

'I know, but—' Berowne shook her head ruefully and shrugged.

'Do you think,' Artia said, 'that they'll be selling that silver leopard of hers?'

'You have to consider your own interests,' Neppie's father said.

'But the poor girl – she's having such a bad time.'

'It's very sad, I agree. But the girl will survive and—'

'She's being sold!' Neppie said.

'Is that so awful? She'll be fed, she'll be clothed, she'll be housed, and she'll learn new skills and an awful lot about herself. Believe me, I've sometimes considered selling you! It'd be the making of you!'

Neppie half laughed, grimacing at the same time. 'I'll stick to school, thank you, sir.' It was comforting, though, to find that his father didn't think Affie's situation so bad.

'In all seriousness, we really couldn't afford to help her in any substantial way. I'm sorry, Nep, but I'm not going to sell the house over your mother and sisters' heads—'

Neppie laughed along with his father. 'No, sir! Mother would have something to—'

'Of course, you can hand over all your pocket money, if you like! Buy back one of her little toenails!'

Neppie laughed again. 'She must be miserable, though, sir. I should give her a call – maybe go and see her.'

'No!' his father said, very seriously this time. 'No, that's just what you shouldn't do. Don't you see how you'd embarrass the poor girl?'

'She must be miserable, sir. And scared.'

'And you think your turning up, all sympathy but no rescue – you think that's going to help? You'll raise her hopes, and then you'll go off home – and the people she has to make her life among now – having seen you – will resent her more. No, Neppie – leave well alone. That's my advice.'

Neppie fell silent. After a long time, he said, 'She could live – I mean, it wouldn't be much of an expense, and—'

'Neppie, stop right there. Think it through. What would her position be? Some kind of pet, a mascot? How humiliating for her. Do I treat her exactly like your sisters? That means depriving them – do they deserve that?'

'No, but—'

'Or do we treat Affie like some sort of poor relation – the smallest room, that no one else wants, the hand-me-down dresses? And what could she do? Has she any qualifications for a job? If she hasn't, who pays for her education?'

'All right, all right,' Neppie said, giving up the argument.

'Who would marry her now? She's penniless. Is she going to be happy spending her life being passed over?'

'OK! I get it. Bad idea. Forget it.'

His father gripped his shoulder. 'I'm proud to discover that you're so compassionate. And it's very, very, sad about poor Affie, but – this is what the Gods have fated for her. Let her learn from it.'

Neppie went off to his room, to play music and think. He felt bad about Affie and *for* Affie, and couldn't stop thinking about how lonely and scared she must be. It took him a long time to fall asleep that night. But he did, and when he woke, Affie's problems seemed much more distant and a lot easier to forget. He became absorbed in lessons and friends and small, everyday things. By that evening, Affie had receded even further from his thoughts. After that – apart from an occasional, piercing memory, soon pushed aside – he forgot her.

Valued

Affie planned to say, very calmly, 'Minerva. I'm really, flaw-lessly sorry. I was overwrought, and didn't know what I was doing.' Tears came to her eyes while merely thinking about what she would say, so she knew that when she was actually speaking to Minerva, she would cry, even if only from fury at having to apologise. Minerva would surely forgive her, and help her. After all, when you *apologised* . . .

But Minerva wasn't in the house. Affie and Pookie searched everywhere: Minerva's rooms, the swimming pool, the gym, the conservatory . . . Minerva was nowhere.

'She's already gone,' Freda said, when Affie asked her. 'A lot of the servants have gone, too – the free ones.' The cook, it seemed, had gone, and the gardener didn't come any more. They knew that the house was being sold, and that their wages for the past few months were unlikely to be paid. They were away to find other jobs.

'They say people are coming to value us in the next couple of days,' Freda said. 'Once they've sold us off, they can sell the house and contents.'

'And you're all going to sit here obediently, and wait for them to come and sell you?' Affie said.

'And what are you going to do, Free Affie?'

'I shall run away.'

'Good luck to you, Freechild,' Freda said.

Affie meant it when she said it, but then started to think. Where would she go? No one had returned her calls or texts, not even her mother, so no one was coming to fetch her. The thought of turning up on Berowne or Neppie's doorstep, after they hadn't answered – well, it made her turn hot and cold.

Even if she had somewhere to go, how would she get there? She couldn't take a cab because she had no credit – it had all been frozen – and the cars were locked in their garage, waiting to be sold.

In desperation, she thought of taking a bus, or even walking – but where to? The thought of walking, alone, in the dirty, dangerous streets; of climbing aboard a public bus in the smelly, sweaty press of dirty bonders and poor people . . . She couldn't. They might attack her, to steal Pookie, and her watch and clothes – or just out of spite and jealousy, because she was designed and they weren't.

So she stayed in her room, her body near paralysed with doubt and fear, but her mind seething with anxiety and sheer terror of the future. Her mood distressed Pookie, who stalked round the edges of the room, bristling and yowling until Affie couldn't stand it, and asked Freda to take her away.

Even left to herself, her heart pounded, her belly heaved. Food didn't sit well with her. She cried for hours, until she was exhausted, sometimes for herself and sometimes for her father.

For the first time in years, she went to her ancestor shrine. The graceful silver tree, with its dangling fruit of tiny, framed photographs, stood on a table in the corner of her bedroom, surrounded by candles and small mementoes. Buttons on its base allowed you to access more detail about each ancestor: their own relatives and place in the wider family, notable events of their lives, their achievements, film of them, their wills . . . Freda kept it dusted and neat, but Affie hadn't done more than glance at it for longer than she could remember. Now she lit candles, and set flowers, wine and cakes before her forebears; looked through all the photos, trying to remember their names, and prayed to them for help. Her father's photograph should be added to it, but she didn't know how that should be done . . .

'Help me, grandfathers, grandmothers . . . Help me.'

There was no sort of answer. The terrifying blank wall of the future remained ahead of her.

I can't face it, I can't, she told herself. I'd be better off dead. But she was still alive, and time still moved forward. The future was something she couldn't escape.

Freda said, 'Come on now, Free Affie. They want to see you.'

Lying face down on her bed, Affie said, 'Who do?'

'The valuers. Come on, don't keep them waiting.'

Affie sat up in alarm, her hair quickly wavering through blues into orange and pink. The bogeymen were here at last. 'I can't, I can't.'

'You have to, Free. They'll send people to fetch you if you don't go. They'll be angry. Better not make them angry.'

No. Affie was afraid of their anger. If she went to meet them, perhaps she could still talk her way out of it? 'I have to shower, and change, and put on my face.'

'Oh, Free,' Freda wailed, as Affie headed for her bathroom. 'You don't have time.'

'I can't go as I am,' Affie said. 'I *can't*. Run a bath.'

'Oh, Free! A bath takes so long! They're *waiting*!'

Affie hesitated. She preferred a bath, or at least a shower, with real water. It was more luxurious, and much better for the skin . . . But it *would* take far longer . . .

They can wait, she thought. Why should I give up my bath and hurry, just to please them?

But she was scared. Maybe, just this once, she should hurry a bit, if it would keep the valuers in a good mood. After all, she wanted them to listen to what she had to say.

So she took a sonic. It would have cleaned both her and the clothes she'd been living and sleeping in for days, but she didn't want to wear those clothes, so stripped them off, and dropped them onto the floor. Freda picked them up, saying, 'Oh, Free, I said I'd bring you right down. They said they'd value us together.'

'I have to change.' A minute of turning in the sonic cleaned her, and she stepped out, and ran to her dressing table, where she sorted through the make-up she hadn't destroyed. 'What shall I wear?'

'Oh, anything, Free.'

'I have to make a good impression. I should look . . . pretty, but – sweet and good!'

So she added no extra eye make-up to the tattooed lines around her lids, but applied pink lipstick. Her hair she bound back with a modest headband, and she put in small stud earrings rather than the larger, fancier ones with the telephone receiver built into them. 'Get my Wolfe skirt suit –

the black one – and the white – no, the shell-pink shirt. No – the silk, idiot! And the camel shoes – the ones to the left, the far left.'

'We've kept them waiting so long,' Freda moaned, as Affie put on the shoes.

'If you'd been quicker – and less stupid! All right. I'm ready.'

Freda led her down the glass stairs and through the house. In one of the reception rooms – the one with the old-world painting of cornfields full of black plastic bags against a sunset – they came to the other bonders of the house, sprawled in chairs. They would never have dared to do that a few days before. All of them stared at Affie in a way that made her feel awkward, and the moment she'd passed them, one of them whistled and said, '*Hel*-lo, Affie.' She almost turned round to see who it was, but stopped herself and walked on. From behind, came quiet laughter.

The valuers were in the large room that Minerva had turned into a dining room for her dinner parties. Three men and a woman sat at the long, glass table, each with a miniputer in front of them. They all looked up as Affie and Freda came in, and the oldest man said, 'Ah. And is this Affroditey at last?'

Affie was taken aback to be spoken to – or of – so carelessly. She waited for someone to rebuke this man and tell him to speak to her more respectfully, but no one did.

The man – he had a long, tanned face and a thick head of wavy dark hair – looked at his colleague. 'We'll value Freda first. The figures?'

'Wait a moment,' Affie said. 'I want to say something.'

'Do you?' said the oldest man, without calling her 'Freechild' or even 'Free'. 'Then you can wait.'

Affie was silent with shock. Then, her hair glowing pink, she said, 'It's important!'

'Then it will keep. Freew'm Peshek?'

The woman said, 'Freda's older now, so her value's down at least ten per cent.'

'More,' said one of the younger men. 'Doubt you'll get a resale.'

The woman cocked her head. 'Are you taking into account her considerable experience managing children?'

'Child-managers are a glut – and she's old. Look at her. Stooped, greying, wrinkled – nobody's going to want her around.'

Freda said, 'Excuse me, Freemen, Freewoman. Please? How does my account stand?'

Looking at her screen, not at Freda, the woman said, 'Haven't paid off the interest yet.'

Freda made a small sound of dread.

The older man was looking at Affie. 'Those clothes – and those earrings! What are they?'

'Studs!' Affie said, surprised he didn't know.

'Zircon? Diamanté? Diamond?'

'Aquamarine.'

'Take them off,' said the man. 'Why are you wearing them?'

'They're mine!' Affie said.

The valuers all raised their heads and looked at her with blank puzzlement. It would have been preferable if they'd laughed. Less cold.

'They're not yours *any more*,' the woman said, and shook her head slightly, as if in disbelief. 'These are yours.' She pushed a cardboard box across the table. 'The only things that *are* yours.'

Affie stepped closer to the table, and opened the box. Inside was the little, silver tree with the photos and mementoes of her ancestors.

'They're quite valuable, with those frames,' said Freewoman Peshek, on a slightly sour, disapproving note, and Affie realised that she was begrudged her ancestors, though they couldn't be withheld from her. 'I'd look after them if I were you.'

Suddenly remembering, Affie said, 'Where's Pookie?'

'Where's what?' the oldest man said, irritably.

'Pookie – my pet.' She turned on Freda. 'I told you to look after her.'

'She means the miniature cheetah,' Freewoman Peshek said.

'Ah.' The man smiled. 'Pookie's considerably more valuable than you are. She'll go to a good home.'

Affie stared at them. 'You *sold* Pookie?'

'Not yet, but she's being well looked after. Now—'

'She's mine.'

'*Nothing* is yours,' said the oldest man. 'Can we move on? Have we a suit of clothes for her?'

'Certain thing,' said the younger man, and reached down to the floor beside him, snatching something up and dumping it on the table. A heap of cheap, green cloth.

'You'll need to change into those before you leave the house,' said the oldest man.

'I won't need to change,' Affie said, her hands still in her box of ancestors, 'because I won't be going anywhere.' The fact that they had dared to take Pookie away without even telling her made her all the more determined to have her say.

They looked questioningly at her, and exchanged amused glances with each other.

'I haven't been able to get in touch with my mother, but as soon as she hears, she'll pay off my bond. So. You see. I won't need those – horrible clothes.'

'Hmm,' said the oldest man. He reached into the flat case that was open on the table before him and took out a piece of paper. 'I think this might interest you.'

Affie didn't want to take it, because she knew it would be something awful, but he kept holding it out. 'What is it?'

The man turned the piece of paper back towards himself and looked at it. 'A communication from lawyers acting for your mother, stating that she is not your legal guardian, and has no interest in your case.'

'*What?*' That was a bit much, even for her mother. Affie took the piece of paper and tried to read it, though her eyes were filling with tears and her hand shook.

Freda, standing beside her, put her hand on her arm with a slight, gentle touch. She had always known that Freewoman Lloyd would let her daughter down. Helping Affie would have stressed her out and given her a migraine.

'This could be from anyone!' Affie said. 'It doesn't mean anything!'

'We have, of course, checked it,' said Freewoman Peshek, sounding personally insulted. 'The firm does exist, they are reputable and, apparently, they handle all your mother's business. And your mother isn't your legal guardian – she signed away her rights in you at the time of your parents' divorce. Your guardian is Minerva Millington.'

'Oh, Gods,' Affie said. Blue waves moved through her hair and shone a blue light onto her face.

'Who instructed us,' said the oldest man, 'to proceed and clear matters up as quickly as possible. You have been bonded. I suggest you resign yourself to it and stop wasting our time. Now – her value?'

They studied her. 'Young and attractive,' said one of the other men, and tapped at his miniputer. What he tapped out must have appeared on the other screens, because they all peered at them.

'Experience?' said the woman. 'Abilities?'

They all looked at Affie again, as if expecting her to list her abilities. She could think of nothing to say.

'That hair,' said the oldest man. 'Genetically altered, I suppose?'

'Yes,' Affie said, glad to have something she could talk about. 'They take genes from—'

'I'm not at all interested in where the genes come from,' said the man, looking away. 'Most unsuitable. It must be cut.'

'Cut!' Affie's hair turned blue and green. 'Why?'

But the man hadn't spoken for her benefit – one of the others was making a note. 'Do you have any skills?'

'I – I don't know! I won't have my hair cut!'

'Presumably, you can read and write. Instrument?'

'What?'

'Say, "Excuse me, Freeman," when you speak to me. Do you play an instrument?'

'No.'

'"No, *Freeman*." Can you cook? – no, of course you can't. Can't do housework, either. Any experience of childcare?'

Affie was so angry at being made to feel small that she could barely speak. Her hair had an orange glow. 'No.' *Her?* Child care?

'Hmm. Note down that she isn't quick to learn. "No, *Freeman*."'

The woman had been studying Affie and now turned to the older man. 'I imagine our Affie's quite the dab hand with make-up and hair.'

Affie trembled with rage that she had to control. '*Our Affie!*'

The older man brightened. 'Are you? Good with that sort of thing?'

What was she supposed to say? Yes, she'd learned to apply her own make-up rather well, and sometimes enjoyed doing it, but . . .

'And you have no other skills at all? Maybe she'll make a lady's maid . . .'

'That's what I was thinking . . .'

'But with no experience, and her unfortunate back-ground . . . Oh, well.' Looking up at Affie, he said, 'I don't suppose you know what happens next?'

'No,' Affie said, '*Freeman*.'

'Your bond is held by the Hera Agency, so you'll be taken to one of their holding stations—'

'A training station, initially, I would think,' said Freewoman Peshek.

'Yes, very possibly. Whatever training you're given, the

cost will be added to your price – that's why it will be greatly to your advantage if you tell us now about any skills you have.'

'I—' Affie said, but her brain had frozen and nothing came to mind.

'The agency has repaid to the bank the money that was borrowed against you. So now you owe that money to the agency, plus the interest that accrues. Do you understand?'

'I think so,' Affie said, feeling scared and baffled.

'When someone hires you, a portion of the price they pay the agency will be offset against the money you owe the agency. If you earn money, in tips, or by taking other jobs, you can repay more. If you improve your skills, you'll command a higher price when you're resold, and that may reduce your debt too. Work hard, and you may be able to buy yourself out. Good news?'

'But—' Affie said. 'If I'm bought by someone – when will I have time to do other jobs?'

'You will make the time if you really want to buy your freedom.'

'And what if the same family keeps me for years? There won't be a resale.'

The oldest man shook his head irritably, as if she was making difficulties where none existed. 'Then you will have to exert yourself a little, and earn tips and make yourself useful wherever you can.'

'There is the matter,' said the woman, 'of a mirror destroyed – and several hundred euros worth of perfume and cosmetics – plus the bill for cleaning the carpet. It will all have to be added to her outstanding loan.'

Affie turned and looked at Freda. 'I didn't tell them,' Freda said, drawing back.

'Ah, yes, thank you. Of course, any other costs you incur – breakages, clothes, food, medical treatment – will be added to your bill.'

Affie had a dizzying vision of her debt madly spiralling up and up, interest piling on interest, and every meal and every item of clothing adding yet more. 'How can I ever pay it, *how*?'

The valuers looked at their screens. 'That is really not our affair,' said the oldest man. 'Our business is to assess your value, which we have done, and then to move on to valuing the house and contents. Now, if you will change out of those clothes . . .'

'There's a small cloakroom across the corridor where she could change,' said Freewoman Peshek.

'Excellent. If you could accompany – er – Affie, Freew'm Peshek, and make sure of those earrings.'

'Certainly.' Freewoman Peshek rose and gathered up the bundle of clothes. She came around the table, holding out her arm to usher Affie along with her. For a moment, Affie thought of refusing to move, but then, feeling helpless, obediently walked out into the corridor.

'Take the earrings off first,' Freewoman Peshek said, as Affie was about to go into the cloakroom.

Affie obeyed. Her eyes filled with tears as she fumbled to take out the studs. Freewoman Peshek held out her hand, and Affie dropped the earrings into her palm. The sight of them lying there, on the creased skin, was so sad. They were *hers*!

'In you go. Please hurry up.'

There was little space in the cloakroom, and it was a humiliating struggle to take off all her clothes, balancing awkwardly on one foot, and having to drape the expensive shirt and suit over the sink or drop them onto the floor because there was nowhere to hang them. The clothes she had to put on were even more horrible than she'd thought. There was no underwear supplied, so she kept her own on, pulling the baggy trousers and loose tunic over them. They were styleless, and a nasty shade of green. Even in the small mirror, she could see they made her look dreadful.

A fit of crying came on. It was as if they were trying to turn her into someone else.

A rapping on the door. 'Aren't you ready yet?'

Affie looked at her crying self in the mirror, and wondered what to do. No point in prolonging things. She would have to go out eventually. Perhaps, because she was crying, pity would be taken on her.

She gathered up her clothes and, snuffling and whimpering, went out.

Freewoman Peshek didn't notice that she was crying. She took the clothes and sorted through them. 'Don't you wear undies? Where are they?'

'I kept them on.'

'Why? I told you to change into what you were given.'

'But – I can't—'

'Go back in and take off the undies you're wearing – they aren't yours.'

'Surely I can keep a bra and panties!'

'No.'

'But what shall I wear?'

'Nothing.'

Affie cried, loudly. How could she go without underwear? It was dirty, it was rude. It was cold. She would get a cold in her kidneys, her boobs would sag and she'd lose her looks.

'For Gods' sake!' said Freewoman Peshek. 'Stop making a ridiculous fuss about every little thing and take them off. If you don't, they'll only be taken off you when you get where you're going, and they'll have to be delivered back to us, and we'll charge you for it. You want to keep your debt down, don't you?'

Sobbing, Affie went back into the cloakroom and undressed again.

She came out, and handed her underwear to Freewoman Peshek, feeling angry, but afraid to show it, and thoroughly humiliated and miserable.

Freewoman Peshek led her back into the dining room, where the man with the little printer handed her a sheet of paper. She folded it neatly into a plastic packet from her briefcase, and pinned it to Affie's green tunic with a metal clip.

'Your paperwork. Don't worry about it. They'll deal with that at the other end.'

Affie felt like a small child.

Freewoman Peshek handed her the box containing her ancestors. 'Come along, I'll take you out to the van.'

She led Affie through the house, through the empty kitchens and out into the yard. At the yard's entrance, a large van was parked, painted black with the Goddess's face picked out in gold. 'Hera Agency' it said, in gold lettering.

A security man was leaning against the van's side. 'Here's the last of them,' Freewoman Peshek said, and the man opened the van's sliding door.

Affie, clutching her box, stood looking at the van's dark interior and the dimly seen people inside.

'Well, *get in*,' Freewoman Peshek said, and, to the security man, 'Honestly, it's a good job she had money because she is *dim*.'

Affie climbed into the van and the door was slid shut behind her. Inside were her father's bonders.

'Hello, Affie. Fancy seeing you here.'

'Where did you get that outfit? That's *your* colour.'

A laugh went up, grating on Affie like sandpaper on skin. They were so cruel.

'Freechild Affie – come and sit by me.'

That was Freda's voice. As Affie peered round for her, there were mocking, 'Oohs'.

'Ooh, Freechild Affie.'

'No need to suck up now, Freda – it can't get you anything.'

'Let the little cow fend for herself like you always had to.'

'Never you mind 'em,' Freda said, reaching out a hand and guiding Affie to her. And as Affie huddled against her and the van started moving, she said, 'It won't be as bad as you think it'll be. Nothing ever is.'

Affie thought it would be worse.

Good News

Affie was in etiquette class when a buzzer sounded, and a voice from the wall speaker said, 'Affie Millington to the manager's office, now.'

A little role-play drama was being acted out at the front of the class: one girl was enjoying herself by being a stroppy, demanding house guest, and the bonder was having to appease her. The bark from the speakers made the actors falter; and there was a stirring in the class as people looked round at Affie. She cringed, hating to be stared at, and embarrassed by her long name. Most bonders were known by one name, and perhaps a number – Kylie 200, Jaylo 80.

The class tutor, Miss Azagury-Becker was glaring at Affie, the cause of the interruption. Like most of the tutors, Miss Azagury-Becker was a bonder, but a grand one. She put people on report for the slightest thing.

'I'm sorry, Miss!' Affie said.

'You had better go, Affie,' the tutor said, quite affably. 'Perhaps it's a purchaser for you. Good luck!'

Affie bowed, and hurried from the class.

She made her way through the centre's narrow corridors, her heart racketing with apprehension, feeling sick, walking as fast as she could, but not daring to run, in case she was seen and put on report. Had one of the instructors complained about her, said she was inattentive or not trying hard enough? Or accused her of showing an unco-operative attitude again? She'd thought that her behaviour over the past six months – ever since her time in solitary – had been everything the instructors could ask for. She'd tried hard: arranging her face carefully into pleasant, willing expressions; running over every word in her mind before she spoke it; concentrating on being good, all the time. It was exhausting.

Maybe one of her fellow trainees had accused her of something – or blamed her for something they'd done or forgotten to do. What had they said? It was useless trying to guess when it might be anything, but she wished she had an idea, even if only to lessen the uncertainty.

Her most insistent hope was that this wouldn't mean another stint in solitary. She'd hated it so much, being all alone with her unhappiness, and it had taken her so long to win back privileges, and a measure of goodwill from the instructors. She passed the door of a toilet block, and almost ducked inside, to lock the door on herself and hide. As long as she stayed there, nothing could happen – then she realised how stupid – and how much like her mother – that would be, and punched herself. She would be locking herself in solitary again, and if it did put off the moment of punishment, it would only prolong the pain of anxiety. Her mother, being free and rich, could count on everyone pardoning her and excusing her. When Affie was eventually found – as she inevitably would be – there would be no excuses, and the longer she'd been hidden, the more she would be blamed. It would be no good telling them that she'd hadn't felt strong enough to face up to whatever was waiting for her in the manager's office. No one would listen or feel sorry for her. She hurried on, as fast as she could walk, to find out the worst.

The manager's office, like all the administrative offices, was in a narrow corridor, with pale green walls, and a shabby beige carpet. Filing cabinets stood along the walls at intervals, leaving little space. Affie came to a halt outside the manager's grubby cream door.

Just knock, she told herself, but couldn't persuade her arm to lift from her side.

She was still standing there, trying to nerve herself to knock, when the door was yanked open and the manager – a short, burly man – charged out, making her jump.

He stopped short and peered at her. 'Who are you?'

'Affroditey Millington, Freeman. You sent for me, Freeman.'

He blinked. 'So I did.' He was still holding the handle of his door, and pushed it wide. 'Go in and wait. You may sit down.' He hurried off down the corridor.

Affie went slowly into the office. She left the door open because she hadn't been told to close it – besides, closing the door would have been like saying that she owned the office. It might have been interpreted as 'inappropriate attitude'.

She didn't sit down, either, though she'd been given permission. She stood beside the armchair that was placed in front of the desk. On the desk sat a computer and printer, with an untidy tray of papers and folders beside it. Against the wall was a large filing cabinet, filling most of the office's free space and, on the windowsill, some drooping potted plants. What Affie liked most were the photographs, on the desk, and on the walls – photos of children, and a hand-fasting ceremony. It was a scruffy little room, but such a change from the bareness of most of the training centre, where it seemed nothing was allowed that was not strictly useful, and even then, it must be the plainest and cheapest thing available.

A long time passed in waiting. No one thought her time important. Affie looked out of the window at a dreary view of a small car park surrounded by walls. Dreary, but it looked like freedom. Could I open the window and climb out? she wondered. She played with the idea for a few minutes, to pass the time, but knew that she wouldn't dare. She might be caught, and punished.

When she'd first been brought here, she'd been so sure of herself. It was like remembering someone else.

When the van pulled up at the training centre, the security man had called out, 'Millington!' Affie had waited, to see what would happen. Looking round, she saw people grinning at her. No one else moved. 'Millington!' the security man yelled again, on an angrier note.

'You have to get out, love,' Freda said. Not 'Freechild', but 'love'. Affie hadn't known whether to be angry or touched.

She'd got up, awkwardly, clutching her box of ancestors, and made her way down the narrow aisle. There seemed to be a lot of feet and legs in her way. Reaching the pavement, she'd stood there, looking at the depressingly ugly, box-like buildings, and wondering what she was supposed to do next. And then Freda jumped out of the van and hugged her.

'Goodbye, sweetheart. Good luck. It won't be so bad, don't worry. Just do as you're told – that'll make everything easier.' Then Freda had got back into the van, while everyone else on board mockingly called, 'Goodbye! Good luck!'

It had been good advice Freda had given her, but she hadn't taken it.

The training centre was a complex of cheap, shabby, ugly buildings, set in the middle of a factory estate, where it was noisy, grimy and often smelly. The security man led her to the door. He'd spoken to someone inside by intercom, and the door had unlocked with a click. They'd gone inside and waited until a woman in a dark uniform came and unclipped Affie's paperwork from her tunic. The security man left without looking at her or saying goodbye, as if he'd dropped off a parcel. The door locked automatically behind him.

'What's that you've got there?' the woman asked.

'My ancestors.'

The woman frowned, puzzled. 'It's a big bloody box, isn't it?'

Affie was puzzled in turn. 'No. No – it's—'

The woman, without asking permission, flipped open the top of the box. 'Blow Zeus!' She reached in and partly pulled out the silver tree with its dangling, silver-framed photos.

Affie, despite her own neglect of her ancestors, was shocked and insulted. To just reach in a big, grubby mitt and grab hold of someone's ancestors like that! 'Do you mind?'

'Not at all, darling,' the woman said. 'You're the rich girl, right? That explains it. I thought it was a big box for a few bits of beads – that's all most of 'em have got. Well, you can't keep this little lot in your personal locker. Too valuable. I shall have to make out a form, put 'em in the safe. Are you going to cause a lot of trouble, little rich girl?'

'You could be civil,' Affie said.

The woman laughed, turned and walked away, saying, over her shoulder, 'Come on.' Affie followed, carrying her box, into a narrow, dark corridor.

The woman turned into a small room where a computer stood on a desk, and the walls were hung with cluttered noticeboards and tatty posters, most of which seemed to be about communicable diseases, which Affie didn't think very nice.

'Put your box on that table,' the woman said. Affie did, pushing aside piles of papers and boxes of leaflets to do so. She turned to see the woman holding up an iris reader. 'Look in here.'

'*Please*,' Affie had said, something that now made her cringe to remember.

'Eh?' the woman said.

'*Please* look in here,' Affie said. 'Or look in here, please. As you will.'

The woman's face turned hard and angry. 'Don't be smart with me. Just look in there.'

Sighing, Affie looked into the reader, while the woman watched as the computer checked the iris pattern against a database, and confirmed that she was Affroditey Millington.

'Now strip.'

'What?'

'Strip. *Strip*. Take off your sodding clothes.'

'In here? Now? Why?'

'Just do as you're told. I'm not paid to listen to your gripes.'

'But why? You can't just tell me to strip and expect me to do it,' Affie said, very reasonably, she thought.

The woman thrust her ugly, poor person's face towards her, all twisted up with sudden and rather frightening anger. 'Listen—' she started, and then the door opened and another woman in a dark uniform came in.

'Oh – is this the new arrival?'

The first woman returned to normal, and nodded towards the box on the table. 'Her, and all her bloody ancestors.'

The second woman went over, looked in the box, and pulled a mock-impressed face. 'Nice.' She looked Affie over. 'That hair'll have to go. Not suitable.'

'You are not,' Affie said, 'cutting off my hair.'

'Not just yet, no,' said the second woman. 'First, you'll have your med. So strip.'

Well, medical exams were good things, Affie supposed, so she stripped, and was weighed. Electrodes were attached to her hands and feet, to measure her body fat and bone density. Her heart was listened to, and her blood pressure tested, as well as her lung capacity. Then she had to shower in a cramped little sonic cubicle, which somehow seemed grimy to her, though how could it be? The sonic waves would clean it, as they cleaned anything inside it. When she came out of the cubicle, she was given an antibacterial fluid to rub over herself, which stung. She didn't enjoy that at all – nor did she like the look of the rough little towel she was given to dry herself. To her, it had a grubby look, and she didn't want to touch her body with it. But it was the only thing offered, so she used it, with distaste, and dressed again in the horrible green trousers and tunic. But she wasn't, she decided, putting up with any more nonsense.

'Now,' said one of the women, 'let's get that hair cropped.'

'I *told* you,' Affie said, 'I am not having my hair touched.' Honestly, with these undesigned people, you had to keep repeating yourself again and again.

The two women looked stolidly at her, more amused than angry. 'Bonders don't have long, jellyfish hair,' said one. 'Now, do they?'

'Bonders might not, but I *do*,' Affie remembered saying.

'Please yourself,' the woman said. 'We'll put the tracer in first, then.' And from the desk she picked up a needle gun.

'What's the tracer?' Affie asked, eyeing the gun.

'You ask too many questions,' said the first woman.

'Drop your kecks and bend over,' said the other.

Affie didn't move. 'What are you going to do?'

The woman with the gun waved it impatiently. 'I've got to put your tracer in.'

'What's a tracer?'

'Just bend over, shut your mouth and pull your trousers down,' said the other woman.

The one with the needle gun said, 'It's just a little ID tag – a tracer transmitter, y'know. I've just got to put it in your bum. Only take a second. Won't hurt.'

'You are *not*,' Affie said, 'injecting *anything* into me!'

The woman sighed. 'I've got to. It's—'

'Enough,' said the other woman and touched her fingers

to studs on her belt. She said, 'Medcalf, Lutyens, to room 3A please.' To Affie, she said, 'So you won't have your hair cut and you won't have the tracer, eh?'

Affie said, 'You can't make me—' Then the door opened and two big men came in.

And they made her. They took her by the arms, dragged her to the desk and bent her over it. Affie yelled; she yelled until her throat hurt and she thought her lungs might be emptied out of her mouth. Her anger didn't intimidate anyone. The women laughed. 'Look at that hair!' The men pinned her to the desk with bored indifference. No one came to find out what was going on; no one came to help.

Affie fought with a desperation partly born of astonishment and partly of disbelief. In her memory, no one had ever laid hands on her like that, and she was amazed to discover that they could. Nor had she realised that there were people in the world so much stronger and heavier than her. The strength of her muscles soon gave out, and they were no more use than wet towels.

'Keep her still,' said one of the women, and Affie felt her trousers pulled down, and the sting as the transmitter was fired into her buttock, followed by the chill of antiseptic.

The men lifted Affie up. Her face was scarlet, and she was sobbing.

'Are you going to let us give you a nice haircut?' asked one of the women.

Affie understood that if she didn't let them cut her hair, the men would hold her down again. She couldn't bear it. She sat down in the chair and tried to speak, but could only sob.

'She's going to be good now,' said one of the women, and the men went off.

All the time her hair was being cut – as it fell in curls and piles on the floor around her – Affie trembled and sobbed. It wasn't just the loss of her hair. It was the realisation that she wasn't safe. That force could, and would, be used against her; and that the people who did it weren't afraid and didn't feel guilty, because they hadn't done anything wrong. They were allowed to treat her like that now.

She realised that she had no defence and no appeal. That she had no choices any more – that if she didn't do as she was told, she would be made to obey, and nobody pitied her, or thought it unjust, or cared at all. This was shattering to her.

The woman used clippers to shave her perfectly bald. 'That's good,' said one. 'Be longer before you need it done again.'

The two women then turned to the computer and, while Affie stood by, filled out a receipt for the box of ancestors, one telling the other what to type. They printed off a copy and gave it to her. 'Keep it safe,' one said.

The other laughed. 'She'll lose it the first week.'

It frightened Affie more, that they could calmly turn to form filling after assaulting her. This place was a terrible place. She hadn't realised. She'd thought it would be uncomfortable, embarrassing, maybe scary – she hadn't known she would be attacked by the people in charge. Who was supposed to protect her from the bonders? She was meek and docile – indeed, meek and trembling – as she was issued with her kit: a change of clothing, sheets, a blanket, a towel, toothbrush and paste.

'Don't lose any of it – you'll be put on a report if you do.'

'We should put her on report, anyway.'

'Ah, give the kid a break – she's new. Daresay she'll be on report soon enough. Come on. I'll take you to your dormitory.'

Affie wanted to ask what would happen to her ancestors – they suddenly seemed very precious – but was afraid to say anything. She gladly followed the woman – who seemed the kinder of the two – relieved to be leaving the angry one behind.

In the dormitory, ten beds were lined up on either side of the room, each with a locker beside it. They looked cold and hard and, like everything else in the centre, grimy.

'Make your bed, and then sit quietly. Somebody'll come and fetch you for assessment when we're ready.'

Affie wanted to ask where everyone else was, but she was still unnerved, and the woman had gone before she could speak. She looked at the dusty, dirty mattress, and the folded sheets and thin duvet. She'd never made a bed. She looked round, as if half expecting Freda, or someone, to come and do it for her. Then she sat down on the edge of the bed and cried. Probably, she would never see Freda again. Or Pookie. It was as if they'd died, like her father. No one here would help her.

She cried for perhaps ten minutes, wiped her eyes, and looked round. No one had come. The bed was still unmade. What would happen if – when someone did come – she hadn't made the bed? She could explain that she didn't know how . . . She remembered what had happened when she'd refused to have the tracer injected.

Jumping up, she looked down at the bed, trying to remember what a made bed looked like. She unfolded the thin, grubby sheets and spread them out over the bed, trying to touch them only with her fingertips, and as little as possible. It still didn't look right. After a moment, she realised that the sheets should be tucked under the mattress, so she did that – hating to have to touch the mattress. Something gritty kept getting under her nails, and she was driven to wipe her fingers on her trousers every few moments. She wasn't looking forward to sleeping in that bed.

With the bed made as well as she could manage, she sat on it, glad to be alone. The people she'd already met had been horrible, and frightening, which gave her no great hope of anyone else. And the mere thought of the other bonders alarmed her. They would be rough, and crude, and dangerous – far worse, probably, than the people who had assaulted her with the needle gun. She felt very scared again. This life wasn't worth living.

After another fifteen minutes, a woman came along, more smartly dressed than the others and not in uniform. She looked at the hologram floating above her palm and said, 'Millington? Come with me.' She didn't seem at all surprised at Affie's baldness, which was both comforting and depressing, because this was a place where people expected shaven heads.

Affie followed her to a small box of a room, painted entirely in grubby cream, with the plainest of tables and chairs. It was all so boring and dreary, it made Affie's heart ache. 'Sit down,' said the woman. 'I'm going to test you. Don't worry.' The woman didn't smile; her manner wasn't reassuring. She was merely passing on information. 'Nothing too difficult, and nothing will hurt.'

The tests turned out to be mildly amusing, and it was an immense relief that they were so easy, but Affie found it hard to see the point of them. She read a passage aloud, and answered the woman's questions about it. She typed out a passage dictated by the woman, and then wrote out, by hand, another dictation – which she managed, but not so well, since she hadn't had as much practice in handwriting.

Then there were some puzzles to solve: look at this series of shapes, or numbers – which of these shapes or numbers would come next? A general knowledge quiz followed, and then a long interview where the woman asked many questions about Affie's life and experience. Affie, still frightened and eager to please, answered as fully and politely as she could.

'Right,' said the woman, at last. 'I'll take you to the dining hall.'

This was another plain, drab room, with ugly, exposed pipes and girders in the roof. People were seated at the tables and queuing at the counter, but there was only a desultory murmur of conversation. Affie's heart beat very fast. All those horrible, undesigned, rough people. All very well when they were your bonders and you could count on them doing as you told them, but when you were thrown in among them, on the same level . . . Who knew what they might do? She was conscious of her own baldness too. Cautiously peeping round, she saw no one else with a head shaved as bald as hers, though a few had a close crop. They would laugh at her baldness – it might give them a reason to attack her.

When she had stood in the queue for a while, and no one had attacked her – or, apparently, taken any notice of her – she calmed somewhat, and was able to peep about her. These people were lumpen and plain, certainly – all gawky shoulders, red hands and pimply skin. Some of them had been shaved bald, too, like her. They seemed docile.

She reached the front of the line and was given her food. It wasn't good. A plate of greasy chips and a thick slice of bread spread with margarine. Yet she heard enthusiasm expressed around her. 'Ooh – chips today!'

With her loaded tray, she looked round for somewhere to sit, hoping for a place by herself, but uniformed supervisors were ushering people to tables, and she had to take a place at one that was already crowded. Ashamed of her baldness and afraid of the bonders surrounding her, she kept her head down and her eyes on the unappetising food. But others were looking at her.

'You're new,' said the person beside her.

Affie, glancing at the speaker so briefly that she didn't see anything about her, nodded.

'What's your name?'

'Affroditey Millington.'

'Ooh. Two names. Are you designed?'

'No,' Affie said quickly.

She was conscious of the stare from beside her, and of someone leaning close from her other side.

'Go on,' said this new person. 'You are. You're designed.'

Affie didn't know what to say, and looked hard at the table.

''S all right, there's lots of designed people here,' said the person to her left.

'Well, a few,' said the person to her right.

'So, what happened to you?' asked Left-hand.

'I – er—' Affie started to cry.

'Ssh, ssh,' Left-hand said. 'Shut up – they'll be coming.'
Affie struggled to keep her sobs quiet.

'Eat your food,' Left-hand whispered. 'You won't get any
more.'

Affie ate, surprised that she'd been given such kindly
advice. Perhaps it was only because she'd seemed so pathetic,
bald and weeping. Give them another day or two, and they
might still attack her.

After the meal, lessons began. In small, bare rooms, with
four or five others, she was given lessons in cutting and
styling hair, using bonders from within the centre to practise
on. The other pupils were bonders between purchasers, who
were increasing or refreshing their skills, and Affie had never
cut or styled hair before in her life, not even her own. It had
always been done for her. She was afraid to touch anything
and, when ordered to pick up a comb, felt her hands become
weak and almost paralysed with doubt and fear. The instructors – bonders owned by the training centre – were
contemptuous of her, and soon ignored her, preferring to
teach the others. Affie would have learned nothing at all if it
hadn't been for her fellow trainees, who sometimes left their
own work to help her. They were not – and she felt great
thankfulness for it – as fierce and frightening as she had
dreaded, these bonders. Many of them were older and, like
Freda, were kind, even if they were ugly, and sometimes
crude.

Affie was thankful to tears for the kindness, because she

spent her days in an agitation of nerves, eager to obey every rule, do well at every lesson and win praise; because this was a place where anything might be done to her if she failed to please. It often seemed that her very eagerness made her clumsy and stupid: she dropped things, she forgot things, she confused things.

She was often so nervous that her stomach was unsettled and she couldn't eat much – the food was always bad. She lost weight, and her hair grew back, and was cropped again. Every night she was exhausted, and she'd long ago given up feeling disgust for her bed. It was often cold, though, and hard to sleep, and she would think of her father, and miss Pookie and Freda, and cry, and wake hungry, tired and sick at heart at the thought of the anxious day ahead of her.

It was with a sort of desperate despair that, one day, she refused to get out of bed. She knew that someone would come to find out why she hadn't got up, and she waited for their arrival with a mixture of fear and defiance.

Along came one of the uniformed supervisors. Was she ill? Affie tried saying that she was. 'Up on your feet and along to Med.'

The doctor was unable to find anything wrong but allowed her a day in bed anyway. Triumph! Affie luxuriated in it, but returned to classes the next day, afraid to push her luck.

After that, she felt that she was learning the ropes, and had relaxed just a little – which led to her shouting at a tutor, 'How do you expect me to learn when you never show me how to do anything properly?' And she'd thrown her scissors onto the floor.

They put her in solitary for 'attacking an instructor'. They took hold of her, dragged her along – she realised anew, with fresh shock, that that could actually be done to her now – and then they bundled her into a small cell, and locked her in.

There was no window, and no bed – just a slightly raised bench along one wall. No pillow, no blankets. Nothing to watch, nothing to do. They left her there for four days. At night, she was too cold to do more than doze, waking miserably to miserable thoughts, again and again. Three times a day, a small door was opened in the large one, and a hand pushed in a flask of water and a thick slice of bread.

No one had told her how long the punishment would last. She thought she would go mad. Hunger became intense, far worse than she had ever experienced. Unhappiness overwhelmed her: why had this happened to her? What had she done to deserve it, why had her father cared so little for her, why didn't her mother love her, why hadn't her ancestors answered her prayers? For days, she raged and wept that it was so unfair, that she'd been so cruelly treated. She cried so much that she was bored with crying, but there was nothing else to think about and nothing else to do.

Perhaps, came the idea, people deserted you, not because they are hateful, but because *you* are. Perhaps you *do* deserve all this. Maybe you're a nasty, unlovable person. That was a jarring thought. It might be true.

The misery went so deep that when they let her out, she was grateful. When they gave her one of the centre's meals, she enjoyed it. It was such a relief merely to be out of that cell, and to see people again, even if they were ugly bonders.

She never wanted to go into solitary again. She was ready to be good, to do everything she was told, to like the centre, to love the supervisors.

The manager came back and looked surprised to see her still standing in his office. 'Sit down, sit down,' he said, as he went behind his desk.

She sat, feeling guilty.

'Good news!' he said. 'There's a purchaser wants to have a look at you!'

Purchased

This was what she had hoped for, almost – to be bought, to be taken out of the hateful training centre. But now that there was a buyer, she felt cold and nauseous. Too much was happening too soon. A buyer wasn't a rescuer, but someone who would own her, judge her, find fault and punish. Someone she would have to please and obey – someone worse than all her instructors put together.

'No,' she said.

'Oh, yes,' said the manager. 'I just have to get back to her.' He clicked buttons on his keyboard and, looking at his monitor, said brightly, 'Ah, Freewoman Perry! Glad to see you again! I've got the girl I told you about right here, if you'd like to take a look.'

'Certainly, if I may,' said a voice from the speakers beneath the desk.

'Putting her on,' said the manager, and he mouthed at Affie, and pointed out the cam she was to look into, perched on a wall bracket behind his desk.

Affie gripped the sides of her seat and stared at the cam, feeling her face set into an expression of terror.

'She's bald,' said the voice from the speakers. 'Why is she bald?'

'Oh – ah—' The manager tapped keys as he consulted Affie's file. 'She has genetically altered hair. It wasn't thought suitable.'

'Genetically altered? A bonder?'

'Oh, this girl wasn't born a bonder. Comes from an excellent background, in fact, very well spoken, very—'

'In that case, I'm not sure I'm interested. And her being bald is very unsightly. It makes you think she's diseased. Would there be a reduction?'

'We're already offering her at what I feel is a very competitive price, but there might be space for a little fine-tuning.'

'She's very *pretty*,' Freewoman Perry said, as if it was a bad thing. 'Despite the bald head.'

'She's designed. Very decorative—'

'I don't want her to be decorative, I want her to work. Is she a hard worker? – she doesn't look it.'

'Her instructors report that she's hard-working, has made enormous progress, and has an excellent attitude – quiet, obedient, keen to please . . .'

Affie had never imagined that being designed and beautiful would be a reason for being passed over. Her eyes burned with tears when she heard herself called unsightly and possibly diseased. But to cry wouldn't show good attitude.

'What can she do?' Freewoman Perry asked.

'Well, her main training has been in hair care and hairstyling, and in beauty generally.'

'Good, good—'

'But she's a bright enough girl. I daresay, with a little instruction, she could perform most tasks about the house.'

'Child care?'

'That comes naturally to most girls, we find. I'm sure you would be very happy with her.'

'I'm sure I would,' said Freewoman Perry, on rather a sarcastic note. 'What's your name, girl?'

Affie had been nervous and restless under the gaze of this woman she couldn't see. Now, suddenly addressed, she found her voice had gone.

'Her given name is Affroditey,' said the manager.

'Oh, no, that wouldn't do at all. That would have to be changed. Thank you – I have some other bonds to consider. I may get back to you.'

'Please do. Always ready to do business. I don't think you'll find anyone selling cheaper than us, but if you do, please come back, and it may be that we can come to some arrangement.'

'Very well. Goodbye.'

'Goodbye, and a pleasure doing business with you.' The manager broke the link and jerked his head at Affie. 'Off you go.'

Affie quickly rose to her feet and, head down, hurried away. Etiquette class was over, and now she had to go to her beauty class and apologise to Miss Vaughn for being late.

Two days later, while she was eating lunch, the buzzer sounded and a voice boomed over the noise of the canteen, ordering Affroditey Millington to report to the office with her basic kit.

Startled, Affie said, aloud, 'Basic kit?'

'You been sold, love?' said the woman next to her.

A painful, sickening dart of dread went through Affie. 'What's basic kit?' The world was so frightening – she didn't know even the simplest things and didn't think she ever would.

'That's like toothbrush, change of underwear if you've got it – your basic kit, you know. Hurry up and finish your dinner and get off, don't keep him waiting.'

Affie gulped down the last of her pasta and, as she was swallowing, remembered her ancestors. She would have to ask for them to be released to her, and that would give the supervisors a chance to be unpleasant and difficult.

Her family had never made a lot of fuss about their ancestors. They'd just had them because everybody else did. At Yule, they went through the customs – had gone through the customs – of setting places at table for the returning dead, and offering a little sacrifice – cakes and wine, usually – but they'd never taken it very seriously. Maybe she should just forget . . .?

The thought had hardly started in her head before she reacted against it: No! They were her *ancestors*! Hers. She had to have them. Everybody did, even bonders, even if theirs were just bits of junk.

Leaving the refectory, she ran back to the dorm, grabbed together her kit, and then ran on to the office, where she tapped politely on the door. 'Excuse me,' she said to the woman at the computer. 'So sorry to bother you, but I think I've been sold, and I need my ancestors. They're in the safe.'

'In the safe?' the woman repeated. 'Your ancestors.'

'Yes. Silver trees and frames. They were locked up for safekeeping.'

'Oh – yes. You're the rich girl. The boss is waiting for you. Go into his office and I'll bring them along.'

'I must have them,' Affie said. 'They're my ancestors.'

'All right! I told you, I'll bring them along.'

Affie went along the corridor to the manager's office, where he was waiting for her, his door open. 'There you are. Freewoman Perry came back. Couldn't find a lower price anywhere. Come on.'

'Wait!' Affie said. 'We've got to—'

As the manager halted in surprise, along came the woman from the office, with a cardboard box in her arms. 'Here you are, as promised.' She put it into Affie's arms.

'What's this?' the manager said.

Affie hugged the box to her and turned slightly away from him, so he couldn't touch it. 'My ancestors.'

The manager laughed and, reaching out, took the lid from the box. He looked inside. 'Your ancestors!' he said, seeming surprised, and then a little put out. He replaced the lid. 'Your car awaits, your majesty. Let's get you delivered.'

It was strange to see real life again after her time in the training centre: the traffic in the streets; the people crowding everywhere, about their own business; bonders and free, designed and undesigned. Everything seemed so bright, so noisy – Affie was glad to see it, but also scared.

The house they drew up outside seemed strange, too: smart and brightly painted and rather small, like a toy house. It wasn't half as large or smart as her father's house had been. She realised that she was coming to be a bonder – a *bonder* – in this small house, and she felt herself shrivel with shame.

She wanted to be anywhere else – or, if she couldn't be, then just staying in the car for ever, crunched up in a ball, hiding her head, would do.

The manager got out of the car and opened the door, waiting for her to get out. When she wasn't quick enough, he said, 'Come on!' So she had to get out, awkwardly, because of the box and kit bag she had to carry. Despair and fear lay like heavy stones in the pit of her belly.

Carrying her things, she followed the manager up to the door. She looked at the sky, and thought of the music she'd played when she'd been able to choose the music she listened to, trying to withdraw from the world around her, to not know what was going on. She didn't really hear the knocking on the door, nor was she aware of it opening. Dreamily, she followed the manager inside, only dimly aware of a narrow hallway, a staircase and doors.

She came to a halt in a room where she tried not to see anything. There was a woman in there, probably Freewoman Perry, but she didn't want to know anything about her.

'So this is the girl. Isn't that bald head awful? It'll have to be covered with a scarf. What did you say your name was? Girl. Hey, girl? What's your name?'

Affie came out of her daze, and saw a pretty young woman with red hair seated in an armchair. She looked young, but probably wasn't – it just meant she could afford rejuvenation, if not a larger house. 'Affroditey Millington, Freewoman.'

'Millington?' The woman laughed. 'I don't think we need bother about surnames.'

Why not? Affie thought. That was my father's name. It's *my* name.

'Affroditey's no good for a maid. I can't talk about, "my maid, Affroditey". No. I think I shall have to call you "Kylie". That's a decent maid's name, don't you think?'

'Absolutely, I agree,' the manager said.

Affie thought: but Affroditey's my name. *My* name. That my mother and father gave me.

She thought about her mother and father. One of them had gone to the other side of the world and forgotten her; the other had killed himself rather than care for her. The name was all they'd left her.

'Your work, Kylie,' said Freewoman Perry, 'will be all sorts, really. Put your things down, girl. No one's going to steal them.'

She waited until Affie put the box and kit bag on the floor.

'As I was saying – you won't be bored. I shall certainly want you to help me with my hair and make-up, especially when I entertain – and you can wait, and take coats. And general housework, when I require it. And I have a little boy. I shall want you to take care of him from time to time. I shall expect you to work hard. Are you prepared to work hard, Kylie?'

Already I'm 'Kylie', Affie thought, but she said, 'Yes, Freewoman, of course, Freewoman.'

'Excellent. I hope she will suit. A month's trial?'

'A month's trial,' the manager agreed, rising. Affie watched them shake hands.

'Wake up, girl!' Freewoman Perry said, and Affie realised that the manager had gone and she was alone with her new mistress. 'I've spoken to you twice! I do hope you're not dim-witted. Come along with me. No – leave your things. I'll show you the house.'

Affie was led along a corridor towards the back of the house, passing closed doors on the way. 'Please remember,' Freewoman Perry said, 'that you are not to speak unless you are spoken to, and then you are to answer as to the point as possible. I do detest cheeky, impertinent girls who think I want to listen to their chatter.' Affie said nothing, and Freewoman Perry looked over her shoulder. 'Understood?'

'Yes, Freewoman.'

Freewoman Perry opened a door. 'This is the kitchen.' Affie followed her inside. 'Can you cook?'

'No, Freewoman.'

'No matter. I have a cook who comes in. But can you at least boil a kettle, make a sandwich?'

'I think – I think I can do that, Freewoman.' She had boiled a kettle, a couple of times in her life, and she knew how a sandwich was made, in theory.

'Good. You may have to feed my little one. Cook will show you where everything is. Whenever you have nothing else to do, I want you to come down here and help Cook. Understand?'

'Yes, Freewoman.'

'Now, when we don't have company, I want you to wait on us at table, so I'll show you to the dining room.' She led the way from the kitchen, back the way they'd come. 'Do you know how to lay a table?'

Affie had eaten at tables laid by others her whole life without ever taking much notice, but said, 'They taught us a little of it, Freewoman.' So they had, but she couldn't seem to remember much.

'Well, I'll show you exactly how I like it done. After meals, of course, you are to clear the table and wash up, and wash the cloth if it's been stained. I like my tablecloths spotless. You are familiar with laundry?'

'No, Freewoman. A bit, Freewoman. Not much.'

Freewoman Perry sighed heavily. 'Well, you are cheap. Ask Cook to show you – she's been doing the laundry for me. This is our sitting room.' Freewoman Perry had opened the door of another room, with sofas and a large television. 'I want all the furniture dusted once a day, upstairs and down – oh, and the carpets vacuumed, too – and everything polished at least twice a week. Plenty of elbow-grease!'

Affie's head was beginning to swim. How was she to fit all this in?

'You'll look after my clothes, of course – I expect you'll enjoy that. You'll be washing the ones that can be washed here, and ironing them –'

Affie gasped. She'd never ironed a thing in her life and had been taught nothing about it.

'– hanging them up, keeping them in repair, sewing on buttons, sewing up hems. I shall expect you to take them and collect them . . .'

Affie was shown Freewoman Perry's bedroom. 'You'll keep things tidy in here.' She was led on along the upper landing to a room painted brightly with cute tigers and cuddly, big-eyed bears. On a small bed lay a small boy, asleep.

'This is my son,' Freewoman Perry said, looking down at him. 'He's having his nap. Isn't he a cherub?'

Affie thought he looked like a child: pretty enough in a greetings card kind of way, but that was all that could be said. Indeed, he seemed rather alien to her.

'His name's Apollo. You may call him Freechild Apollo. I shall require you to look after him, keep him out of mischief. You won't find that too hard. Come along. I'll show you to your room.'

There was a door on the upper landing that opened onto a steep, narrow, uncarpeted stair, leading up to what had been the loft space. Up there was a tiny room, with a sloping roof and a dormer window. There was a bed covered with a counterpane, bright blue, but old and worn. Beside the bed was a straight chair and a small, cheap table. A small, old wardrobe, too. None of it fashionable or pretty.

'You have your own little bathroom, too,' said Freewoman Perry, 'so you see, you'll be quite comfortable.' She opened the door of the bathroom. It was tiny, holding a basin, a toilet and a shower. It was all white, clean, and inexpressibly bare and depressing. Looking around at her room, Affie felt like crying. There wasn't anything wrong with it – indeed, it was ten times better and more comfortable than the shared dormitories and washrooms at the training centre. It was the realisation that this was probably the best she could expect for the rest of her life that was so disheartening.

'Do you like it?' Freewoman Perry asked, smiling, and obviously wanting to hear her say, 'Yes'.

'Yes, Freewoman,' Affie said, her eyes full of tears.

Freewoman Perry sat down on the chair. 'Run down and get your things. I'll wait here.'

When Affie came back, out of breath, carrying her box

and her kit bag, Freewoman Perry was still sitting calmly on the chair. She rose, moved to the wardrobe and took out some clothes on a hanger. 'Here's your uniform. Change out of those things now – I'll have them sent back to the agency. There are two of everything, and I expect you to wash your clothes when you do the laundry and be well turned out at all times. Wear the heavy cap and apron for dirty work, but when you answer the door, put on the fancy ones. Understand?'

'Yes, Freewoman,' Affie said, putting her box and kit on the bed in order to take the clothes. She wondered how on earth she was to change cap and apron quickly enough to answer the door.

'When you wait at table, you are to put on this velvet dress and a clean fancy cap and apron. I shall be most displeased if you appear at table in anything stained or grubby. Understand?'

'Yes, Freewoman,' Affie said, feeling quite desperate.

Freewoman Perry calmly went to Affie's box, opened it, and took out the ancestors inside. 'But these are solid silver!'

What are *yours* made of? Affie thought. Plastic? She had to clamp her mouth shut. Bonders weren't allowed to be angry.

'They're very showy things. Not at all suitable.' She looked at Affie, as if expecting her to agree. 'Why don't you sell them, and put the price towards your freedom?'

'Sell my ancestors?'

'Not the *photos*, silly girl.' Freewoman Perry had shocked herself. 'Keep the photos, sell the frames.' She was suddenly embarrassed and in a hurry to go. 'Take your agency things down to the kitchen when you've changed and make them up into a parcel – a *neat* parcel. Cook should be there by now. She'll tell you where to find the paper and tape. Then leave the parcel in the hall. After that, I'm sure Cook can find you some work.' She stepped out onto the tiny landing at the top of the steep stairs. 'I do hope you'll like it here,' she said, and clattered away down the bare steps.

Affie was left to look at her clothes. They were all black and white, not colours that she would have chosen to wear. There were two dresses of a plain, unrelieved black, a little faded from washing, and two of black 'velvet', which she suspected was synthetic, but the lettering on the label had all worn away. She put one of the plain dresses on and looked at herself in the narrow mirror inside one of the wardrobe doors. There was no style or fit to the dress at all: it hung straight down from her shoulders and reached to mid-calf, making her legs look short and thick. Above it, her shaved head was ridiculous, and even more ridiculous when she put on one of the 'fancy' caps – a strip of lace-edged white cloth that tied behind her head with strings, but kept slipping down.

She started to cry as she put on the apron for dirty work – it was more like a coat than an apron, with sleeves, and strings to tie round her waist. It was thick, coarse, heavy, and more grey than white. The cap that matched it was of the same material, and fitted like a hat – a sort of pudding-bowl hat that, at least, covered her baldness. She looked at herself in the mirror, and sobbed aloud. Her figure was swamped in the thick, bulging apron; her face made clown-ish by the awful cap. She saw, in the mirror, an ugly lump.

No one would ever have guessed that she was designed, and very beautiful. Still sobbing, she gathered up her agency clothes and went downstairs to the kitchen.

There was a woman there, working at the table and moving between sink and fridge. An *old* woman, which meant she was poor. A fat, ugly old woman, with badly-dyed hair – too black, too flat – shambling about in downtrodden shoes. Her clothes were cheap and baggy, in harsh, over-bright colours. Affie thought: imagine being so poor that you had to go about looking so old and ugly. Then she remembered the image of herself that she'd just seen in the mirror, and wanted to lie down on the floor, she felt so despondent. Everyone who saw her would think that *she* was ugly and poor too. And she wasn't! Not really. She didn't have any money just now because – because she'd been robbed of it. And she was beautiful, she still was, if she could grow her hair long and wear prettier clothes. It was all so unfair.

The old woman looked up from chopping vegetables, and saw Affie. 'Oh,' she said in a voice as thick and gruff as a man's. 'Yome new bonder.'

For a moment Affie thought she was speaking a foreign language, but then, thankfully, belatedly caught the sense. 'Yes, Freewoman.'

The woman laughed, a thick, phlegmy sound. 'I'm free, right enough, but no need t'keep telling me.' She saw the clothes in Affie's arms. 'Brown paper and tape's in that drawer over there.' She pointed with her knife.

'Thank you – er—'

'Call me Cook,' said the cook. 'No need to learn names. I doubt yo'll be here long enough to mek it wuth t'bother.'

That didn't sound friendly or hopeful, and a few more tears slid from Affie's eyes as she opened the drawer and found the paper and tape. She tried hard to make a neat parcel, but she'd never made a parcel before. Someone else had always done it for her, or she'd paid to have an item gift-wrapped. Now, she couldn't make the paper fold properly – it buckled, crumpled, and made lumps. The tape twisted and stuck where she didn't want it to stick. As she sweated over it, she worried about why Cook thought she wouldn't be with Freewoman Perry long, but was too shy to ask. Once, she wouldn't even have noticed a woman like Cook. Now she seemed awesomely capable and frightening – and also vulgar and rude and tough.

Fortunately, Cook didn't need to be asked. When she'd finished chopping vegetables, she said, 'I've lost count of how many bonders Her Majesty's gone through. Gets 'em in, expects 'em to do three jobs at once, wears 'em to a frazzle, then chucks 'em back and gets another. And the poor little buggers, 'course it's their fault.'

Affie was gripped by a panic. Sent back to the agency in disgrace – what would happen to her then? Sold on to someone worse?

She felt a rush of hatred for the people who hadn't helped her – Minerva, the bitch; her mother – her own mother, the useless, idle cow; and Neppie, the utter bastard. But she could not reach any of them, not even to yell at them. She tried to hold it back, but her sobs broke through her gritted teeth.

'No use snivelling,' Cook said. 'If yo've finished that parcel, tek it up to hall table, and then come and wash some pots for me.'

So Affie spent a long time washing horrible, greasy pots and plates, covered in cold fat and congealed sauces. It turned her stomach.

'Ar,' said Cook, seeing this. 'It could all goo in t'dishwasher, o' course – we got a dishwasher, naturally. Gods forbid there should be a gadget we haven't got. But our precious things must be *hand*-washed, mustn't they? Much more swank. "Oh yes, I always has my bone china washed by hand, by my bonder." Except when her ladyship's got no choice but to wash 'em herself. *Then* they goz in dishwasher.'

Affie was washing the floor when Freewoman Perry came into the kitchen, holding the parcel of Affie's agency clothes. 'Kylie,' she said. Affie had forgotten her new name and went on mopping.

'*Kylie*. Girl, I'm talking to you.'

Affie started. 'I'm sorry, Freewoman. What?'

'Don't say "what?" in that rude way. Didn't they teach you any manners?' Affie, who thought her manners perfect, gaped. '"I'm sorry" would have been sufficient. What do you call this?' She held out the brown paper parcel.

Affie couldn't think of anything to say that wouldn't be obvious or, worse, sound sarcastic.

'I call it a mess,' Freewoman Perry said. 'Now please undo it and wrap it again.'

Affie did so, watched by Freewoman Perry. All her muscles became tight and she sweated, unable to make the simplest movement. Freewoman Perry tutted, snatched the parcel from her, folded paper, snipped through tape. 'You are a clumsy girl! Good grief, I hope this isn't a fair example of your abilities.' At last the parcel was wrapped to Freewoman

Perry's satisfaction, and she left, carrying it, saying, 'Buck yourself up, girl!'

Affie felt mangled and sore, too much so to cry. She stood by the kitchen table and hugged herself. 'You'll have to get used to worse than that,' Cook said.

A buzzer sounded, making Affie jump.

'Front door,' Cook said. 'Answer it. Your job.' As Affie started for the kitchen door, she called, 'Don't forget to change your cap and pinnie.'

Affie stopped, aghast. 'They're upstairs, in the loft.'

'Silly girl,' Cook said. 'Yo should have brought 'em down with yer, had 'em to hand. Goo on, hurry up.'

Affie ran. In the hallway, she wondered if she dared answer the door as she was, just this once. But Freewoman Perry had been so specific about changing her apron. Affie ran straight past the front door and up the stairs, along the landing and up the loft stairs. She tried to untie the apron strings as she ran, but it wasn't easy. Once in her little room, she tore off her cap and threw it on her bed, struggled out of the big apron and threw that down too. At least the fancy apron was easy to tie, but the fancy little cap . . .! She tried to fasten it as she clattered back down the stairs, but it kept falling off. As she came rushing down the last stretch of stairs, the cap in her hand, she saw Freewoman Perry just closing the door as another woman went through into the sitting room.

'Kylie,' said Freewoman Perry, 'I didn't buy you so I could answer the door myself. Nor do I want my guests kept standing on the doorstep.'

'Oh, I'm so sorry, Freewoman.' Why couldn't you have a

door cam, and buzz people in yourself, you old cow? But that wouldn't show her guests that she could afford a bonder, would it?

'Where on Earth were you?'

'Changing my apron, Freewoman.'

'Oh, good grief! Buck up your ideas. Now put your cap on, and bring in tea. And please don't make an idiot of yourself in front of my guest.'

Affie ran back to the kitchen, where Cook tied her cap on tightly. Cook set out the tray and gave her careful instructions on what she was to do and say in the sitting room.

'I can't do it – I shall drop something – I can't.'

'Get on with it,' said Cook. 'Nobody's going to do it for you.'

No. For the rest of her life, Affie realised miserably, nobody was ever going to do anything for her. She picked up the tray in hands that shook so much, the teacups rattled. Feeling sick, she walked down the hall to the drawing room. But she managed to open the door without dropping the tray balanced on her hip. She crossed the floor without dropping anything, though her knees shook. And though the cups and plates rattled when she set the tray on the table – and Freewoman Perry gave her a short, sharp glare – she didn't spill anything, either. Then she was able to flee the room – and run upstairs to change into her work apron, and run back down to the kitchen, taking her fancy apron and cap with her. There, Cook gave her bewildering instructions on how to use the washing machine and how to do the washing – 'Just quick, afore I goo.' It was a sonic machine, but much more complicated than a sonic shower. The length of time it operated depended on how big the load of washing was; and how dirty the items were, and how delicate they were. Some things mustn't go in it at all, but must be washed by hand, in water; some could only go in for a few seconds, which meant they must be washed by themselves. Affie felt panic rising again: she would never remember it all, she was going to make mistakes. Before Cook had even finished, another buzzer sounded, and Freewoman Perry's voice said, 'Kylie. Clear the tray, please.'

'Quick, change your pinnie,' Cook said. 'See you tomorrow.'

'Don't go! I don't know what to do!'

Cook grinned. 'Think I'm going to stay here a minute longer than I have to? Think again, blossom. Don't worry. Her Majesty'll let you know when you goo wrong. Er – don't you think you'd better change your apron and get up there for that tray?'

Affie changed, and ran up to the drawing room, and was reprimanded for running. 'We could hear your great hooves clattering all the way. A little more decorum, please.'

Back down to the kitchen, a change into her work apron, and then she washed up the tea things. What to do, *then?* She was terrified of being found idle – but Freewoman Perry arrived, to supervise her in the laying of the dining room table, and to ask why the day's laundry hadn't been done.

Because there hasn't been time! Affie wanted to shout, but didn't dare speak.

The table laid, she was left to do the laundry, afraid every moment that she was making mistakes and ruining clothes – until Freewoman Perry came down to supervise the heating of the meal Cook had made, and the serving of it in the dining room to herself and her husband – a man Affie wouldn't have recognised again because she didn't dare look at him. Afterwards, she was lectured for being slow, for dropping cutlery, for having dribbled gravy on the edge of the plate. Then, back to the kitchen, to do the washing up, finish the laundry and eat a sandwich.

She had just taken a mouthful when Freewoman Perry came in. Affie leaped to her feet, trying to chew without it being noticed.

'Well!' said Freewoman Perry, looking round. 'It needs a good tidy-up in here! When you've done that, Kylie, you may go to bed. There's a little bed made up in Apollo's room – I want you to sleep there tonight because he's not well. If he wakes in the night, you can get him a glass of water or take him to the bathroom or whatever. If he's really unwell, of course, come and fetch me. So! And have you enjoyed your first day with us?'

'Yes, Freewoman.'

'Very good! That's what I like to hear! A bright and early start tomorrow, then. And do try to buck your ideas up.'

And if I do, Affie thought, my reward will be years and years of more days like this.

The Woman in the Street

'Apollo, you brat, you stinking brat, I hate you, hate you!'

Freechild Apollo had, again, pulled free of Affie's hand and gone running off down the street, laughing wildly and looking back over his shoulder because this was such a wonderful game. Affie, terrified of him getting hurt, or lost, had to pick up her leaden feet and run after him. She did hate him. She hated his rosy, chubby cheeks and his bright eyes, his blond hair and button nose and every last cute thing about him. She loathed him.

She loathed his mother too, and his father; and every millimetre of carpeting in their house; every millimetre of paintwork; every cup and plate, spoon, fork and knife; every step of the stair; every window. She hated hearing her own voice saying, 'Yes, Freewoman; no, Freewoman; sorry, Freewoman,' when she really wanted to scream, swear and throw things. She hated her own thoughts when she caught herself planning how to please Free Sodding Perry, she hated her own cringing and cowardice. She hated answering to the name of 'Kylie'. She hated her life. From the moment she woke at five in the morning to the moment when Free Bloody Perry allowed her to go to bed, she hated her life. And there seemed no prospect of it ever changing – except for the worse.

She could not remember ever being so tired before. She had learned to keep her fancy cap and apron close at hand and could change them in moments before running to answer the door or wait on her mistress. Although she'd spoilt a silk shirt – the cost of which had been added to her price – she had finally mastered the complications of laundry, and seldom now made a mistake. She could wait at table more or less in the manner that Freewoman Perry demanded. But somehow, every day, there seemed to be more and more work to do, and Freewoman Perry was never quite satisfied. When she washed all the windows, from the top of the house to the bottom, and finished, soaking wet and exhausted, Freewoman Perry pointed out all the smears.

She was set to weed the garden – after doing a lot of work around the house – and finished with a back aching, as if it would break. Freewoman Perry pointed out all the weeds she'd missed, and sorted through the pile of weeds to find the one or two garden plants she'd pulled by mistake.

She washed all the paintwork in the house – fitting it in around her other work. It took her days, and she ached all over, and had grime under her nails. Freewoman Perry went all over the house and found every little groove and corner where she hadn't quite removed all the dust.

'Really,' Freewoman Perry said, 'I thought the girl I had before was bad, but sometimes I wish I'd never sent her back.'

Affie heard: I sent her back; I might send you back too. It always sent her into a flurry of distress because she dreaded that a bad reference from Freewoman Perry would get her a worse place. Cook had told her of miserable sweat-shop factories, where the bonders slept in cold dormitories and caught TB and died in a year.

The few minutes she could find for herself between jobs, when she might sit down or have a cup of tea, had become extraordinarily precious. It was precisely at those moments – as if she had a sixth sense – that Freewoman Perry appeared and set her to look after bloody darling Apollo. Take him for a walk, play with him, read to him . . . When she just wanted to sit quietly, she had to put up with the brat squealing and running about and making a mess, which she then had to pick up, her tired muscles twanging.

And he was such a brat. *And* he was simple-minded. It would have made her laugh – had she dared – to hear Freewoman Perry going on about how intelligent he was, and what a unique mind he had, when he couldn't even talk properly. It was galling that the simple-minded brat didn't like her at all, and made it plain he didn't. He was always pushing her away and running off from her. The last thing she wanted to do was run after him. He could run and run until he reached the edge of the Earth and fell off, for all she cared. But she had to run after him because of Freewoman Perry.

Catching him, she shook him by the arm, which was all she dared to do, though she would have liked to smack his legs. But then he would certainly tell his mother, and she would be in worse trouble than ever.

'*Don't* run away! You might get lost.'

He laughed in her face, and she longed to slap him.

'I won't take you to the park if you don't behave!' He liked going to the park, because there were swings and slides and ducks.

He laughed at her again. That was one of the most infuriating things about him – you couldn't talk to him, you couldn't explain things to him or reason with him or make a deal with him at all. He just giggled, made monkey noises, and pranced. He wasn't like a human being. He was an alien.

'Oh, I *hate* you!' she cried again, before she could stop herself, and once more shook him hard.

She felt a touch on her arm and started violently, thinking Freewoman Perry had caught her in the act of abusing her child.

When she saw who it was, she took a step backwards and gaped. A small woman, more chic than Freewoman Perry could ever be, stood beside her. She was dressed all in black: a tight-fitting black jacket, a black skirt, black stockings and high-heeled black boots. The small hand that was still stretched out to Affie after touching her arm was covered with a black glove. Best of all was the tiny black hat perched at a tilt on the small head, with a veil obscuring the face. Pictures and headlines – 'Shares Down', 'New Deal Agreed' – drifted across the veil, constantly changing, completely hiding the wearer's face.

'Poor child,' said this beautiful but faceless woman, in an odd voice. 'Are you tired?' The voice was quite soft, even childish, but would suddenly catch and grate on a rough note, like a child with a cold. Somehow, it sounded foreign, though Affie couldn't place the accent. 'Are you exhausted?'

For a moment, Affie thought she was speaking to Apollo, the brat – but no. The woman was looking at her, speaking to her. She almost cried. This woman, this gentle, wonderful stranger, had *seen* her. Despite the expensive, lovely clothes she wore, here was a woman perceptive enough to see through Affie's dreadful, cheap bonder clothes, to see past the headscarf that covered her cropped head. She had noticed Affie – *Affie*, not a mere bonder – and had understood.

The woman reached up and tore a corner of her veil loose from its velcro. Lowering it slightly, she looked at Affie above its flickering headlines, revealing a pair of dark, Japanese eyes that stared at her steadily and deeply. Affie, mesmerised, stood quite still, staring back.

The woman reached out and lightly touched Affie's arm. Leaving the slight weight of her fingertips there, she said, with certainty, 'There is love for you.'

Affie cried. She couldn't help it, the tears just burst out of her. She had been feeling so tired, so lonely, so ignored, so unimportant to everyone.

The woman let her veil drop, revealing an oddly round and snub-nosed, childish face, though with strongly marked black brows. Stepping forward, she embraced Affie with a tight clasp: wordlessly squeezing her.

It had been so long since anyone had touched her fondly – or touched her at all. Affie, to her own bewilderment, sobbed and sobbed.

'I'm sorry, I'm sorry,' Affie said, at last, pulling away. Apollo was standing nearby, staring at them with his fingers in his mouth, baffled. 'Thank you,' Affie said, hardly knowing what she was saying. 'Who are you?'

The woman put up her veil again, fastening it to her hat, hiding her face. 'Someone who loves you,' she said, and then turned to Apollo, holding out her arms. Apollo ran to her, was picked up and cuddled. Affie watched, surprised – but then, the woman had come from nowhere and hugged Affie, telling her she loved her. Why wouldn't she embrace even bloody Apollo?

The woman looked over Apollo's shoulder as she held him. The black veil, with its shifting headlines, hid her face, but the dark eyes looked through it, fixed on Affie. Affie felt herself tingle, felt as warm as if she was still being cuddled. The veil moved as the woman spoke. 'Will you come and see me?'

'I—' Affie remembered how difficult it was to get out of the house, with Freewoman Perry constantly finding her work to do. True, she was often sent to take Apollo for a walk, but could never be sure when that would be.

'You must come and see me,' said the woman. 'Please say you'll come and see me. Can you read?'

Affie withdrew for a moment, insulted despite herself. 'Of course I can!'

Again came the light touch on her arm, beseeching, comforting, apologising. 'Forgive me. How was I to know unless I asked?' The woman put down Apollo, who wrapped his arms round her legs.

The strange woman reached inside the cuff of her black glove and drew out a small card, which she handed to Affie. 'Please come and see me here.'

Affie looked at the card. 'A temple?'

'Come any Wednesday, morning or evening. I shall look for you. Please come.'

'Why?' Affie asked. 'Why me?'

The woman reached out and touched her cheek, lightly, briefly. Affie almost recoiled, because the touch was so unexpected, and intimate – but then she remained still, accepting it.

'Because you are loved.' The woman put Apollo down, touched his head and quickly walked away, crossing the road and climbing into a waiting car.

As the car drove away, Apollo said, 'That was Mummy.'

Affie, distracted, didn't realise what he'd said at first. Then she said, 'No. Your mummy is Freewoman Perry.' And you deserve each other, she thought.

Apollo looked up at her, sucking his fingers, seeming puzzled. 'Lady Little Mummy.'

Stupid brat, Affie thought. As if a woman like *that* would be the mother of a nasty object like you. If that had been what he meant – but who knew what the idiot meant? She couldn't be bothered to argue with him, or to try and find out what he was thinking. Taking his hand in a firm grip, she said, 'I suppose we've got to go to the park.'

The park could be paved over, for all she cared. The only important thing was: how could she find a way to go to the temple of Odin, on Wednesday?

The Temple

Holding Apollo's hand, Affie looked across the street at the heavy, square building of wood, steel and glass. Its tall, wide double doors, covered with sheets of polished bronze, shone and glared in the sunlight.

'We're going in there,' she said to Apollo. 'You'll have to behave. It's where a God lives. You will behave, won't you?'

Infuriatingly, Apollo looked up at her and grinned. It was impossible to tell if he even understood, let alone whether he was going to co-operate. Affie would rather have had charge of a dog. At least, when she kicked it, it wouldn't be able to tell tales. Hoping for the best, Affie led Apollo across the road and up the steps.

The sheets of bronze that covered the doors were engraved and embossed with many pictures, bordered with intricate, entwining bands, showing scenes from the myth of Odin. Apollo stopped dead when he saw them, dragging Affie to a halt. 'Horse!' he said, pointing, and then, 'Bird!'

He wouldn't move. Affie picked him up and carried him through the partly open doors into the dimly lit lobby beyond. He seemed to accept this as one of the trials of life and bore it good-humouredly, without screaming as she'd feared he might.

On the wall at the back of the lobby, glowering over a small table set with leaflets, was what Affie thought a very ugly sculpture, carved – hacked was a better word – from a lump of wood. A bearded face looked out of the wood, and some of the rough bark of the natural wood had been left, to suggest the texture of hair. One eye watched those entering the temple. In place of the other eye was merely a roughly gouged hole. The mouth below gaped and a thick tongue emerged from it.

On either side of this carving were more doors, and Affie, still holding Apollo, leaned on one of these and entered the temple. She felt shy, conscious of her awful clothes and her shorn head covered with an ugly cap. She hadn't looked her best since she'd been bonded. She was even glad to have Apollo in her arms, so she could duck her head and hide behind him.

The main body of the temple was a long, high hall, dim and shadowy, though it was daylight outside. In the half light, the long-fire that burned the length of the hall flickered and danced with blue and yellow flames, shooting washes of warmth into the corners and up among the rafters.

At the far end of the hall, towering towards the roof, were three statues, of the three main Nordic Gods. The largest, in the centre, was of Odin, and had the same ugly face as the sculpture in the lobby: bearded, one-eyed, a swollen tongue lolling from its mouth. The hulking body of the figure was roughly outlined, as if covered in a cloak. It held an iron spear at its hip, pointing at the roof.

To its right was a smaller figure, also male, also bearded, though its beard and hair was the red of copper and rust.

Rising from its hips and grasped by both its hands, was a hammer. This was Thor.

To the left was a figure of Frey, its hair and beard glimmering gold in the firelight. It had a more human shape than the others – a very human shape, since it had an enormous erect phallus.

There were people gathered near the feet of the three statues, where offered candles glowed in racks, and computer screens glimmered as people typed in their prayers. Affie put Apollo on his feet, and led him down the hall by the hand. She studied the people at the computer screens, or those lighting candles, hoping to spot the woman who had spoken to her in the street. 'There is love for you,' the woman had said, and Affie had repeated that to herself many times since. She had come because of that promise. But she couldn't see the woman.

Affie stopped at a distance from the people, too timid to go closer. Perhaps if she waited, the woman would come.

'What this place, what is?' Apollo asked.

'Ssh. It's a temple. People come here to worship the Gods.'

'*Hel*-lo, sweetheart.' A woman had come close and was stooping to speak to Apollo. 'And how are you today?'

Apollo simply sucked his thumb and smiled. Affie felt a stab of jealousy. Just because he was little, everybody loved him, and he was a brat. What about *me*? I'm here too.

Straightening, the woman looked at her, and smiled.

She was tall and slim, and her clothes were very good – good cloth and beautifully tailored. But her face was wrinkled and she'd let her hair go grey. If she could afford clothes like that, Affie wondered, why didn't she get her hair and face fixed?

'I've not seen you here before,' said the woman. 'Is it your first time?'

'I was invited,' Affie said. 'By a woman in the street.' She looked round again. 'I was hoping—'

'Ah,' said the elderly woman and, to Affie's surprise, took her by the arm. 'You've come to see our Odinstoy.' And she led them both down the hall towards the statues.

The next few minutes were full of introductions, hand-shaking and air kisses. Apollo was being fussed over and given sweeties, so Affie didn't have to worry about him, and for a few moments she felt that she was back in her old life, and she smiled and nodded and said she was *so* pleased to meet people. It was such a relief. Then, one of the women whispered that she was not to worry: in Odin's house, all were equal before the God. Affie fell back a little from the gathering then, realising that they had known all along that she was a bonder: had known by her close cropped hair and scarf, and by her clothes. Their friendly welcome had been an act, demanded by their faith. Outside the temple, they would treat her like any other bonder.

'You are so lucky,' said another woman, leaning over to speak to her. 'Odinstoy is here today.'

Glancing up, Affie saw many people looking at her, smiling and nodding. They were all eager, expectant, keen to see what she was going to make of it all. They were creepy. Affie tried to look round again, without being too obvious, looking for the woman in the chic black outfit, the one she'd met in the street. Of course, the woman's face had been covered by a veil, and she might be wearing different clothes, but Affie thought she would know her again. There had been something about her—

Apollo was gone! A spasm of panic seized her, making her heart pound and her skin turn cold, as she feared, for a moment, that Apollo was lost. She would be in such trouble! She looked round frantically, and shoved through the people, still looking and – with a rush of relief – saw him. He was at the foot of the big statues, holding a man's hand. They seemed to be looking at the statues together.

Affie made hurriedly towards them, to take Apollo back. If he had nightmares about those ugly statues, she'd be in trouble again. She was supposed to be taking him for a healthy walk in the park, not bringing him to a temple of Odin. Freewoman Perry and her husband went to the temple of Zeus and Hera.

The man holding Apollo's hand looked round. It wasn't a man, but a woman dressed as a man. Not simply a woman with short hair, wearing trousers, but a woman dressed like a man. Her face was round and childish, but had a thin moustache, and Affie experienced a few moments of bewilderment as her eyes told her she was looking at a young man, but some deeper instinct told her otherwise. A man's suit, a man's heavy shoes – but the neck was thin, the hand that held Apollo's was small.

As if guessing that Affie had come to fetch Apollo, the man-woman picked him up and carried him away. Apollo was quite happy in his-her arms, and they nuzzled their faces together, laughing, as they went.

Affie stopped short, dumbfounded. Sensing someone at

her side, she looked round with a slight start, and found it was the older woman who had first welcomed her.

'I have to take care of that little boy,' Affie said.

'He's perfectly safe,' the woman said. 'No one here will hurt him.'

'That – person he's with,' Affie said, lowering her voice. 'Who is that?'

The woman by her side seemed mildly surprised. 'A priestess. A völva, we say.'

'She's dressed like a man!' Affie said, and then put her hand to her mouth, afraid she'd been rude.

The woman smiled. 'Well, sometimes our priestesses do. And sometimes our priests dress as women. Animals, too. Odin is a shapeshifter, you see. We think of Him as male, but He was female too, at times. So the Eddas tell us.'

Strange people, Affie thought, hardly reassured. She started after the cross-dressing priestess who had abducted Apollo. Freewoman Perry would have her head, if anything happened to the brat.

The man-woman was carrying Apollo up a short flight of steps, onto a small stage in front of the central statue. Behind Affie, someone clapped.

The desultory chatter turned to an eager buzz and everyone in the temple turned and walked to the front, to gather beneath the statues and the little stage, looking up at the man-woman who held Apollo in her arms. Affie, unhappy, stood among them. Some performance was about to begin. She couldn't rescue Apollo now.

The man-woman did nothing except gently sway to and fro, balancing Apollo on her hip, smiling at him and humming. Yet everyone watched, rapt, with bright eyes and grinning mouths as if, any second, this freak might do something amazing.

Affie stared too. She didn't know the man-woman, yet there was something familiar about her. Her face was round and babyish, with a snub nose and heavy dark brows; not pretty at all. And yet – somehow attractive, almost Japanese in looks, but not Japanese. Affie looked round and saw that everyone there was gaping at the man-woman: fascinated, admiring.

'Polly, Polly, Polly,' sang the man-woman, dancing round with Apollo on the stage. Freewoman Perry hated him to be called 'Polly'. It was ignorant, she said. 'Together again, He's brought us together again,' the man-woman on the stage sang. Her voice was distinctive – soft and childish, with an odd accent that was difficult to place. Then it would catch and grate, suddenly rough, like sandpaper. It could have been a woman's voice or a boy's.

'Give thanks!' the man-woman cried out, throwing back her plain head. 'Oh, give thanks to the great God!'

Affie felt a passage of electricity through the air, like the static that sometimes tingles from your fingers when you touch a metal door handle or tap. It jumped from person to person and, as she looked round, startled, a whisper was dragged from the throats of all there. 'Oh, thank the great God, thank Him, thank Him.' Affie felt that rough, awed whisper tingle down her spine.

'He has given back to me what I most wanted!' cried the man-woman from the stage, her voice cracking. 'I asked and He heard! I asked and He gave!'

Affie knew that voice. That voice had said to her, 'There is love for you.' She stared, unbelieving. This odd creature – plain, awkward, neither male nor female – was the chic woman in black who had touched her arm and lowered her veil.

The man-woman turned in her dance and looked down at her audience. For an instant, her eyes flashed on them as they'd flashed from behind the veil. It *was* the chic woman. Affie's heart leaped up towards her, unbidden, as if the woman had once more touched her arm and promised her love. It was as if the woman had performed a miracle, had changed shape before Affie's eyes.

Turning to the person beside her – a young woman – she said, 'Who is that?'

The woman gave her an astonished look and said, proudly, 'That's Odinstoy!'

'Oh, great God,' Odinstoy called out, 'look on this world with Your sighted eye, and on the other with Your blind eye, and tell me, tell me, tell Your toy what I am to know! Tell me, tell me!' Odinstoy danced in a circle, her voice panting, drumming her heels, spinning Apollo round, making him shriek.

The young woman leaned close to Affie. 'She's trancing.'

'There is one,' Odinstoy called out, and stopped dancing, putting Apollo down. She scanned the audience, her finger poised to point. 'There is one here called Kylie.' Affie's heart barely had time to skip before Odinstoy pointed, with straight arm and forefinger, right at her. 'But her name isn't Kylie, it isn't Kylie, it's—'

Affie held her breath.

'It's Affroditey.'

Affie gasped, and put her hands to her mouth. The people near her turned to her eagerly, eyes gleaming, drinking in her astonishment and shock. They plucked at her, whispered, 'Is it true? Is it true?'

'How did she know?' Affie asked. 'How does she know?'

The woman smiled a huge, beatific smile. 'Because she talks with Odin. She's Odinstoy.'

Affie felt stunned, exposed, vulnerable – and loved.

'Affroditey, Affroditey, there is love for you,' crooned the scratchy, childish voice. 'Remember, believe, there is love for you, love for you.'

It was, above all, what Affie wanted to hear. Tears ran down her face; her breath came between sobs. The people around her hugged her, and it was so nice, so good, to be held warmly.

'Welcome, Affroditey, welcome, Affroditey,' Odinstoy chanted. 'Odin welcomes you, Odin calls you home . . .'

The woman hugging Affie drew back and looked at her. Tears were on her face. 'Will you stay? For the feast? Please stay, sister.'

Sister. Affie nodded. She would stay, no matter how late it made her, no matter what trouble it made for her. More than anything, she wanted to be close to Odinstoy again, to be touched by her again, and to be told that there was love for her . . .

After the service, the gathering went into another, smaller room, for the feast. Here, there were low tables in the centre, surrounded by broad, shallow benches, each covered with soft rugs and cushions. It was lit by dim, warm lights, set to flicker and change like firelight. Odinstoy led them into the room, carrying Apollo, and was already seated, with the little boy on her lap, when Affie entered. As soon as she saw her, Odinstoy held out her hand and called, 'Come and sit with me! I want Affie to sit with me.'

People moved aside to let Affie go forward, and she felt her face flush and her chest fill with warm, trembling joy. She was chosen, acknowledged – in her real name. She was loved.

She sat down by Odinstoy – careful not to sit too presumptuously near – but Odinstoy leaned close to her and kissed her cheek. From the corner of her eye, Affie saw others watching, seeing her kissed and made special by Odinstoy. She looked back at Odinstoy and received another tiny shock. Odinstoy had pulled off what must have been a wig and a false moustache. Now, above the man's suit, her face was sharp, gamine, framed by her own, spiky, tufty dark hair. Affie wondered how she'd ever thought her plain, even ugly. The slanting, Asian eyes that watched her so intently were hazel – but as the light changed they were green and gold flecked – or they were slate-grey-blue. Together with the round face – its wide cheekbones and narrow, pointed chin – the soft, smiling mouth, strong brows, and the oddity of the short, black hair, Odinstoy was unique. Words like 'beautiful', 'plain' and 'ugly', meant nothing when applied to her. She was herself, and that made her beautiful.

Odinstoy was holding something out to her. It was a

small bowl, full of brown liquid. Affie, honoured, took it. Others around the table were handing bowls to each other.

Raising a bowl, Odinstoy called, 'Health!'

'Health!' everyone bellowed back, and drank from their bowls. Affie raised her bowl and smelled a yeasty, malty smell. The drink wasn't Coke, as she'd supposed, but beer. How very – unsophisticated. But, eager not to offend anyone, she took a gulp, and shuddered. It was horrible.

Odinstoy patted her on the back, stroked her shoulders, and she looked up, eyes watering, to find people smiling at her encouragingly and sympathetically.

'You'll grow to like it,' a man said.

'It's the blood of the God,' said a woman, and held out a dish of small biscuits shaped like birds. 'Ravens and eagles,' the woman said. 'Odin's birds.'

Feeling shy, Affie took a biscuit.

'Take two, take two!'

'Take several!'

She felt so lucky to be sitting here among these lovely people; smiled on, talked to, accepted as an equal. It was almost like being free again. No one was going to scold her, or order her to do some horrible, dirty chore. A heavenly respite. And she had Odinstoy to thank for it.

She looked at Odinstoy and saw her kissing Apollo, who sat in her lap. She cuddled him, giving him a sip of beer from her cup, and another biscuit. He was looking up at her, smiling, and both were flushed and glowing with happiness.

Odinstoy looked up and saw Affie watching her. 'You must come again, Affroditey, you must.'

'I can't get away very often.'

'Come whenever you can – whenever you take Pollo for a walk.'

All around the table, smiling people murmured that, yes, she must come, they would love to see her again.

'I'd love to come,' Affie said, honestly. It would give her something to look forward to. 'But I don't know – how often do you meet here?'

'Never mind the gatherings,' Odinstoy said. 'Come to see me. At my flat. Bring Pollo. Any time.'

There was a gasp from the others and Affie realised that this wasn't an invitation extended to everyone: that she was being honoured. Perhaps even making some people jealous. 'Thank you,' she said. 'I'd love that.'

Odinstoy reached out and gripped her wrist. Affie was very aware of everyone watching. 'I knew you were special,' Odinstoy said, in that crooning voice, now soft, now rough. 'When I saw you on the street, I knew you were special. I felt it.' She touched herself over the heart and gazed intently at Affie with those beautiful Japanese eyes, as if seeing her specialness again.

Everyone gathered round the table gazed at Affie too; some smiling, delighted; some seeming dazed by what Odinstoy had said; some perhaps just a little grudging that Odinstoy had singled Affie out instead of them. It was all wonderful to Affie, after the miserable time she'd had lately. She was elite again, she was favoured, she was smiled on by the Gods. She loved it.

'I know,' Odinstoy crooned, 'I know, because I was a bonder too. A slave!' There was a slight flutter among her

141

audience as she used the offensive word. 'I was born a slave – I am a slave still!'

Affie was puzzled, but the others were rapt. They murmured, perhaps in denial, perhaps agreement.

'I am Odin's slave – I am Odin's toy. I work for Him with all my heart—' Her audience whispered again, gleefully agreeing, thrilled. 'But He is my only master now, the only one I obey!'

Her audience all but applauded.

'And you,' Odinstoy said softly, her hand holding Affie's wrist, her eyes on Affie's face, 'who is your true master – or mistress?'

'My—?' Affie didn't want to think about being a bonder just then.

Odinstoy's grip tightened on her wrist. 'Your *true* master?'

'I don't – I don't know.'

The Japanese eyes stared. They were all that Affie could see. 'Come to me again, Affroditey – come to me again.'

The Man From Mars

Earth. Mother Earth. The sleeping goddess – the sleeping beauty. The dreamer and giver of all life.

In the park, Thorsgift was surrounded by green, and the white and red and blue of burgeoning flowers, his ears full of the sound of trickling water and birdsong. He set himself to feel reverent.

It wasn't difficult there, with such abundance of leaf and flower all about him, and thick-trunked trees growing out of the untreated regolith, straight out of the beautiful flesh of Mother Earth Herself; with the weight of her pulling at him and compressing his long spine, with the air full of scent, with bees buzzing and squirrels skedaddling across thick grass strewn with white daisies and hazy blue speedwell. His heart swelled and lifted. Oh, Gods! He was on Earth itself, Earth, the first home, the womb, of all humankind. He was so lucky. So lucky to have been given this job and this chance, so lucky to have his feet on Earth. He would remember this all his life – the life he might so easily have spent contentedly on Mars, never seeing Earth except through Mars's pink-tinged atmosphere, as a purplish dot in the sky. And now he was here – and could look up and see Mars – and all his family, friends, everything – as a distant, reddish dot in the sky! Gods, life was strange. Thank the Gods. Thank the Gods for the strange complexity of life!

He looked at his watch. Time to stop sightseeing, and find a cab.

Outside the park, in the open air of the city street, it was harder to be reverent about Mother Earth – or, harder not to be angry about what mankind had done to Her. The awful roaring din, the crowds, the traffic, the pushing and shoving, the beggars calling out, whining, pleading – it was not a good place to be. Mars was better.

And everyone looked at him, of course, stared at him: because of his height, pallor and clothes. He'd been told that almost everyone on Earth spoke English, so not to worry, but he'd found it hard to make himself understood. His accent was difficult, he was told, and he used strange words. 'Where are you from?' he'd be asked. If he told them, or they guessed, there followed many jokes about men from Mars and invasions from Mars and, 'Take me to your leader, Earthling . . .' After three hundred years, he thought, Earthers should have got over it.

It was a relief to find an empty cab at the stand and to get into it, away from the noise and crowd of the street, and not to have to speak to anyone, but simply programme his destination into the cab's computer.

Odinstoy sat in the swivel chair, with one leg crooked over the arm, and the toes of the other foot on the floor, pushing her from side to side, sometimes spinning her right around as she watched the various screens. She was dressed in loose, baggy, grey trousers, and a loose, grey top. Her short dark hair was mussed and spiky, while her eyes were still darkened with yesterday's eyeliner, not quite washed off. She watched the screens, her face serious and absorbed, her fingers playing with her ancestor string, counting the beads and trinkets over and over as some people counted prayer beads.

The dimly-lit security room, with its banks of screens, was one of her favourite places. The cameras covered all areas of the temple, and the streets outside it. They were connected to computers which identified faces, and even iris patterns, and matched them against a database. They analysed body language too, picking out individuals showing markedly high levels of agitation and stress.

Odinstoy didn't need a computer for that. She'd been born bonded, and the bonded need to please those who hold power over them. She had learned to identify moods keenly, and could tell a lot about people by looking at them and observing their movements. She liked to watch the people in and about the temple on the silent screens. The bonded stood out, to her, as if they were illuminated. They could put on their best clothes, they could stand up straight and walk with heads held high – she still knew them, often by the very fact that they held their heads high and stood up straight. They made too much effort.

She could pick out plain-clothes members of the security forces – impossible to say how, in words. The signals were visual, not verbal, and it was a matter of many tiny details taken together: details of their dress, their stance, the way they watched others.

She could pick out lovers – that was easy, anyone could do that, but she could pick out lovers who had quarrelled, and weren't standing together or speaking. She could pick out lovers whose relationship had cooled; identify those about to break up.

Degrees of friendship, parents and grown children, pick-pockets, people who were unhappy, even depressed – there was so much you could tell, just by watching, and the more you watched, the more you learned.

'Want a Crunch, mate?' Bob Sing held his bag of snacks towards her.

She peered into the bag. 'No.'

'Please yourself.' Some might have thought his words and tone disrespectful towards a God-speaker; and Bob knew it, and revelled in it. Not many people could say they were a friend of Odinstoy, and called her 'mate'.

Bob's given name was Thorhart, but he had grown tired of being confused with every Thor, Thorsday and Thorshammer. In his class at school, he'd told her, there had been one other 'Thorhart' and seven other boys and five girls whose names began with 'Thor'. So he called himself Bob instead.

'Haven't seen you around much lately, Tat-head.' When Odinstoy didn't answer, he said, 'None of the socials, noth-ing. Thought I'd see you at Sif's party, but no.'

Odinstoy, her eyes on the screens, still swinging her chair from side to side, said, 'Haven't seen you about, either.'

'I've been busy,' Bob said. 'Had to sort out a program for, like, the day before yesterday. Clients all in a lather.' Bob free-lanced in computers and programming, specialising in security. He kept the temple's security network up to date and running smoothly, as well as worshipping there. But this was his lunchbreak.

He kept glancing at Odinstoy. 'Want a swig of beer?'

She shook her head.

'Sure you don't want a Crunch?'

'Sure.'

'You can have half this chocolate if you like. 'S got chili in it.'

She ignored him.

Bob finished his Crunches, glanced at her, drank beer, glanced at her . . . She was intent on the screens. He sighed. There was something he wanted to know. He knew he shouldn't ask, that it wouldn't do him any good, that he shouldn't want to know. It shouldn't bother him at all. But it did.

'Sure you don't want any chocolate?'

Odinstoy, watching the screens, flipped her hand at him impatiently.

He knew that asking would make him look and feel a fool. But it irritated like an itch. Carefully pitching his voice to sound casual, he said, 'I suppose you've been seeing Markus?'

He'd got the voice wrong. It sounded too thin, too accusatory – and he had no right, no right whatsoever, to accuse her of seeing Markus. Even if she had.

At least he got her attention for an instant. She looked at him in surprise, her cat's eyes a slate-blue in the light from the screens. 'What makes you think that?'

'Oh—' He hunched the shoulder nearest her, shrugged.

'Markus has been busy. Working. Or with his family. Kids' birthdays. Wife's birthday. Something.'

He wondered if her indifference was as feigned as his.

It sounded genuine, but perhaps she was better at acting than he was.

Maybe she'd dumped Markus, and so didn't care what he was doing. The question, 'Have you dumped him?' rose into his mouth, but he firmly swallowed it. None of your business, he told himself. Be too nosy, and she'll dump you too.

'Affie's been coming over a lot,' Odinstoy said. 'She brings Apollo.'

'Oh,' Bob said. Of course, she'd drop anything to see Apollo. Bob felt enormously bucked up as he remembered all that Odinstoy had told him about Apollo – had told him, and asked him to keep a secret. He thought he might be the only person who knew apart, possibly, from Affie. He must be special to Odinstoy, or she wouldn't have told him that, would she? 'How is the little sprog?'

'Look at him,' Odinstoy said, and pointed to one of the screens.

Startled, Bob looked at the screen, but didn't see Apollo. 'Where?'

'Him. There.'

The screen held a tall, lanky man – very tall, very lanky. He moved clumsily, stumping along, but he had a big grin on his face as he looked round, even though he was alone.

Odinstoy watched him as he progressed to another screen. She'd noticed him, not because of his height, but because he was excited. Not agitated, not afraid – it wasn't the sort of excitement someone feels when they're about to steal, or smash a statue. It was a happy excitement, but it marked him out because he had so much more of it than anyone she'd seen for a while. His grin was one of sheer, spontaneous happiness. A happy man.

Bob studied the screen too, feeling a slight pang of jealousy. What was so special about that long length of string? 'What about him?'

'He's happy,' she said.

'No law against that, is there?'

'Who is he?'

'Just some punter.'

'Who is he, Bob?'

Bob tapped his computer keyboard, requesting the happy man's identity. Obviously, he was not a happy known criminal, or the computer would already have alerted them – though also reminding them that there was no law against known criminals, happy or otherwise, worshipping their chosen God at their chosen venue.

'Ha! Another cussed Thor,' Bob said. 'Thorsgift, this one. 'Course, all we really know is that the *database* says these irises belong to somebody called Thorsgift. A lot of people think that—'

'What's his other name?' Odinstoy asked.

Bob grinned, acknowledging that he'd been riding off on one of his hobby-horses. 'Thorsgift Blackmore. Hey, he's a Martian! He's a man from Mars!'

Odinstoy rose abruptly, and left the room without a word. Bob was surprised and wondered if he'd offended her. He spent some time checking back through everything he'd said, and even the way he'd said it, but remembered nothing that could have given offence. He decided that it was just her way. Half the time she lived in another world altogether.

Odinstoy emerged from the narrow, dark corridor that housed the temple offices, onto the balcony overlooking the great hall. Leaning on the wooden rail, she looked down at the long-fires redly lighting the darkness, and the great, looming, half lit bulks of the statues. The security screens had shown her the temple in brighter, clearer detail – their computers compensating for the temple's atmospheric darkness.

It took her a few minutes to spot the Martian. There were people writing prayers on the glowing computer screens, or reading the prayers of others, their faces catching the light; and there were people standing before the statues with their hands held in the air, praying. Others, that she knew, were sweeping, or polishing; and there were a few tourists wandering aimlessly about and pointing, curious to see a temple of Odin, but not quite sure what to expect.

And there was the Martian. He'd been in a particularly dark corner near the statue of Frey, and now emerged from it, stumping along like a toddler not used to walking. In fact, all his movements were slow, clumsy, over-controlled.

She started down the stairs to the main body of the temple. He was half expected, this man from Mars. There had been e-mails from him, introducing himself because he was travelling and wanted to visit temples and meet the gatherings. At the time of his first e-mails, months ago, if not a year ago, Odinstoy had hardly paid attention. She had been missing Apollo too much to be interested.

But here he was, and something flickered in Odinstoy's brain, too quickly even for her to know what it meant – but *befriend him*, was the gist of it. Befriend him, and more – captivate him. Why it was important that she should, she didn't yet understand, but she didn't question. Such half-understood compulsions were, she knew, the voice of the God. Some people didn't hear it. Some heard, but ignored it, because the orders seemed senseless or inconvenient. She had learned both to hear and to obey. It was that voice, far more than any attraction to them, that had led her to single out both Markus and Bob.

She reached the great hall, and hung back in the shadows against the wall, knowing that someone in the centre of the hall, looking through the light of the long-fires, wouldn't easily be able to see her – she was a small and insignificant figure. No one would ever be so struck by her face and figure that they would turn their heads to give her a second look. No one had paid for expensive genetic fiddling to ensure that she would be born beautiful, like Affie. But she knew that she could make someone remember her for longer than they would ever remember Affie.

The lanky man was still hanging around by the three huge statues of Odin, Thor and Frey; but even if she could have got closer, unseen, she felt it was clumsily obvious for Odin's toy to appear to him from the shadow of Odin's statue.

He stopped to study the statue of Freya. Of course he did. He was a man, and Freya was the Goddess whose power was, above all, sexual. The statue made no attempt to show the Goddess's beauty – how could any statue do that? The statues in the temples of Aphrodite and Venus tried, and the result was a series of tritely posing, blandly pretty girlies, like so many genetically-engineered teenagers.

The statue of Freya conveyed Her power. It was a piece of tree, old and gnarled. The upper part had a suggestion of a head and a turned away face. Below that, the withered and rotted wood suggested a neck and part of a hollowed-out torso, a full breast, the line of a narrow waist. Then the wooden stump swelled out into hips, and split into two parted legs. The hips tilted towards the onlooker, and between the legs was a deep hole.

The artist had done little to embellish this natural, forest-grown Freya, except for the addition of the Goddess's famous girdle, Brisingamen, which, according to myth, had increased Her already divine beauty and desirability whenever She wore it. The several strands of the golden girdle described the curve of the statue's waist, belly and hips, touching the wood where there was wood to touch, standing free in the air, seemingly unsupported, where there was none.

It was not a pretty statue, but it was made from a tree, once living, that had naturally embodied the Goddess's shape. Now dead, it suggested Her power over death, and Her immortality. It held all of the Goddess's age, power, strength, and, finally, even beauty. Thorsgift was studying it, somewhat dubiously, when Odinstoy stepped from the shadows beside it. Startled, he looked full at her, and she smiled and said, 'Thorsgift!' Reaching out, she touched his arm. 'You've come a long way to see us!'

Thorsgift drew back sharply, startled by her sudden appearance, and by her closeness and hand on his arm. He hardly took in her words, except that she called him by name.

He looked at her again, wondering: did he know her? And then, annoyed with himself: of course he didn't know her, how could he?

'People are missing you in Mars,' said this small, odd person, looking up at him with long, dark eyes. He wasn't sure if it was a boy or a girl.

'I – ah – yeah. Do I know you?' *In* Mars? he thought.

She leaned close and touched his arm again. He almost pulled away. 'Odin welcomes you,' she said. 'There is love for you.' And with a cheerful wave, she turned and walked away, towards the three great statues at the end of the hall.

An eccentric, he thought. A strange Earth person.

Some people nearby were standing very still and, he found, staring at him. He thought of snapping: 'I'm from Mars! Get used to it!' But then he realised that they were gazing at him with deep respect. One smiled timidly, as if hoping they could be friends.

One, a young man, took a half step towards him. 'Will you join us? The gathering is beginning.'

Thorsgift smiled, pleased by the friendliness. 'Thank you.'

There was a small, raised platform in front of the three statues, and the people gathered around it. A small figure in loose grey clothing climbed the steps to the platform – it was, Thorsgift saw, the person who had touched his arm and known his name. He stared again, noticing again the small face under the dark, spiky hair, and the long, dark eyes.

Feeling a nudge, he looked down, and found beside him a woman from the group who had invited him to join the gathering. 'That's Odinstoy,' she said, nodding towards the stage. 'What did she say to you?'

Stooping towards her, he said, in a loud whisper, 'That I'd come a long way. She was right. I'm from Mars.'

The woman laughed. Her eyes turned towards the stage.

'She knew my name,' Thorsgift said.

'She speaks with Odin.' The woman looked up at him again. 'She's famous, you know.'

Thorsgift looked up at the stage, and the small figure, arms outstretched, praying, and he felt – gratitude. Gratitude, because, among all the people in the temple, Odinstoy had spoken to him. He felt warmed, and loved and favoured; and he wanted to know more about Odinstoy. He wanted to know anything and everything he could learn about her.

It was days before it occurred to him that she might have discovered his name and origin by other means than a whisper from Odin – but he dismissed the thought as soon as it occurred.

Martian Cake

Affie was loading still more clothes into the washer. Every day, more clothes to wash. Freewoman Perry changed every single item she wore every single day, and put the worn items to be washed.

Freeman Perry, too, changed all his clothes every day, and Apollo, dratted Apollo, changed his – or had them changed for him – even more often, because he was always spilling things down himself, or rolling on grass, or stamping in puddles. One little splash of mud, that was all it took, for Freewoman Perry to declare the clothes dirty and in need of washing. And then there were Affie's own clothes, and the tea towels, and hand towels, and bath towels, and bedsheets, curtains, tablecloths, tray cloths, face flannels, mats, scarves, shawls, throws – it was amazing how many things Freewoman Perry could find to wash.

Affie could remember when she herself had changed all her clothes every day – and had often put clothes to be washed after trying them on for a few seconds before deciding that she didn't want to wear them. Now she wondered who had done her washing then. She'd never known, or wondered, or cared. Some poor, weary, bored, dispirited bonder. If I could have that life again, she thought – and she'd take it again immediately, she yearned for it – she'd be more considerate, she really would. Oh, Gods; Oh, ancestors: if you let me have that life back again, I'll be kinder, I promise. She'd wear clothes twice before having them washed. Not underwear, of course. And her sheets and pillowcases would have to be changed every day. And blouses and dresses and stockings. But skirts and jackets and trousers could be worn twice.

Every day, even when Affie was faced with washing down the woodwork, or the windows, or polishing, and washing up and helping Cook, and cleaning shoes, there was another load of washing to be done. And then sorted, perhaps ironed, and checked to see if anything needed repair. Then the things had either to be put aside for repair – when she had time – or taken to the various places the articles were stored or hung. It wasn't that it was hard work, or took long, now that she knew how the washer worked. It was the tedium, the annoyance. *Every* day, another pile of washing. *Every* day. No matter how well or quickly she did it, the next day there would be yet another load. Affie felt sick sometimes, when she found herself loading the same things into the washer that she'd loaded in only the day before. The sheer repetitive monotony seemed to bruise her mind.

So when Freewoman Perry came in, just as she was opening the washer door, and said, 'Leave that for now,' it was an unexpected joy.

Obediently, hiding her pleasure – which wasn't suitable in a bonder – Affie dropped the clothes back in their basket, straightened and waited.

'Apollo is rather excitable today,' Freewoman Perry said,

'and I have things to do. Take him out, please, and let him run about and tire himself.'

'Yes, Freewoman Perry,' Affie said, keeping her face solemn while, inside her, a bubble of happiness and excitement swelled. She stood still, waiting for permission.

'You'll find him in the garden.'

Affie still waited, having grown wary of doing anything in the wrong way or without permission.

'Go on!' Freewoman Perry said. 'Time is passing!'

Affie pulled off her cap and apron and almost ran from the kitchen. Apollo, in the garden, was wearing his little Roman helmet, made of gold plastic, with a crowning fringe of fine red plastic shreds. With a short sword of gold plastic, he was determinedly destroying his mother's flowers – which was no doubt why she wanted him distracted, being unable to control or discipline him herself.

'Freechild Apollo . . .' Affie hated the very feel of those words in her mouth, but she had to call him that. Freewoman Perry might be listening. You never knew when she might be listening, because there were web cams and mikes everywhere, even in the garden, connected to the house computer. It helped to make sure that servants and bonders weren't stealing, or doing or saying anything they shouldn't. When Affie had been rich, she'd never bothered to watch the web cams, or the footage they recorded either, but maybe Minerva had – or she'd employed someone to do it for her. '*Brat*,' she called Apollo, in her head, and '*pain*'. 'Listen – I'm to take you out – we're going out—'

As she came near, Apollo turned and thrashed her legs with his sword, and laughed. The blows stung, and she caught the sword in her hand, which also hurt. Stooping over him, and smiling a fixed smile of hatred, she said, 'Listen, *listen* – be good and we'll go and see –' She lowered her voice, hoping the web mikes couldn't pick up her words. '– Odinstoy.'

That caught his attention. He stopped trying to wrest the sword away from her, and looked up into her face. 'Stoy?'

'Yes – if you're good. Don't tell Mummy.'

But he knew that he mustn't tell Mummy about their visits to Odinstoy. Odinstoy had told him so herself, and her word was law with him. And he was a bright little boy in some ways, though backward in his talking. He let go of the sword and put his hand in Affie's. 'Hurry!' he said.

Affie, as eager as he, dragged him into the kitchen to wash his hands and face – because Freewoman Perry would be annoyed if he 'went out publicly looking like a street child that no one loves or owns'. When he complained, she reminded him, in a whisper, who they were going to see.

Next, she quick-marched him into the hall, where she bundled him into his coat, put on his hat – putting it on again when he took it off and threw it on the floor – and changed his shoes while he kicked her. At the third kick, she whispered, 'If you do that again, I'll hit you.'

'Cameras. Tell Mummy,' he said.

'Kick me again and I shan't take you to Odinstoy. I shall take you to the park, like *she* wants me to.'

Apollo understood much better than he spoke. He thought about it, and then nodded. He even sat patiently while she put on her own drab coat, and the headscarf seemingly made of sacking, which covered her growing curls.

They were shimmering pink with excitement now, even quivering into magenta. Soon, Freewoman Perry would notice them and order Cook to shave them again. And Cook would do it, without caring, because although quite friendly and pleasant – in her own way – she was pragmatic. 'The freewoman pays me,' she said, though her inflection on 'free-woman' was not all that Freewoman Perry would have liked, 'and what the freewoman asks me to do, I do.'

'Come on, come on,' Affie said to Apollo, and hustled him into the kitchen again, and out the back way. She was afraid that Freewoman Perry would change her mind.

Once in the street, they ran in the direction of the park. Freewoman Perry wouldn't like it if she saw them running, but Affie could always say that she had been dutifully tiring Apollo out. Her real intention was to reach the taxi rank near the park as quickly as possible.

There were a couple of cabs waiting. Affie fumbled in her pocket for the card that Odinstoy had given her, gripping it tightly for a moment as she caught sight of Odinstoy's picture on it. What trouble that card had given her – always carrying it about with her, changing it from outfit to outfit, afraid to leave it anywhere that Freewoman Perry might find it. She'd managed to keep it hidden for more than two months now.

She slotted the card into the cab's door to open it, and gave the computer the account number for payment. She lifted Apollo inside, climbing in after him. He bounced on the seat and crowed – he liked cabs. So did Affie. It was bizarre that she'd once taken them for granted. The door of the cab closed, sealing them safely away from the dirt, unpredictability and danger of the streets, which Affie feared more than ever now.

The programming board was set into the roof, out of Apollo's reach, but he watched closely as she pressed in their destination – indeed, he called out the address she should enter. She was in such a good mood, she smiled at him instead of finding him infuriating. The cab moved away from the kerb, pausing to allow other traffic to pass, then gliding into the stream.

Affie sat back with a sigh. Odinstoy was an angel! It was only because of Odinstoy that she could ride in this cab at all. Odinstoy was so beautiful, so talented, so special, and yet so kind – and she didn't have to be. If she ignored people, or did only as much for them as she had to do – or even if she was unkind – she would still be beautiful, and talented and special. How many people could speak with a God? But no, Odinstoy was always kind. She remembered people, she remembered their mothers and their sick children, even their pets. She helped people, she gave them lovely presents, like cards for riding in cabs.

Affie sat staring straight before her, daydreaming, while Apollo clambered about the seats, peering through the windows and chattering about what he saw. Affie didn't hear him. She smiled at the air, dazzled by the wonder of Odinstoy. Why, Odinstoy even loved Apollo! She was always glad to see him, and played with him, and would look after him so that Affie could take a shower, with lovely gels and lotions, or dress up in Odinstoy's clothes, or take a look round the shops, or the internet. But Affie liked to be with Odinstoy as much as Apollo did – more, because what did that brat know? He had no appreciation. Being with Odinstoy made Affie feel beautiful again, and special –

because, despite the fact that her parents had thrown her away, abandoning her to bondship, she must be special somehow for Odinstoy to notice her.

She thought about Odinstoy all the time now, while she was working, in the moments before she slept, and in the few minutes she had to herself after waking.

She remembered how Odinstoy had looked the last time she'd seen her, and what she'd said. She imagined conversations they might have, and things she might say to surprise and delight Odinstoy and make her laugh.

Everything seemed to remind her of Odinstoy, and she wanted to talk about her all the time. She couldn't, because she wasn't supposed to be seeing her, but it was a compulsion. The words struggled into her throat, they filled her mouth and pushed at her teeth, wanting to throw themselves into the air. She once told Cook all about Odinstoy, and kept saying, 'I heard that she . . .' and, 'Once I read that she . . .' and, 'Someone told me that she . . .' She became excited and pink as she spoke, and so did her hair. Cook had noticed, she could tell by the way the woman smiled, but Affie couldn't stop herself talking. Luckily, Cook wasn't a bit interested – though that was hard to understand – and probably forgot everything as soon as Affie stopped speaking.

That was how it was when she wasn't even with Odinstoy. When she knew she was going to see her, she was fizzy with excitement and happiness. Her head seemed full of light that shone out of her eyes, and ears and mouth. And when she was actually with Odinstoy, sometimes it was like sitting in sunshine: warm and contented and peaceful. Sometimes it hurt, the happiness spoiled with disappointment and frustration –

because other people were there, and she got too little of Odinstoy's attention, or because Odinstoy was taken up with Apollo, or because some little conversation she had all planned out in her head went completely wrong when she tried it. But she still had hope that at their next meeting, things would be better – so even their worst meetings were like sitting in the sunshine, surrounded by nettles and thorns.

It was like being in love – but more than love, because she'd never felt so deeply and wildly for Neppie or any other boy – and Neppie had let her down, just like her father. Just like her mother. Now and again, she wondered if she was going mad, because surely it was a bit crazy to feel like this – it wasn't as if she wanted to sex with Odinstoy – she never thought about her like that at all. Never. Surely that was crazy? To be so obsessed with someone, and it wasn't even about sex?

Or did that mean it was something deeper and more spiritual, that she and Odinstoy were soul mates, or sisters-in-spirit or something?

She held her breath, contemplating that beautiful thought, which had surprised her. Maybe that was why Odinstoy thought she was special, perhaps she saw that Affie was going to change in some wholly new way, like a bug turning into a beautiful butterfly – and she'd fly away from bondship and be free . . .

The cab pulled into the kerb outside the block where Odinstoy lived. Affie grabbed Apollo, ready to heave him out onto the pavement. She was suffused with happiness. 'We're here,' she said. At her soul sister's door.

They were in a side street behind the temple. Odinstoy's flat could be entered from the street or from inside the temple, but Affie always preferred to enter it from the street. That seemed more special than going through the temple, where any member of the gatherings might see her and guess where she was going.

'Toy! Toy!' Apollo said, as Affie looked into the iris scanner beside the street door – which might have been the dirty, neglected rear door of some industrial building. It wasn't a nice place to be, even by day. At night it was frightening. Only for Odinstoy would Affie have come there.

The temple's computer recognised her, and there was a clank as the door unlocked. The hallway behind the door was an ugly, nondescript brown: a cold, dusty place. Affie followed Apollo inside, pulling the door shut after her and making sure it locked. She didn't like to think of intruders finding their way inside.

Apollo was already climbing the stairs, and she hurried after him. The landing at the top was drab, too: the same dull brown, but a little cleaner, lit by a row of small windows. There, next to the caretaker's flat, was Odinstoy's.

Affie wanted Odinstoy to live in a place approached through gardens dripping with roses – blue and silver and iridescent roses – in a large, open, airy flat where diaphanous white curtains floated from windows overlooking, far below, the dazzling lights of the city: a sparsely furnished, but tasteful place, where they would sit on cushions on the floor, drinking wine and eating little treats and snacks from a low glass table. Apollo would not be there – no one would be there, except Odinstoy and herself, laughing together. She imagined it so vividly that she often remembered Odinstoy living in this place, and was slightly confused by the reality of her ordinary door in a shabby corridor.

Affie looked into another iris scanner, and the door opened, letting her into a narrow hallway, saved from gloominess by being painted white: walls, ceiling, floorboards and all. She called, 'Odinstoy! It's us!'

Apollo ran down the corridor into the room at the end, and immediately returned, saying, 'Not here.'

It didn't matter: if Odinstoy was out, they would make themselves at home and salve their disappointment by being in her flat, surrounded by her things.

'Maybe she's in the sonic,' Affie said. She shooed Apollo back into the flat's main room. It was small, and dully square, made even smaller by walls painted deep red, except for the one painted black. On that wall was tacked a poster of Odin's strangling, one-eyed face, emerging from darkness and storms.

A big, comfortable sofa took up most of the space, covered with a blood red throw. Rune stones were scattered on a small coffee table. Anyone with the patience to learn the symbols could read the runes, after a mechanical fashion, but of course, when Odinstoy read them . . .

A sound, a patter, and the door from the bedroom opened. In came Odinstoy, naked. Affie wanted to think her beautiful – she tried to make her eyes see her as beautiful – but had to admit, after a struggle, that Odinstoy's body was rather thickset, and childish. She was slim, but had hardly any waist, and very small breasts. It was a child's body, strong, sturdy, but with no grace of line. Affie's own body, she well knew, was far more shapely and attractive. It had been designed to be.

She pulled her thoughts together, marshalled them. This was Odinstoy. Ordinary standards didn't apply to Odinstoy. Her beauty – depths of it – shone from within. (But still there was a part of Affie's mind that whispered: She's plain. You're beautiful. She's not.)

Odinstoy smiled at Affie, but held out her arms to Apollo, who ran to her and was picked up. That gave Affie a sharp jab of jealousy, and she was quick to remind herself that Odinstoy *had* smiled, she *did* love her . . .

'We can't stay long,' Affie said, 'but we both wanted to come and see you.'

Odinstoy kissed Apollo's cheek. 'You'll be wanting something to eat. Let's go and get our Affroditey something to eat,' she said to Apollo, and Affie felt warmed at being called 'our' Affroditey, even if it meant belonging to brattish Apollo as well. 'Coffee or tea? Or wine, or mead or beer?' Odinstoy delighted in feeding people and giving them things. She was so kind.

Odinstoy walked towards the kitchen, Apollo in her arms. She called, 'Thorsgift! Stop hiding! Come out here – come out now!' To Affie she said, 'He stopped to get dressed. He's shy.'

Affie followed Odinstoy into the kitchen. Something spiked and sharp seemed to be moving in her chest. 'Is he good-looking?' she asked, trying to sound light-hearted and girlish, while hating Thorsgift, whoever he was, for being in the flat at all, when she wanted to be alone with Odinstoy; and hating him even more for being in Odinstoy's bed. He might be someone Odinstoy would come to love, and that would take her attention away from Affie. He might be the love of Odinstoy's life, and it wasn't fair: he didn't deserve to be.

Odinstoy gave Affie a quick, sidelong glance, and smiled slightly. Affie's jealousy was as clear to her as if she had broadcast it. 'He's Martian,' she said, and then put Apollo down while she looked into her fridge. Apollo laughed and slapped her bare bum.

'A Martian?'

'From Mars? Do you want chicken? Peaches? Ice cream? All of it?' she asked Apollo, laughing, as she caught his hands and tried to tickle him. 'I'll take all your clothes off and tickle you – all your clothes off . . .'

They started giggling and tussling with each other and Affie, sighing, turned and went back into the other room. Apollo was a brat and a pest. She wished she had another excuse for getting away to see Odinstoy. Maybe, next time Freewoman Perry told her to take him out, she could tie him to a tree in the park and go back for him later. Or program a taxi to take him on a round trip of the city, and jump out, leaving him locked inside.

As she went into the main room, a man – a very tall man – was just ducking in from the bedroom. He started at the sight of her, and almost turned back.

'Oh, you must be Thorsgift,' Affie said, and held out her hand. 'I'm Affroditey, Odinstoy's friend. How are you? I hear you come from Mars?' And I wish you were back there, she thought. Go away! Just leave!

Thorsgift fidgeted on the spot, still apparently toying

with the idea of going back into the bedroom. He was so tall that he had to keep his head bent slightly, or he would have hit it on the ceiling. He blushed a little, she thought, which she didn't think becoming in a grown man – decidedly grown. 'Oh – er – aye,' he said eventually. Awkwardly, he reached over and briefly shook her hand. 'Where is Odinstoy?'

For a moment, Affie didn't understand the garbled sounds; then sense filtered through. 'In the kitchen. I think she's getting us all something to eat. So – how do you know Odinstoy?' She thought: I've known her longer, my claim is better!

'Oh—' He seemed embarrassed. 'I – only met her – recently.' He tried to edge by. 'I just need to say goodbye.'

'Going so soon?' Affie said, while cheering inside her head. Yes! He was going! If only he'd take Apollo with him.

Odinstoy came in, still naked, carrying a cake on a plate. Apollo was behind her, carrying four plates so carefully that he seemed to be holding his breath. 'Thorsgift, you are stay-ing!' Odinstoy said. 'I haven't finished with you yet.'

Thorsgift looked shocked, but then smiled at her, delighted. Affie saw at once that she had a serious rival.

'Odins,' she said, so that Thorsgift could see how close and easy she was with Odinstoy. 'Don't make him stay if he doesn't want to. Maybe he has appointments.'

'He's got to stay,' Odinstoy said, 'and tell us about Mars.' She pointed at a chair. 'Sit down, Thorsgift, and cut the cake. Give me the biggest slice.'

'No, me, me!' Apollo said, and they went into one of their silly games, pushing each other and giggling. Affie only just saved the cake, snatching it from Odinstoy's hands.

'Give it to Thorsgift,' Odinstoy said, picking up a wriggling Apollo. 'Only he is to cut it – if he doesn't cut it, we can't have any!'

'Cut it, cut it!' Apollo shouted, and Thorsgift was obliged to sit down on the big settee, in front of the little table, and cut the cake.

Odinstoy sat down beside him, Apollo on her lap. Affie remained standing, at a distance: hating Thorsgift, hating Apollo. This brief visit was to have been her treat; and it was ruined.

'Tell Pollo about Mars,' Odinstoy said. 'It'll be good for his education.'

Thorsgift shuffled plates and slices of cake. 'I don't know what to tell you. What would you say if I asked you to tell me about Earth?'

'I'd say it was a stinking pot of shit.'

Thorsgift paused in his task of serving cake, and both he and Affie stared at Odinstoy, surprised by the bitterness.

'People say it's red,' Odinstoy said. 'Is it? Is the sky red?'

Thorsgift grinned, and shook his head. 'You Terrans. The Red Planet.'

'Is it red?' Odinstoy demanded. 'Apollo wants to know.'

'Not as red as it was,' Thorsgift said, speaking to Apollo. 'There's a lot of green now. And – the sky isn't blue yet – it will be – but it's not as pink, either.'

'Oh, not fair,' said Affie, plumping down in the other chair, a little apart from the others. If Thorsgift hadn't been there, she would have been sitting beside Odinstoy. 'Mars *should* be red. If it's not red, what good is it?'

Odinstoy looked from Thorsgift to Affie, and laughed.

She took a plate, with a slice of cake, from Thorsgift, and held it for Apollo, while he picked up the cake and took a big bite.

Thorsgift seemed offended. He passed a slice of cake to Affie, but looked at her seriously and said, 'We've been terra-forming for centuries.'

Goddess! Affie thought: I was joking.

'Mars isn't just a little, far-off copy of Earth any more, you know.'

I never said it was, Affie thought, and who cares anyway?

Thorsgift turned suddenly to Odinstoy and said, '*You'd* love Mars.'

'Would I?' Odinstoy asked.

Affie, watching, realised that Thorsgift wished her gone every bit as much as she did him. She felt hurt, snubbed. Why should that be? It was unfair. She was much more beau-tiful than Odinstoy.

'Outside the city, it's so – everything grows – it's very fer-tile. The Goddess is good to us.'

'Which Goddess?' Odinstoy asked.

'Oh, she's worshipped under so many names – as Affroditey, and Venus, and Freya, Sif and Yorth.'

'Odin?' Odinstoy said.

'Oh yes, certainly Odin – but I was talking about Goddesses.'

'I serve the God. Do you have cake on Mars?'

Thorsgift smiled. 'We have everything you do.'

'Martian cake!' Odinstoy said to Apollo, and they started to giggle again.

This is tiresome, Affie thought. It's Thorsgift's fault,

being in the way and making Odinstoy skittish. Normally, she made some time for Affie, instead of just giggling with the brat.

So it went on, the minutes of the precious visit frittered away by Thorsgift grinding out stuff about Mars – oh, domes and big volcanoes and canyons – and who *cared*? And Odinstoy would say something really childish and unfunny like, 'Martian domes!' and she and Apollo would fall about laughing. It was unbelievably tedious, and Affie began to dislike Odinstoy. Honestly, she could be as big a pain as Apollo.

So she stood abruptly and said, 'Is that the time? I've got to go! I've got to get Apollo back or I won't be able to come again.'

Odinstoy rose, took Apollo by the hand and led him away. 'I'll wash him.' He had cake and jam and chocolate plastered round his face and hands. 'I'll put him in the sonic.' That would clean his clothes and body.

Affie was left alone with Thorsgift. There was a silence, a little sulky on Affie's side. Then Thorsgift said, 'You're a good friend of Odinstoy's?'

'Oh, yes.' Better than you, for sure. 'I'm here *all* the time.'

'Do you think she'd come to Mars?'

Affie stared at him. 'Why would she do that?'

'To be a priestess. She'd do well there.'

'She's doing well here. No, she wouldn't. She'd have to leave all her friends.'

'Oh,' Thorsgift said.

'I don't think *anything* could persuade her,' Affie said.

Odinstoy came back with Apollo, as clean as when he'd left his mother's house. 'Bring him again,' she said.

'I always have to bring him,' Affie said. 'I can never get away without him.'

'Come whenever you can,' Odinstoy said, and put her arms round Affie, hugging her tight as if, Affie thought, she wanted to keep her there. She kissed Affie's cheek. 'You're *always* welcome.' Then she started saying goodbye to Apollo, crouching down and hugging and kissing him until Affie, irritated, said, 'We have to go – we'll be late!'

They got out into the hall, but Odinstoy waved them off from the top of the stairs, until they went out onto the street. Then she went back to Thorsgift, Affie supposed. It had been a most thorny, nettling day. Affie thought she would finish with Odinstoy. She'd seen through her, tired of her.

But when they passed the front of the temple, on the way to the taxi rank, she couldn't resist looking in, and there were some new leaflets, with a really wonderful picture of Odinstoy, one that made her look amazing.

Affie was going to leave it. She reminded herself that she'd finished with Odinstoy. But in the end, she took several of the leaflets. She might want to remember this part of her life, and it was a wonderful photo, a piece of art, really. It would cheer up her bedroom a bit . . . She wanted that picture. She couldn't have left it behind.

A Favour

Affie didn't sleep well. She went through her visit to Odinstoy again and again, reliving her disappointment, seeing again every look and word that passed between Thorsgift and Odinstoy, even inventing some. She swore that she really wouldn't ever go to see Odinstoy again, because she saw now that Odinstoy didn't care for her at all. Then she sobbed herself to sleep because, without Odinstoy, there would be nothing in her life except her hated work.

When she woke, she felt quite differently, and laughed at herself. After all, there'd been disappointing visits to Odinstoy before. The next visit might be the best ever. They might leave Apollo to play a computer game – or tie him to a tree in the park – and Odinstoy would give all her attention to Affie, and they would talk about everything, and laugh and grow closer.

While she was dressing, she saw the leaflets she'd taken from the temple lying on her chair. Odinstoy was so beautiful in the photo, with dark hair drifting across huge, dreaming eyes and the slightest smile on her mouth, making the onlooker wonder what those dreaming eyes were seeing. Looking at the picture almost made her late beginning work. She would have been late if it hadn't occurred to her to take one of the leaflets with her. She'd taken several from the temple so that she could keep one pristine, and have a few spare, in case of accidents. She could risk crumpling one. So she stuffed a leaflet down the front of her uniform and ran downstairs to start her drudgery.

There were all the usual chores: washing to be put in the sonic, the table to be laid and the breakfast made. Luckily, it was just cereal and toast and fruit today, which meant no cooking. Affie hated it when she was asked to cook bacon and eggs, or kippers or – even worse – kedgeree. She'd never cooked before she'd been sold, and she wasn't good at it, and every time she tried, it meant nerve-straining lectures from Freewoman Perry. The food was cold. She'd broken the egg yolk. The scrambled eggs were too hard, or they had shell in them. The toast was burned. Freewoman Perry could never simply make her complaint and leave it at that. She had to go on and on, with long pauses, as if she was waiting for Affie to do or say something, and Affie didn't know what was expected of her. Sometimes, as Freewoman Perry stood with folded arms, staring at her, waiting, she felt quite desperate, and ready to burst into tears.

But even the washing up wasn't too bad today – there wasn't all that disgusting grease and dried egg yolk. She even slipped half of it into the dishwasher. That way, she had a few things to be washing or drying if Freewoman Perry came into the kitchen suddenly, but less work. It was worth the risk that Freewoman Perry might spot what she'd done on the web cams.

Then it was off to distant corners of the house, to dust and polish and wash windows. There was less chance of

Freewoman Perry suddenly coming upon her, and she broke up the long hours of monotonous work by sitting down on the attic stairs, where there were no cams, and taking out her photo of Odinstoy.

She was warmed by a sense of wonder as she looked at the picture: she actually knew this glamorous, famous person! Freewoman Perry might think her lower than a resistant cockroach, but Freewoman Perry couldn't call Odinstoy 'Odins'. Freewoman Perry – that stupid old cow (she could think such things inside her head; no web cams could film her thoughts as yet) – that stupid cow, who wasn't as rich or as stylish or as clever as she liked to pretend she was, might think Affie was just a bonder, but Affie knew differently, and this photo proved it. She was best friends with Odinstoy.

At noon, she went to the kitchen, where she was glad to see Cook – she was *glad* to see that ugly, stupid old woman! It wasn't that once she would have laughed at a woman like Cook – she wouldn't even have known of her existence. If Cook had been drawn to her attention, she wouldn't have thought her worth laughing at – any more than the pavement underfoot was worth laughing at. Now, she was so glad to have Cook's company for a few minutes.

Cook put a cup of tea and a large cheese sandwich in front of her. 'Get yourself outside of that, me lover.'

Affie sat and, gratefully, ate. Cook, on her side of the table, poured herself another cup of tea and stared at nothing. Perhaps she was thinking; perhaps her mind was vacant. Affie worked her way through half of the enormous sandwich, waiting for and expecting Cook to start a conversation, but nothing was said.

She hunted through her mind for small talk. 'And how does today find you, Cook?'

'Hmmm,' Cook said, on a note that meant, 'As well as can be expected.'

'Are your legs any better?'

'Hmmm.' This time it meant, 'A little.'

Affie thought of a favour she could do Cook, a treat she could give her. She took the photo of Odinstoy from inside her uniform, and smoothed it on the table beside Cook's hand. Cook's gaze returned from the distance and sharpened on the square of paper. 'What's this?'

'*That*,' Affie said, 'is Odinstoy.' (A dim memory tickled in her head. A long, long time ago, hadn't someone – Neppie? – said almost exactly that, in the same proud tone?)

Cook smiled and picked the paper up, holding it at various distances to get her focus right. She frowned. '*Who* is this?'

'Odinstoy.'

Cook looked again. She put the leaflet down, then picked it up again, and carefully studied the photo once more, making sure. 'Odinstoy? That whajamacallit yo'm barmy about?'

'She's a priestess.'

'Her's our old bloody bonder,' Cook said, and dropped the leaflet on the table.

Affie was startled, but realised that Cook must be joking. She didn't find the joke funny. 'Oh, of course, yes. I should have known. Odinstoy was your bonder.'

'I'm telling you, that's Kylie, that is; our owd bonder. The one afore yow – no, I tell a lie. There was two or three after her that didn't last long. It was, "I'm not paying these extortionate fees to have my things ruined." Know why you've lasted so long? 'Cos you're cheap.'

'*Odinstoy* worked here?'

'I don't know nothing about no Odinstoy. But her can grow her hair and put on make-up and do what her likes – I *know* that face. Funny-looking little chuck, her always was, and that's her. Yow've told me yourself that your Odinstodge was a bonder once.'

'Odins*toy*.' Cook was dim, and could never get the name right. '*She* worked *here*?' It was like hearing that Odin Himself had dropped by on His way to the shops.

'I'll tell you what it was. Her Majesty was jealous on her. And I don't care if you hear!' Cook shouted out, to the web cam in the corner. 'The great thing about a shitty, low-paid job like mine, Free, is I can get another shitty, low-paid job any time I like. There, now,' she said to Affie, 'if her watches that, her'll pretend her didn't. We don't like home truths or having to find a new cook. Servants are such a problem. But her couldn't stand having Kylie around.'

'Why not?' Affie whispered. She had to ask.

''Cos the little boy thought the world on her, didn't he? It was, "Where's Kylie? Want Kylie." And Kylie loved *him* from here to there and back again, didn't her just. Kiddies love the folk as love them, that's what I say, and they know who loves 'em. Only to be expected, really, when you know the facts on it.'

'You mean, *Apollo*?" Affie said.

'No, the five other little boys in this house! Who else?'

'She used to have to look after him, like me!' Affie said. All her chores and drudgery, and even the task of minding that brat, took on a lovelier glow, were sanctified, by Odinstoy having shared them.

'Her was a lot handier than you, all round. Trained up to it from a kiddie, see. I reckon Her Majesty's been kicking herself ever since her got rid on her. But her couldn't stand having her in the house, with Freechild Apollo tagging after her all the time. Hurry up and finish your food and get back to work, I should.'

Affie dusted and polished in the dining room, doing places she'd already done, in a daze. As she sprayed polish, as she rubbed, she thought, Odinstoy did exactly this, in exactly this place. Odinstoy stood here, breathed this air . . . It was almost like being Odinstoy.

It explained why Odinstoy never complained when she arrived dragging the brat Apollo along with her. Even when they'd first met, Odinstoy had known Apollo, had known him better than Affie did. And Apollo had known her.

Affie came to a dead halt, remembering how she had first met Odinstoy in the street, how Odinstoy had said, 'There is love for you.' And Apollo had said, 'That's my Mummy,' and she'd told him off for talking nonsense . . . But Apollo had recognised Odinstoy – and Odinstoy had recognised Apollo. She hadn't singled Affie out because of anything special about Affie, nor had Odinstoy been showing any great compassion. She'd come to her simply because Affie was with Apollo. 'Her loved him from here to there and back again,' Cook had said. She would have approached anyone who happened to be with Apollo. She would have told anyone with him that, 'There is love for you.'

Affie froze to her marrow. Odinstoy had only befriended

her because of Apollo. It wasn't *Affie* Odinstoy wanted to see, it was Apollo. 'Bring Apollo along . . .' Odinstoy was always saying that. Affie had thought it was part of Odinstoy's kindness, that she didn't want Affie to feel bad about always having to bring Apollo with her. But what if – what if – Odinstoy only welcomed Affie when she was alone because she knew that next time, almost certainly, she would have to bring Apollo. Did Odinstoy only tolerate Affie as a way of seeing that brat?

It was too much. She would not believe it – but the thought was in her head now and there was no ridding herself of it. She couldn't vomit it out of her system, or poison it as she might microbes or nits. It was lodged in her mind, sore, and irremovable.

She went furiously at her polishing, as if she could rub the horrible idea away, but she only polished it brighter.

Her hands rubbed harder and harder, until she was panting, sweating, but the painful thought was still there. She could not live with it.

Freewoman Perry came into the kitchen as Affie was finishing the last of the washing up that night, and said, 'Well! You've almost finished. I do believe that you might be getting a grip on things. Dare I hope so?'

Without thinking, Affie turned from the sink and said, 'Freewoman Perry!' so commandingly that the woman stood to attention and listened. 'Freewoman,' Affie said, softening her tone, 'I haven't pleased you, I know. I'm not used to this work, and I know I'm not good at it, but I have been trying very hard to do everything just as you like, and I've been working very hard, for very long hours, and Freewoman – I'm exhausted.'

'Yes. Well.' Freewoman Perry was uneasy. She wasn't used to being the person on the receiving end of lectures. 'If you were a little quicker, and a little more organised—'

'Freewoman, I'm not making excuses. I know my work is poor and, honestly, I am trying to improve . . .'

Freewoman Perry coughed. 'Well, yes, I think there has been a slight—'

'But it's very hard, Freewoman, to struggle on, with nothing but work to look forward to. It's not the life I'm used to, Freewoman.' Freewoman Perry looked away, embarrassed. 'I wanted to ask you, Freewoman, for permission to go out tonight.'

'What?'

'I need a little time off, to relax. We all do, Freewoman, and we're all better for it. I promise, I'll work all the harder if you let me go out this evening.'

Freewoman Perry stared. 'I never – I. Where would you go?'

'You don't have to worry, Freewoman. A friend from before – from, you know, *before* – has invited me to visit her.' Freewoman Perry looked shocked and puzzled. 'She's offered to pay the cab fare – so, you see, I shall be going and coming home in a cab, and we shall only be talking and catching up. I shan't be late. It would do me so much good – would be so refreshing. Please let me go, Freewoman.'

It took Freewoman Perry a while to answer. She cleared her throat. 'How – ah. How did your friend get in touch? There have been no calls or—'

'She found out where I was living, Freewoman, and had a note delivered by hand – to the kitchen door here. You were out.'

'May I see the note?'

'I'd happily show it to you, Freewoman, but I threw it away. I didn't think there was any chance of my going, and it upset me, so I ripped it up and threw it away.' Affie listened to the flow of her own words with admiration. She thought: this is inspired. 'But then I thought I would ask you, because you've been kind enough to put up with all my clumsiness, and I thought you might be kind enough to let me go.'

Now refuse me, after that.

Freewoman Perry again took a long time to answer. 'May I at least ask the name of this friend and where she lives?'

'Berowne Poole,' Affie replied promptly. 'She lives in St Paul's Square.'

The name might mean nothing, but Freewoman Perry drew back her head at the mention of one of the most expensive districts in the entire county. Affie was hoping that she wouldn't actually contact the Pooles – how would she, after all? Their numbers and addresses were ex-directory.

'I'll allow you to go this once,' Freewoman Perry said. 'Please make sure that I don't regret it. And please tell your friend that this is a one-off visit.'

Freewoman Perry left the kitchen, and Affie turned back to the sink with a wide smile of pure triumph.

She finished her chores and then left the house, openly, without having to worry about the web cams. But it was dark in the streets, and she was scared – even though she was now poor herself, she was still frightened by the thought of poor people prowling ferociously in the dark, seeking for people to murder, rob and rape. So, though she'd been working all day and was tired, she ran towards the park and the taxi rank. There were cabs on the rank, and she opened the door of one with Odinstoy's card, and gratefully sealed herself inside.

She directed the cab to the front of the temple, because the street behind it would be too dark and frightening. Even the temple itself was disturbing, with its firelight, and deep shadows, its glowing computer screens lighting the faces of late worshippers, and the hulking figures of the Gods. Affie went through it quickly, and gained the side door that led to Odinstoy's flat.

This time, she knocked on the door. She had to see Odinstoy, but didn't want to walk in on her and Thorsgift again – though she hoped Thorsgift had gone, even died, caught some horrible disease or fallen from a high building.

The intercom clucked. 'Yes?' said Odinstoy's voice.

'It's Affie, Odins. Let me in, please.'

'OK, sweetheart.' And the lock clicked. With relief and gratitude, Affie entered Odinstoy's flat. How lovely to hear herself called 'sweetheart'.

Affie went in, hurrying through to the main room. Odinstoy came to meet her, dressed in a long, loose tunic, her legs and feet bare. She embraced Affie in a big, warm hug, which Affie happily returned. Odinstoy kissed her cheek. 'I'm so glad you came! How did you know I wanted to see you? Odin must have sent you!'

Affie was confused – flattered, but confused. It was pleasant to be told that she was so welcome, and in touch with the

God – but why did Odinstoy want to see her? It couldn't, surely, be for the same reason she wanted to see Odinstoy.

'Come and sit down,' Odinstoy said, drawing her to the couch. Thorsgift didn't seem to be in the flat, and of that Affie was glad. 'What will you have to eat? And drink?'

'Nothing, I—'

'Nothing? But there's chicken, and biscuits, and wine—'

'Odinstoy, I have to ask—'

'Oh, I have something to ask you! It's so wonderful—'

'No, Odinstoy, I have to—'

'Would you like to come to Mars?'

Affie was stunned. Her mind scrabbled for meaning. Had she misheard? 'Mars?' Her voice was dry, and she had to cough.

Odinstoy pulled her down on the couch. 'Mars! Thorsgift – do you know, he came here, looking for a priestess for his temple. They want a God-speaker to lead them.'

'Mars?' Affie said again. She was thinking: it's so far. Her mother was in America, on the other side of the world, but that was next door compared to Mars.

'He's been to lots of temples, but he's asked me! He wants me to go to Mars and speak for Odin there! And I'm going.'

Odinstoy's eyes were huge, fixed on Affie.

'You're going?' Affie said. Just like that? Someone said, 'Come to Mars,' and Odinstoy said, 'OK,' as if they were proposing a trip to a club?

'I'm going. I knew Odin was speaking to me when I first saw Thorsgift. And Mars was the God of war, wasn't he?'

'The Roman name,' Affie said. 'The Greek is Ares.' Her

parents had worshipped the Gods in their Greek form, when they'd bothered to worship at all. It was considered an older, purer practice than the Roman.

'Odin is a God of war too,' Odinstoy said. 'But of death, and magic and healing and wisdom, too – He is the greater God. I have to go. Odin wishes it. You see?'

Affie had nothing to say. She felt sorrow rise in her throat, choking her. 'I shall be left on my own.'

Odinstoy grabbed her and hugged her. 'No, no, no! You are coming with me. That's what I wanted to tell you. Ask you.'

Affie could say nothing.

'Think of it! I shall be a famous priestess, a God-speaker, the greatest in Mars. Because I am going to be. And you – you'll be my sister. Earth will be nothing to us – and good riddance to it! You'll come, you'll come! It'll be wonderful!'

'I'm bonded,' Affie said. They were hard words to say, but – her father had sold her. She belonged to the agency and Freewoman Perry. 'How can I go to Mars?' She didn't think she *wanted* to go.

'I have a good friend,' Odinstoy said. 'He's very good at getting into things. Computer things. Files, and websites and databases.'

Affie stared at her. Why was she talking about databases?

Odinstoy put one finger against her eye, pointing to it. Affie looked at the eye: large, and, in this light, green-hazel. 'Security,' Odinstoy said. 'Everywhere you go, security. Reading your eye, printing out your name. If a bonder runs away, sooner or later they pass a camera that reads their eye and tell-tales who they are.'

'Yes,' Affie said. 'And I'm a bonder.'

Odinstoy grabbed her hands. 'But how does the camera know who you are? A camera isn't clever, Affie. A computer isn't clever. Not that kind, anyway. They're just fast. It only knows who you are because it matches your eye pattern to a database – *poof*! Fast as that. And the database has everything about you.'

'Yes!' Affie said, exasperated. 'And it will say that I—'

'What if the database said that your eyes belonged to – Freewoman Perry?'

Affie was silent, her mind racing through the possibilities. If the web cams picked up Freewoman Perry – or someone they thought was her – there would be no alarm. A freewoman, no criminal record, plenty in the bank . . .

'What if the database said you were – a free girl? You make up a name. A free girl who could go to Mars, anytime she liked?'

Affie sat with her mouth open, thinking of this. 'But it doesn't. It—'

'My friend can get into the database. He can make it say anything he likes about you. He can make it say you're free – that you're my sister.'

Affie was silent again, overwhelmed, as the fields of Mars rolled out before her. Leaving everything behind – Freewoman Perry, bondship, Earth, everyone who had let her down – flying away to a new life with Odinstoy. Her sister, Odinstoy. And free – she would be free again. Everything she did would be for herself.

She struggled to hold onto good sense. 'But – there's a tag. You know. In my – bottom.'

'We can have it turned off,' Odinstoy said. 'Mine was turned off when I was freed. You know the thing they read it with?' She meant the hand-held scanner that could be passed over the skin. 'It can be turned off with that as well. Or you can have it cut out, if you like. It isn't in deep. It's only a small cut, and a stitch.' Odinstoy shrugged. 'I didn't bother. Though maybe I will before we go to Mars.'

'But who would do it?' Affie asked.

'Who would do what?'

'Turn off the tag – or cut it out. It would be illegal.'

'Oh.' Odinstoy laughed. 'I'm a God-speaker, sweetheart, the voice of Odin. There are all sorts here at the temple – doctors, lawyers, programmers, van drivers, nurses, carpenters, plumbers – anything I want done, I can get done. Some of 'em would sell their children and give me the money if I told 'em it was the will of Odin.'

Affie said, 'And you'll tell them that my – that our going to Mars is the will of Odin.'

Odinstoy stared at her with huge eyes. 'That *is* the will of Odin. You will come?'

'I – ah – I – how would I pay? For my ticket?' She didn't know how much a passage to Mars cost, but supposed that it must be very expensive.

'You won't pay. I won't pay. The temple will be paying. They want their God-speaker!'

'Yes, but what about me? I don't talk with Gods.'

'They want me to be happy,' Odinstoy said. 'I need you, I want you with me. They'll pay for you too. We share a cabin, go second class. And it's one way. Not so expensive.'

One way. The words struck a chill. If she went to Mars to

be free of one bondship, might she not find herself in another?

'Say you'll come, say you'll come.' Odinstoy shook her arm. 'Say yes, say yes! What do you have to stay here for?'

What indeed? Her old life was gone, her mother might as well be as dead as her father. All she had here on Earth was Odinstoy, and if Odinstoy went to Mars . . .

Affie took a deep breath and said, 'Yes. If you can arrange it all, yes, I'll come to Mars.'

As soon as she said it, a great sense of relief rolled over her. She felt light, and full of light, loose and relaxed and ready to float. She knew she had said the right thing.

Odinstoy hugged her. 'Good, good! I'm glad!' She drew back to arm's length and looked at Affie seriously. 'Affie, I'll arrange everything. I'll tell Thorsgift. We'll buy you the things you need. I'll get my friend to alter your details in the security bases. I'll get someone to turn your ID tag off. I'll take you to Mars with me. But there's one thing I must ask you to do for me in return.'

Affie looked back at her, surprised. 'What can *I* do for *you*?'

'Steal Apollo.'

Freedom and Revenge

Affie's thoughts were thrown into confusion again, flapping and whirling about her head like a flock of birds startled by a thrown stone. 'Steal Apollo?'

'He's coming to Mars with me.'

'Apollo? Mars?' It wasn't going to be her and Odinstoy together for ever, then. 'You only want me for Apollo.' She tried to get up, but Odinstoy was holding onto her arm. Affie shook her off. 'You only made friends with me because I was looking after that *pain*. And you don't want to take *me* to Mars. It's only—'

Odinstoy gripped her arms with a strength that hurt and stared her, with those Japanese eyes, into silence. 'He's my *son*.'

The conversation seemed, to Affie, to grow more strange with every word. 'He's Freewoman Perry's son.'

'*Mine*.' Odinstoy put her hands on her belly. 'I was as full of him as the peach is of its stone. *I* pushed him out. Not that thieving bitch.'

'But—' Cook had said that the former maid had 'loved Apollo from here to there and back again'. And he didn't look like Freewoman Perry. But then, he didn't look like Odinstoy, either.

'I was her bonder. Not even my own finger-ends belonged to me. Apollo was pretty, she fancied him. So she took him. The only thing I had, that I ever had, and she took him.'

'But if he was *your* son,' Affie said, 'then he belonged to the agency. Surely?'

Odinstoy laughed. 'He *belongs* to Freeman Perry. Freeman Perry made him.'

It was a moment before Affie understood what she meant. '*Freeman Perry?*'

'And all I ever got out of it was Apollo. He's *mine.*'

Affie was aghast. She lived under Freeman Perry's roof now, and she was far more attractive than Odinstoy. Had he already noticed her, looking at her legs as she went upstairs, her backside as she walked down the hall? It made her skin creep. How much longer was she going to be safe from him?

'*I* changed his shitten nappies,' Odinstoy said. It was a second before Affie realised she was talking about Apollo, not Freeman Perry. 'She wouldn't touch that job. I taught him his first rhymes. *I'm* his mother! But if they have their way, he'll never know I existed. They'll teach him that bonders are dirty and stupid. When they've finished with him, he won't even look at me.'

Affie was embarrassed, and turned away. She still thought, if she was honest, that all bonders except herself and Odinstoy *were* dirty and stupid. And, if she was even more honest, she thought Odinstoy was probably dirty, and a bit stupid, but she was prepared to overlook it.

Odinstoy, thinking that Affie's turning away meant disagreement, said, 'Help me. To get my son back. Once we're

in Mars, no one'll ever be able to take him from me again.'
She waited for an answer but there was none. She said, 'This
is Odin's will.'

Affie's face twisted. 'Why should I? You don't love me.'
She was aghast to hear herself talking about love, but then
said, 'You never loved me. It was just—'

'Not true! All right, yes, it's true, I watched Apollo. Yes,
I spoke to you because you were with him, because I knew
you were Perry's new bonder. Yes, I wanted to know you
because, if I knew you, I could see Apollo. Yes! That is all
true! Do you blame me? Do you think I should have forgotten my son, and never tried to see him?'

Affie, accused, rejected, confused, began to cry. All this,
and the memory that her own mother had abandoned her,
finding her too much trouble; and her father had killed himself to avoid the difficulties he'd made for himself, hadn't
bothered to think about her need for him. And yet here was
Odinstoy, a bonder, without the education or self-respect of
Affie's parents, determinedly keeping in touch with her son,
plotting and scheming and managing . . . Odinstoy was wonderful. Affie felt guilty for having questioned her motives,
but even more hurt and disappointed that this wonderful,
loving Odinstoy's affection had never really been for her.

Odinstoy came close and, despite Affie trying to fend her
off, hugged her tight. 'Oh, love, I never meant to make you
cry! What I was going to say is, even if I made friends with
you to see Apollo, that doesn't mean I don't love you! We
make friends with people for all different reasons – and
there's always something in it for us. Isn't there?'

Odinstoy looked into her face, and Affie had to nod. It

was true. You made friends because you wanted a companion, or because you wanted richer, prettier friends, or because you wanted an 'in' – there was always something.

'And some of those friends don't last long, but with some of them, we find more and more reasons to be friends, and they go on and on. And you're bright, and funny, and make me laugh – and this will bring us even more together. We'll be sisters in Mars! Martian sisters!'

Affie giggled. It was as if they were playing the silly game that Odinstoy had played with Apollo. It made her feel close to Odinstoy, and special.

'Will you do it?' Odinstoy asked. 'All you have to do is find a way of bringing Apollo to me when I ask. I'll fix everything else.'

Freedom, Affie thought, and revenge on Freewoman Perry. I'll go to Mars and get rich. Somehow. Richer than my father. Her old, easy, comfortable life again; and she would be Odinstoy's sister. Sister to the greatest priestess on Mars. Sister to the most special, intriguing person in the Universe – moon to Odinstoy's sun.

'I'll do it.'

At the time, she meant it. Later, when she was frightened at what she'd promised, she told herself that nothing would come of it. Odinstoy would find out that it couldn't be done, and they'd all be stuck here on Earth, in misery.

They couldn't actually do it – what if they were caught? Taking Apollo would be kidnapping. What would a bonder get for kidnapping the child they'd been bought to look after? She wasn't sure but she suspected, with a horrible lurch of her heart under her breastbone, that it would be hanging.

Odin's Runes

Odinstoy watched the others enter the feast room. They came through the low, narrow door with the wooden pillars on either side, into the room with its wooden-panelled walls, and its heavy, embroidered wall hangings, which showed oak trees and deer hunts.

She was already seated at the centre of the long, low table, on one of the low, cushioned benches. And there was Thorsgift, bending almost double to come through the door, and still having to keep his head ducked low even when he was in the room. He looked vexed because the places next to her were taken.

There was Freewoman Atwood; there were other regulars, smiling at her, nodding, taking their places, some of the older ones struggling with the low seating. Affie wasn't among them. Odinstoy watched the door for her, as she had looked for her in the temple, but soon the places were all taken, and still there was no Affie. She hadn't been able to come. So, she wouldn't see Apollo today. Still, it was a relief to be without Affie and her jealousy of Thorsgift.

Odinstoy poured beer, handed round the cups, and offered people bread, while they congratulated her on the gathering.

'I *felt* the God.'

'Yes. He was here, among us. It was good.'

'He always comes for Odinstoy, doesn't He?' She was sitting among them, looking like a wild thing, dressed like a völva, a priestess of the ancient North, in a long robe decorated with bones and feathers, her dark hair wild and spiky, and her eyes painted round with black and red. They still smiled on her indulgently.

She looked across the circle at Thorsgift. 'Did *you* enjoy it, Thorsgift?'

He grinned at her. 'The gathering?' He nodded. 'Wonderful. I felt the God. I hope to hear you lead many more.'

People looked at him curiously. Freewoman Atwood offered him the plate of bird-shaped cakes. 'Oh? Are you extending your stay, Thorsgift?'

'Thorsgift has asked me,' Odinstoy said, and the eyes and attention of most people moved to her, 'if I will go with him to Mars, and lead gatherings there.'

A silence came over them. At length, someone said, 'To *Mars?*'

Freewoman Atwood cleared her throat and said, 'What an opportunity for you!'

'Opportunity?' said Freeman Kane. 'No offence to our young Martian friend, but Odinstoy could do much better than *Mars*, if it's opportunity she's seeking.'

'You're not *leaving* us, Odinstoy?' asked young Sif.

Odinstoy looked around at them, her hair standing out around her head, her long eyes blazing against the thick, dark paint around them. 'I shall ask Odin.'

That silenced them. There were those who thought, secretly, that, since they'd contributed money to buy Odinstoy's freedom, she was now obligated to them, despite talk of freely giving her to herself, or of her being owned by Odin. But what Odin willed must be.

'I shall ask Him here, now, and you'll all see.' Odinstoy leaned forward, pushing aside dishes and cups to clear the table top. People put dishes and cups on the floor beside them. 'Many of you have studied the runes, you know their meaning—'

'Not like *you*, Odinstoy,' Sif said, and there were nods and whispers of agreement. It was one thing to know the meaning of the different runes – it was another to grasp instinctively, as Odinstoy did, the combinations and connections of the symbols, the interplay between them, the meanings within meanings, the poetry of them. To hear the voice of Odin.

'It's a simple question,' Odinstoy said. 'The answer won't be hard to understand.'

She touched buttons beneath the table's edge, and the room's lights dimmed, shadows leaning in from the corners. A touch on another button, and the table's glass surface lit with a blue, opalescent glow. Everyone around the table leaned forward, and their faces were strangely lit from below by the bluish light.

Silver shapes rose from deep within the table, as if rising through depths of water. The runes caught the light as they rose, firelight shimmering across them – or they were lit by a sudden harsh, lightning flash glare. There was music: drumming, and the melancholy creak of a fiddle.

'The question,' Odinstoy said, 'is, "Odin, do You wish me to go to Mars? Do You wish me to speak for You on Mars? Odin, what is Your will?"'

As she pressed the button that activated the program, her free hand, hidden in her robe, curled into a fist. Be with me, Odin! Give me the answer I want – that I need. But she knew that Odin might already have given her all that He intended to give her. Perhaps, now, He would turn on her.

The runes spun and whirled, falling back into the depths and rising up again. After some seconds, one rune rose to the surface, shining silver, and steadied at the table's left side, showing a straight line with two chevrons attached at its upper right side.

There were gasps of astonishment, and several voices whispered, awed, the name of the rune: 'Mouth.'

'Odin's rune,' someone whispered excitedly. The computer chose the runes at random. The only influence that could be brought to bear on its choice was that of the God's. And, from thirty runes, the first to appear, in answer to the question, was Odin's rune – Odin's mouth, Odin's voice.

'It's *you*,' Sif whispered. 'The voice of Odin.'

'Maybe,' Odinstoy said. Another rune was rising from the depths and steadying beside the first. Shining as if lit by fire, it was a hollow diamond, with the sides of the diamond, at top and bottom, extended beyond its points.

'Ing,' Sif said, naming the rune, but her voice was puzzled. The others round the table were puzzled too, and looked at each other. Ing was another name for the God Frey, and the rune named after Him stood for fertility. They didn't see what two God runes, appearing together, could mean.

Another rune rose from the depths and settled into place at the right hand. A straight, vertical line surmounted by a crooked line. A stormy, indigo light flickered across its silver.

'Grave,' Sif whispered, naming it. People drew back, looking at each other. In the table top, the three runes gleamed against darkness.

'The meaning's clear to me,' Odinstoy said, and sat back. Her heart was thumping, and she had to be careful not to let them hear her slight breathlessness. 'The first stands for me, as you guessed, and for Odin. It's Odin speaking to us here and now, and it's what He wants me to do – speak for Him. And Ing – Ing is a rune of good fortune – you all know that – and it speaks of spring and fertility – but of rebirth too, and recovery and *new beginnings*. But there's more. What does the story of Ing say?'

She waited. The people at the gathering wriggled in their seats like guilty, inattentive schoolchildren. 'What does the story tell us about Ing?' Odinstoy prompted.

Thorsgift half raised a big hand. 'That he was a traveller?'

'He was a traveller. And he sailed away from us in a ship. And I shall go to Mars in a ship.'

Thorsgift looked round the gathering, grinning. Everyone was looking at their friends.

Odinstoy touched the dimly glowing table with one finger. 'The runes are speaking of travel – by ship – for the mouth of Odin. And blessing the journey with fortune.'

'But – the last one,' Sif breathed.

'Grave,' Odinstoy said. 'We all must die, and our Lord is Lord of the Dead. But, "*Let Death be a spur to courage.*" And, "*The great names will never die of those who win themselves fame.*" Grave comes to tell us not only that we must die, but that *all* things end. Your dearest friend, your dearest love – no matter how faithful, no matter how loyal – will one day turn from you and enter the grave . . .'

In the dim room, the great oak trees loomed from the folds of the hangings, and there was a scent of wood from the walls; of wood, and of lavender and thyme.

A chill crept over their skin as they listened to the low voice – a voice now soft and warm, now hoarse and grating, as it rose and fell over the words.

'Every love affair will end. Every part of your life will have its end. Youth leaves us. Children grow away. Nothing goes on for ever. Times of sadness end. Times of happiness end. All is change. This is the promise Odin makes us – "Whatever I grant you, I will take away." Seize His favour while you have it. It will not last.

'And so the message here is clear to me. My time on Earth is over. My happy time here, as your God-speaker, is over. I must take ship and speak for Odin in Mars. I may have good fortune in Mars, I may have bad – but I must seize this chance offered to me while I have it, and go. It is Odin's will, and I am Odin's toy.'

She looked around at them. Thorsgift's face was eager, delighted; and young Sif's face was rapt, awed – but many others were not convinced. They dared not say they didn't believe in this message of the runes but, by their faces and the looks they gave each other, she could tell that they resented it, and didn't want to believe. They enjoyed her growing fame, and still thought they owned her. They wanted her to stay on Earth and be their tame priestess.

'You don't believe,' she said.

'No – no!' It came from all sides.

'If it's Odin's will . . .' someone said.

'*If*?' Odinstoy said. '*If*? You do not believe.' Touching a pad, she dismissed the runes that glimmered in the table top. They watched them sink into deep, dark water. Odinstoy took a deep breath. 'Freewoman Atwood. Call up a single rune. You do it. Ask Odin to tell us whether I should go or stay.'

Freewoman Atwood reached for the table's edge, but drew back her hand. She looked round guiltily at everyone. 'But no – Odinstoy. It shouldn't be me . . .'

Odinstoy folded her hands in her lap. Unseen, her fingers knotted tightly together. 'Freewoman Atwood. Ask the God.'

Freewoman Atwood reached out her hand again, clearing her throat. 'Odin – look on this world with Your sighted eye, and the next world with Your blind eye, and give us our answer.' She touched the table's edge, and a single rune rose from the darkness, turned and twisted, then settled, like a silver lightning flash, at the table's centre.

A gasp, of astonishment, awe, and even fright, went up from those around the table. The single rune – randomly chosen from thirty – was sun.

Odinstoy laughed, and quoted, "*Sun is a joy to seamen when they cross the seas until the brine-stallion brings them to land. Sun brings good faring and good luck!*"

The gathering sat silent, humbled, staring at the rune. Everyone there had enough rune knowledge to know that the chief meanings of 'sun' were good fortune and journeying. But there were other runes that stood for travel – horse, or riding, or water. Odin had shown them the only one that was in the sky. There was no rune for Mars, so He had shown them sun.

They were shaken. 'I am sorry,' Freewoman Atwood said. 'Sorry that I doubted. I did doubt. I must learn to have faith. It's His will, then, that you go to Mars. You must go.'

'He inspired us to free her, so she could go to Mars!' said Freeman Kane.

'We must do all we can to help you.'

'Everyone who can contribute . . .'

'Vote money from the temple funds.'

'She must go.'

Odinstoy looked into Thorsgift's eyes, and smiled.

'You've never heard of the space elevator?' Thorsgift said. '*Never?* Honestly?'

Odinstoy lay curled into his side, her head on his shoulder. He found it amazing and touching that she, who was so powerful, could lie with him like that, so small and gentle. Her shoulder under his big hand, with its tiny sharp bones under the smooth, slippery skin, almost broke his heart. 'No,' she said. 'What is it?'

She had a sly, odd sense of humour. Remembering that made him cautious. 'You're joking me.'

'No.' She looked up at him, tipping her head back in the hollow of his shoulder. 'I know what an elevator is, but the space elevator?' Her dark hair stuck up spikily. 'What is it?'

Aghast, he contemplated her ignorance. 'Just the biggest engineering project ever.' Astonishment made him eloquent. 'Only a triumph of nanotechnology. Possibly the biggest,

most audacious project ever completed by humanity. Cost –
I don't know – can't even guess. Unimaginable amounts.
How can you not have heard of it?'

Irritated, she reared up on one elbow and looked down at
him with a scowl. One little, pointed breast dangled, amusing him. 'I never went to school, friend. Not a proper school.
I was a bonder. I was only taught to clear up other people's
shit. Why should I know anything about anything? Are you
going to tell me what it is or not?'

He felt a ridiculous alarm at her annoyance, and also
amusement and delight that someone so small and cute
could scowl and speak so gruffly. It was like being mauled by
a kitten. He stroked her arm soothingly. 'I'll tell you! Cool it;
I didn't mean anything – I was surprised, that's all.'

'So what is it?'

'The space elevator. It's – well, it's how you leave Earth
on your way to Mars. And the moon, too. They take tourists
up to the space stations and the moon, and they lift up – oh,
supplies, and materials for building and repair. And imports
and exports. It's a passenger and freight line. But the thing
itself, it's a – well, it's a huge, huge, tall – cable. Or tower. It's
the longest cable ever, anchored to the tallest tower ever. It
goes up – right up into space. It's amazing. Incredible.
Wonderful. Wait till you see it.'

'Into space?' Odinstoy said, frowning.

'Space, yes.' He could tell from her expression that she
didn't understand. 'Into space. Out of the Earth's atmosphere. Into space.'

She looked even more baffled, and he found himself sitting up in bed, naked, giving a God-speaker a basic science

lesson, explaining about the Earth being a spherical planet that circled the sun, enclosed in a layer of gases, which was the atmosphere, and which made the sky look blue by refraction. He couldn't tell how much, if any of it, she understood.

She pointed at the ceiling. 'This cable goes right up through the clouds?'

'Yes, but much higher too. Right out of the Earth's air, up to where there's no air, no up really, no down . . . Into space.'

She said, 'Mars is in the *sky*?'

He gaped at her. 'Well . . . When you're on Earth it is. Where did you think it was?'

She stared at him, stared at the bedsheet under them, then shook her head. 'Across the sea?'

He opened his mouth, but found nothing to say. He gaped at her, realising that she had no conception at all of the journey she'd agreed to undertake. 'Mars is a planet. Like Earth. They're both planets.' Did she know what a planet was? Or the solar system? He realised that, when he'd been talking about the sky of Mars no longer being so red, she'd had no idea what he was talking about. What had she imagined? Another country on Earth, with a red sky? 'Odinstoy – Mars is a long way off.'

'How far?'

What was the good of telling her when she wouldn't understand? 'It depends. Sometimes it's further away—' She looked annoyed again, and he quickly said, 'At its furthest, it's one hundred million kilometres away. At it's closest, it's about fifty million. At the moment it's nearer a hundred than fifty.'

She accepted this placidly because, he suspected, she had no concept of what a hundred million kilometres meant.

'The diameter of Earth is only about thirteen thousand kilometres,' he said. She didn't respond. That number meant nothing to her either. How could it? She had been raised and educated as a bonder. Her own native sensitivity and intelligence, plus the favour of the God, might have made her a priestess and a God-speaker, but she was still untaught and ignorant. She needed somebody to look out for her and guard the merely human side of her.

'Does this cable go all the way to Mars?' she asked.

He laughed. She really had no idea. 'A hundred million kilometres?' He laughed again at the idea of Mars orbiting on the end of a tether. 'No – the cable's only twenty-six thousand kilometres. It goes up to a space station. But we shan't go there. Our ship will be released from the cable and *flicked!* towards Mars. You know how you whirl something round on a string very fast, and then let it go? And it flies off? A bit like that.'

She looked at him, her frown puzzled, not annoyed.

He grinned at her. ''S true. Honest.'

She seemed to think about what he'd told her for some time, in silence, her small head bowed. 'How long will it take to get to Mars?'

'About two months.' He took her question as a request for more information generally. 'First we book your ticket—'

'And for Apollo and Affie.'

'What? Oh – yes.' He became serious. This was going to be awkward. 'I heard – is it true what I hear – that Affie is bonded?'

'You can tell she is. By looking at her.'

'I'm Martian,' Thorsgift reminded her. 'I can't always tell these things. If she's—'

'Well?' Odinstoy demanded.

'I know she's your sister, but I don't see how we can take her – or her son – with us if she's bonded. I can't afford to buy them, Odinstoy. The committee would never authorise it.'

'I won't go to Mars without them.'

Thorsgift opened his mouth to say, well, then she wouldn't be going to Mars. There were other God-speakers. His mouth stayed open, the words unspoken. He had visited other God-speakers. None were as remarkable, as compelling as Odinstoy – none that were willing to go to Mars, anyway. If she stayed on Earth, he would lose her. She would no longer be in his life, making it larger, making it significant. And he would no longer be taking back to Mars a God-speaker who excelled, who surpassed, all expectation. He would no longer be the Thorsgift who did that. It would be hard to give it all up.

Odinstoy turned to him and put her hand on his chest, stroking the hair there as if she was stroking a cat. It amused him, made him feel like some big, powerful, shaggy creature, being petted by its little mistress. She said, 'You think bondery's a good thing, I bet.'

'A good thing?' he repeated. He'd never thought much about it at all, any more than he wondered whether the ground under his feet was a good thing, though he supposed it was. He'd miss it if it wasn't there. Life, he supposed, would be a lot harder without bondery.

'Why should I be bonded?' Odinstoy asked.

'You're not. You're – well, you belong to the God. But you would, anyway.'

'I was bonded.'

'Some people are suited to it,' Thorsgift said. 'They're happier that way.'

'I wasn't,' she said. 'I was born bonded. I didn't choose it. Nobody asked me if I'd be happier free.'

'Some people are born free, when they'd be happier bonded,' Thorsgift said. 'They have to put up with it too.'

Odinstoy moved in a blur. A blow, a sharpness, struck him at the side of the face, filling his head with noise, buzzing, stinging. She sprang from the bed, away from him, spinning to face him, crouching, defensive, feral.

Amazed, scared, he was still recovering from the blow. He put his hand to his face and found blood where her nails had dug in. He looked at her, her face set and snarling with rage. Small as she was, he didn't dare approach her. Even the small, in a rage, can bite and gouge and kick – and he wouldn't want to hurt her, while trying to stop her hurting him. 'What was *that* for?'

Something came hurtling through the air, another blur. He flattened himself on the bed and it crashed into the wall above him. A wooden box, things falling, clattering from it. Some of the things fell on his head with painful, noisy blows.

'I am going to Mars,' she said, leaning on the edge of the bed, her small breasts dangling. Her spiky dark hair was on end, her eyes blazed, her mouth grinned with rage. 'It is Odin's will. Hear that?'

Odin's will. The Raging One's will. The name – or title – Odin meant the Raging One.

'I am going. And I am taking Apollo and Affie with me. Hear that!'

Thorsgift, awed, curled on the bed, his hands protecting his head. She not only spoke for the Raging One. She embodied Him.

'You know why I'm taking Apollo with me? He's my *son!*'

Cautiously, Thorsgift uncovered his head a little. 'Yours? I thought he was Affie's?'

'No!' Odinstoy was impatient with her own lies and those fool enough to believe them. 'He's *my* son. And I'm not leaving him.'

Thorsgift uncoiled a little more. A mother's refusal to leave her child was understandable, even admirable – if it was true. 'I thought . . .' He hesitated, fearful of setting off another rage. 'I thought – the little boy – was – free?'

'He is.' Odinstoy sat on the bed. 'Listen. I'll tell you. Freewoman Perry owned me, right? She was my last owner. Old bitch. And she had a husband.'

Odinstoy fell silent, sitting naked on the edge of the bed, staring at the wall.

'Yes?' Thorsgift said. He relaxed from his defensive curl, even sat up, his feet among the trinkets that had fallen from the thrown box. 'So – she had a husband?'

Odinstoy gave him a contemptuous glare, as if he ought to have known everything from that mention of a husband. 'Bonders are for doing housework, aren't they? You don't want to shag your husband, send him to your bonder. Your bonder's got no choice.'

'Oh,' Thorsgift said.

Odinstoy continued to glare. 'Don't tell me you've never shagged a bonder. Don't tell me your dad hasn't. That's what they're for.'

Thorsgift looked down at the sheet, rubbed it between his fingers. He couldn't look at her, as heat flowed through him. Because, yes – his first sex had been with his mother's bonded girl, and yes, he knew his father and his brother sexed with her too. And – he grew hotter – he'd always thought he'd done her a favour. He'd given her a present, been kind to her. Cheered her up a little. He was a nice guy.

'Some people are suited to it, they're happier that way,' Odinstoy said.

'All right, all right.' Thorsgift crouched lower to the bed. The anger was rising in her voice. He was afraid she would hit him or throw things again.

'He duffed me.'

'What?'

'Duffed. Stuffed.' Exasperated, she explained. 'I was having a baby.'

'O-o-h.'

'Lucky me, the old bitch thought. Two slaves for the price of one. Then, when Pollo was born, she liked him. Decided she wanted a kiddie to play housey with. So she took him, didn't she? He grew in me, I birthed him, I fed him. I had all the trouble of waking in the night with him – you can bet she wanted none of that. I had the shitten nappies. But I still had to do all my work. I was dead on my feet.'

Thorsgift felt his ears were on fire. Never before had he realised the depth of his own insensitivity, his callousness, as he recalled all those faceless, well-nigh invisible bonders who had cooked his meals, tidied his room, cleaned his clothes, and generally made his life smooth and comfortable. And he had always assumed they were happy. He'd never asked if they were. It had always been obvious. Some people were suited to bondery. They were happier that way.

Now here was one telling him she had never been. Angry. Hurt. Her words were like barbed wire lashes.

'She adopted him. Took him away from me. Called him Apollo. But she's not having him.'

She stared at Thorsgift, who didn't dare say anything.

'Affie's her bonder now. Affie'll bring him to me – if she can come to Mars as well. Affie doesn't want to be a bonder either. Do you know about Affie? She was free. And rich. Ask her if she's happier being a bonder.'

'But, Odinstoy,' Thorsgift said, wondering if he should take cover before he said any more, 'you'll have to pass medical tests first.'

'Medicals?'

'Anybody going to Mars has to pass a thorough medical first. They won't let you on the ship until you do. It's a long trip, and – there's a medical room on board, but it's a cupboard, and the doctor's not a specialist. They try to ensure that nobody on board is going to develop any serious medical condition.'

Odinstoy shrugged. 'We're all healthy.'

'Yes, but you'll have to go through ID checks before you get the medical. They'd find out Affie's a bonder – and not *your* bonder – straight away.'

'There are ways,' Odinstoy said.

'None that I know of.'

'You don't know everything. You don't know much.'

Certainly, he hadn't known how bonders felt about bondery. 'I know that taking Affie to Mars would be theft. And taking Apollo would be kidnapping.'

'How can I kidnap my own son?'

It was an awkward question to answer. 'Legally, he's not your son. Legally, he's Freewoman Perry's.'

Odinstoy allowed a silence. Then she raised those dark, Japanese eyes, their edges still darkened with smudged eyeliner, and stared him out. 'Whose law is that? Odin's? Or Freewoman Perry's?'

A still more awkward question to answer.

'Who made me a bonder?' she said. 'It wasn't my wish. Who made Affie a bonder? It wasn't her wish. Is it Odin's? Or just the wish of people who want to make money out of people who can't fight back?'

He knew he was risking another clout, but he said, 'It must be Odin's will. Isn't everything Odin's will?'

'No,' she said. 'Watch the vids at the temple. *Think* about them. Old age isn't Odin's wish. The end of the world isn't Odin's wish. The Gods are wiser and more powerful than us, but they fight and struggle against fate and evil too. Saying everything is Odin's will – that's lazy thinking. That's cowardly thinking.'

Again, that lash of barbed wire. His head sank.

'Do you believe that I speak for Odin?'

He didn't answer.

'Do you believe,' she demanded, 'that I speak for Odin?'

Of course he did. Everyone here, in the community of the temple – none of them fools – believed that she did, knew that she did, and had known and believed it before he had arrived. He had felt the presence of the God when she had called for Him. He had witnessed her uncanny reading of the runes. She was Odin's toy. He knew that.

So what was he to say now? Was he to deny what he knew, because it would cause him difficulty? Did he only believe and keep faith with his God when it was easy? The old ones had kept faith with Him even when it meant dying for Him.

'Yes. I know you speak for Odin.'

'Then listen when Odin speaks. I am to go to Mars, and Apollo, my son, is to come with me. And Affie. That is His will. You must help me.'

Now Thorsgift looked straight and hard at her. 'Are *you* hearing Him clearly? Do you hear Him saying Apollo and Affie must come because that's what *you* want to hear?'

'No,' she said.

'I think, yes. If He wanted Apollo and Affie to go, He'd make the way clear for them, wouldn't He?'

'He's testing your strength.'

'Maybe He's testing *yours*. Maybe He wants you to go to Mars alone, to see if you're strong enough. Ever think of that?'

They stared at each other. 'Apollo and Affie must come with me. You must help me. That is His will.'

They went on staring at each other.

'Have you rune casting on your phone?' she said.

Thorsgift reached for his jacket from the floor beside the bed, and took the thin flat screen from its pocket.

'Then ask Him.'

He hesitated. If he asked, and the answer was clearly: *Yes, this is My will*, then he'd have no excuses. He would have to believe, and obey. He would have to become a thief and a kidnapper – or, if he didn't, he'd be a faithless man, a fool, a coward, a hypocrite.

'Go on,' Odinstoy said. 'Ask.'

Most of the time, when he consulted the runes, the answer was meaningless, or unclear. 'What if He says He wants you to go to Mars alone?'

'Then I'll go. But He won't.' Odinstoy unclenched her fingers, made herself breathe evenly. This could be the time when Odin turned on her, betrayed her. She didn't think so. She didn't think He'd finished with her yet. But there was no certainty. 'Ask Him.'

Thorsgift touched the screen and it lit, lighting his face. 'Command. Rune casting,' he said. The light on his face flickered as the runes shifted, fire-lit, on the little screen. 'Odin. Look on this world –'

Odinstoy joined him in the prayer. '– with Your sighted eye, and on the next world with Your blind eye –'

'– and tell me, please, is it Your will that Odinstoy takes Apollo and Affie with her to Mars? Even though it's against the law? *Cast.*'

The light danced on his face as the runes tumbled and shifted, then settled as the chosen runes stilled. Thorsgift stared at them.

Odinstoy's fists were clenched again. 'What does He say?'

'Mouth, torch, yew.'

Odinstoy's clenched muscles relaxed. She sagged on the bed. She laughed.

'Mouth – is Odin's voice,' Thorsgift said. 'I know that, but—'

'Odin's voice, speaking to us, telling us that wisdom and knowledge and learning is often hard-won.'

Thorsgift nodded. 'And torch?'

'You know the rune verse,' Odinstoy said.

'"*Torch burns bright,*"' he recited. '"*It burns where leaders gather. It is a beacon calling brothers together. Wisdom and hope are the flames of leadership. Courage makes it burn more fiercely.*"'

'To gain wisdom, be a leader, you must have courage. And the last, yew. You know what it means.'

Thorsgift said, 'It's the World Tree. It grows through all the worlds. Its roots in the Underworld. Its trunk here in our world. Its branches in the world of the Gods.' He frowned. 'But I don't see what it means with the others.'

'The spirit, and the growth of the spirit,' Odinstoy said. 'Odin hung on the Tree for nine days to learn the meaning of the runes. The Tree was the horse he rode into all the worlds, to search for knowledge.'

Thorsgift nodded. He knew this, but was unable to recall it, or bring it together as she did.

'Odin says to you: to learn wisdom, to be a leader, to burn with courage, go into new worlds, ride new paths. Don't follow the old ones. You can't steal a slave? A mother can't kidnap her own son? Old paths. Paths made by other people.'

She sat on the edge of the bed, looking steadily at Thorsgift.

He stared at the runes on his phone, until it switched itself off. Those were the runes that answered his question, randomly chosen. But were they to be understood as Odinstoy said, or could they be interpreted another way?

Or was he just trying to escape Odin's will?

Lifting his head, he stared back at Odinstoy.

Casting the Runes

Bob Sing, dressed in underpants and T-shirt, sat on his sofa, scratched his head and yawned. The sofa, the floor around it, the low table in front of it, and the other chairs in the room were covered with used plates, cups, cutlery, print-outs. Books and magazines were scattered among the other litter, their thin plastic pages flickering as they picked up fresher news. Discarded clothing tangled around chair legs, and shoes lay hidden among it all.

The door buzzer sounded, and Bob grinned, stretched to the tips of his fingers and toes, then clapped his hands to alert the computer. 'Command. Open the door. End command.'

He turned and looked over the back of his sofa, grinning more widely as Odinstoy came into his room, holding up a paper bag. His grin weakened, almost disappeared when a tall figure loomed behind her and that Martian, Thor-something, ducked into the room. Bob had been aware that Odinstoy had been paying the big beggar a lot of attention, but he'd been trying to ignore it, since there was nothing he could do or say about it. It didn't make him want to sing and dance.

"Morning, Toy. Oh, it's a party. If you'd said you were bringing somebody, I'd have baked a cake. And tidied up a bit.'

Bob leaned from his seat, throwing things from the nearest armchair onto the floor, to make room for his visitors to sit.

Odinstoy climbed over the back of the settee, and kicked stuff from the seat before sinking down, cross-legged. 'No, you wouldn't.'

'No, I wouldn't,' Bob agreed. He finished emptying the armchair's seat, and said, 'Sit down, sit down!' to Thorsgift, who was standing beside the sofa with his head bowed and an expression of distaste. Fussy sod.

Bob leaned back into the corner of the sofa, and Odinstoy gave him the bag. From it he took his breakfast: a large pastry full of minced meat, onions, carrots and peas. She took another from the bag for herself. Thorsgift had one of his own – or something, anyway – in a bag that dangled from his big hands.

Bob bit into his pasty and chewed for some minutes. The pastry was thick and greasy, and took some chewing. He sighed. 'Best hangover cure there is. Thanks, pal.' He looked at Thorsgift for a long moment. 'You're swanning off to Mars, then?' He spoke to her, but still looked at the Martian.

Odinstoy licked crumbs from around her mouth. 'Who told you?'

'Everybody. Everybody knows. We aren't good enough, eh?' He still looked at Thorsgift.

'It's Odin's will,' she said. 'He knows best – it's best that I go far away.'

'So what's wrong with Addis Ababa? Los Angeles? Edinburgh? All strange and alien places.'

She was silent, but then fixed him with her dark eyes, still rimmed with the remains of black paint. 'I'm taking my son.'

Before Bob could say anything, Thorsgift broke in, speaking slowly in his comical Martian accent. 'Odinstoy has a son. He was adopted by a free couple, so he's free. He's the little boy—'

'Apollo Perry, who comes here with Affie,' Bob said. 'I *know*. Toy *told* me. Ages ago.'

Odinstoy put her hand on Bob's knee and squeezed it gently, a confirmation of their special friendship.

'Oh,' Thorsgift said, and drew back into his armchair.

'Toy,' Bob said, speaking to her as if they were alone, 'I know how you must feel. But how do you think you're ever going to take Apollo with you?'

'I told her it's theft and kidnapping,' Thorsgift said.

Bob ignored him. 'How are you ever going to get away with it?'

'It's not theft,' Odinstoy said, 'because Affie should be free. It's not kidnapping, because Apollo is mine. It'll only be called theft and kidnapping if we're caught.'

'Which you will be!' Bob said. 'You will be.'

'Odin is with us. Thorsgift is going to buy tickets for us all—'

'You have to have a medical,' Thorsgift said.

Odinstoy looked at him. 'You said you could take a form signed by a doctor.'

'Yes, but—'

'Markus will do it,' Odinstoy said.

Thorsgift looked blank.

'Markus,' Bob said. 'He's a doctor, comes to the temple. He's a – friend of Toy's.'

'I shag him,' Odinstoy said, and stared at Bob until he

looked away. She turned her stare on Thorsgift. 'He'll sign the papers if I ask. So download them, and he'll make them out. But what's best to say? That Affie's my sister, or my bonder – or nothing to do with me? Do we say that Apollo's—?'

'Affie will have a tag in her,' Bob said. 'Apollo might have too: a lot of kids do. As soon as they go missing, they'll be able to locate them exactly, anywhere on the planet.'

'Turn them off,' Odinstoy said. 'Mine was turned off.'

'Yours was turned off at the agency, when you were freed,' Bob said. 'They had the scanner to do it with. Do you have one? No. Because you can't just reach out your hand and get hold of one.'

'Cut them out,' Odinstoy said. 'They aren't in deep. You can feel them.'

'Oh, and who's going to cut them out? I hope—'

'I would,' Odinstoy said. 'But Markus will do it.'

'Three cheers for Markus.'

Thorsgift said, 'You'll still have to get through security checks at the airports and the elevator.'

'Yeah!' Bob agreed. 'They'll pick you up as soon as you set foot in the place.'

'You're always telling me,' Odinstoy said, 'that security is only as good as the database, and that you know how to get into databases. And change them.'

Bob drew back from her with a gasp. 'Odinstoy!'

'You said you could do it.'

'I could do it, I could. But – I was just talking! If I was caught . . .! I could never get work again!'

'And then you'd have to bond yourself,' Odinstoy said,

and left the silence hanging. Bob looked nervously from her to Thorsgift.

'Do it properly,' Odinstoy said, 'and who will find out?'

'There are people who'd know how to trace it back to me . . .'

'Why would they look?' Odinstoy said. 'One missing bonder, one missing child – they don't belong to anybody important. Only Freewoman Perry. So Freewoman Perry's bonder, and Freewoman Perry's adopted son – who was born a bonder – so they vanish. Who cares?'

'And after you're clear,' Bob said thoughtfully, 'I go in and put everything back the way it was.' He grinned. 'It'll be a paranormal mystery!'

'You'll do it?' Odinstoy said.

Bob shrank into his corner again. 'I dunno. I dunno.'

'I have to go to Mars. It's Odin's will. You saw me read the runes.'

'I know,' he said. He'd seen. He knew there was no way she could have influenced the computer's choice of runes. It had to be a sheer fluke – or the voice of Odin. 'I know, but—'

'We won't be caught,' she said. 'Odin wishes this. Odin is with us.'

'Odin is treacherous.'

She pulled something from her wrist and held it out to him. When he looked closely, it was nothing more than a home-made bracelet, a bit of grubby cord, strung with cheap trinkets.

'My ancestors,' she said.

'What?' He glimpsed Thorsgift leaning in for a better

look. Bob's own ancestors were mounted in an elaborate, gilded wall setting, each with their photograph, and an account of their lives held in the computer. A small lamp burned in front of it. He had no doubt that Thorsgift had something similar, back on Mars – and probably a concise version with him.

'Your ancestors?'

'This is how bonders remember our ancestors.'

Bob had never before wondered how bonders remembered their ancestors – or even if they did. He sent a quick look to Thorsgift, seeking fellowship.

Thorsgift gave a slightly smug smile. 'The bead is for Odinstoy's great-grandmother.'

'Oh?' Bob said. 'What was her name, Thorsgift?'

Thorsgift looked aside.

'I don't know her name,' Odinstoy said. 'This locket here is for my grandmother. It opens, look. That's a picture of her inside.'

Bob looked. The picture was indeed of a bonder – but of a celebrated one, who'd performed in vids, famous for her beauty, her singing and her comic talent. He knew because one of his own ancestors had been a fan. He doubted if that bonder had been Odinstoy's grandmother. There had once been many such cheap trinkets made, sold, even given away by the actress's owners. But who knew? It was possible, he supposed.

'This Freya medal, this is my mother. She worshipped Freya. She tied this on the string for me, and put it on my wrist, before she was sold.'

Bob was astonished to find his throat drawn tight and his eyes stinging with tears. This bit of string with its cheap trinkets, the photograph that probably wasn't Odinstoy's grandmother, this image of loss, powerlessness and yearning, seemed to have given him a shock. 'Do you—' He had to pause and steady his voice. 'Do you remember your mother?'

Odinstoy was silent – thinking, remembering. 'I remember the nurse in the crèche telling me about her. She was a bonder too. This stone – this is what I tied on. For Apollo.'

'It's not a stone,' Bob said. 'Well, it is, but – it's an arrowhead. Like, a Stone-Age arrowhead. Where did you get it?'

'I didn't steal it!'

'I didn't say—'

'This should go to Apollo. *These* are his ancestors. Not the Perrys! Not their ancestors! That would be all lies! Apollo is mine!'

Bob looked at the grubby cord and the chipped bead, the tarnished locket, the dented medal, and the bit of grey stone – it was all so cheap, so inadequate, so sad. And so precious. The only way that Odinstoy, the voice of Odin, had of teaching her son about his lineage.

'If I leave him behind, I can't leave him this. It's junk, isn't it? You think it's junk. You both do.'

Bob and Thorsgift murmured that, no, no, they didn't.

'You do. I saw your faces. It would be thrown away. Rubbish. No value. But to Apollo it's not rubbish – not if he's told what it is. But if I leave him behind, he'll never know. He'll never know of me – or of my mother, my grandmother, my great-grandmother.'

For a moment, just a moment, Bob thought: well? Is that so bad? He'd have a better life, an education . . . What he never knew, he'd never miss.

But then that was swept away by a fierce, warm feeling that rose up from his guts, into his chest. To have a mother like Odinstoy, and never know of it? To have that fierceness and inborn talent, that courage to speak out with the voice of Odin, to have the courage to say: I was born a bonder but I'm better than you all, because Odin has chosen me . . . To be an inheritor of all that and never to know it? Of course, the boy would never know of his own ignorance – but Bob would know, and he felt the injustice, the loss, on the boy's behalf.

He looked at Thorsgift. 'Are you going to help her?'

Thorsgift gave a long, slow nod. Yes.

'Have you thought about what you're risking? Really thought?'

A pause; then another nod.

'Then why?'

Thorsgift spread his big hands. 'It's Odin's will.'

'Right!' Bob jumped to his feet and took down a box. He opened it and held it out to Odinstoy. It held rune stones. Not the virtual runes generated by a computer, but flat, smooth pebbles, carved with the signs. 'I'll throw them, and you read them.'

Odinstoy caught back a sigh. Every time she was asked again to prove herself, the risk was greater. This time could be the time that Odin betrayed her. 'You saw me read the runes in the temple. You know it's His will that I go to Mars.'

'But not that you take anyone with you. Read them for me.' He pushed the low table aside, to clear a space on the floor. 'The question is,' he said, 'should I help? Should I do this and break the law? Risk my job, my future. Should I do this?' He gathered the runes into his hands, and cast them.

The runes scattered in a rough fan shape. Odinstoy and Thorsgift left their seats to crouch over them.

The technique of reading them differed from the computer runes. Some stones had landed face down, their sign hidden – they were to be ignored. Those nearest Bob were the most significant – as they fell further away, they weakened. In some cases, if they were upside down to the viewer, their meaning was altered or reversed; but the meaning of one or two was so strong, for good or ill, that it could not be changed.

Four stones had landed near Bob in a cluster: the others were all much further away. Obviously, those four held the answer. Bob frowned and pursed his mouth as he studied them. He could name the runes, and give a meaning for each – but interpreting their meaning as they lay together, and in answer to his question, was too much for him. He looked at Odinstoy. '*You* know what it says!'

She did, and, within herself, was silently, fervently thankful. Thank you, Odin, thank you, All-Father, thank you. She looked at Thorsgift. He was staring at the stones too, his expression stunned.

Odinstoy touched the first stone. The rune was shaped like two small triangular pennants on poles, meeting each other point to point. 'Mankind. "*Man is loved by his friends, yet each will betray his dearest friend when he goes to the cold clay . . . Value friendship, tend it well . . .*"' She looked into Bob's eyes before touching the next stone, so close beside the first. It was shaped like a forked stick, the fork downwards. 'Torch. "*Brightly the torch burns where leaders rest . . . It is the fire of leadership: courage makes it burn fiercely.*" And then, gift.' Gift was an 'x'. '"*Giving is glory . . . Be generous always . . .*" And the last is Odin's mouth. These are the words of the God. But mouth has a deeper meaning too. Odin paid dear for His wisdom. He gave an eye for a drink from the well. To learn the runes, He hung nine days on the Tree, stabbed by His own spear. He thought it well worth the price. It says, risk is worth the gain.'

Bob shook his head. 'It isn't clear . . .'

'Bob,' Thorsgift said, 'Bob . . . These came up for me too. When she read for me, last night. Odin's mouth and torch. They came up for me too.'

Bob stared at him thinking: the runes were mine . . . I threw them . . . There was no way, no way at all that the fall of the stones could be fixed . . . His scalp prickled, he felt cold. He felt the God in the room with them, taking up space and air, looming . . .

But he was still afraid.

Odinstoy leaned over, kissed his cheek and rose to her feet. Thorsgift rose and followed her as she left the flat.

Bob remained kneeling, looking at the runes. There they were, hard pebbles. He couldn't ignore them. He could pack them away in their box, but would he be able to forget them? Cling to your friends while you may, for all companionship ends; have the courage to stand out like a torch, to be a leader; be generous. And then Odin's deep and frightening rune.

He saw clearly what he was to do. Help his friend. Ignore the law, which was unjust and cruel, and help the mother regain her son. It was clear, simple – and terrifying.

If he ducked this he would know, every day for the rest of

his life, that he was a coward, and not a leader, and no good friend.

And Odin, a treacherous, vengeful God, would know it too.

He caught Odinstoy and Thorsgift as they were going down the stairs. 'I'll do it.' She came running back up the stairs to embrace him.

Planning

Markus took a thin, silver wand from his pocket, and held it up. A soft click, and a sharp blade sprang from the wand. He licked his lips. 'Let blood flow.'

Affie gave Odinstoy a look of pure panic.

Odinstoy was playing some finger game with Apollo. Hardly glancing up, she said, 'Markus, don't tease.'

'Got to be done,' Markus said. 'No good doing it on runaway night – too much else to do then. We can't count on Affie being able to get away before—'

'I'm always looking after Apollo,' Affie said. 'I often come over with him, don't I, Toy?' She needed Markus, and couldn't afford to fall out with him, but his ebullience – his bright magenta hair and his green cravat, his embroidered waistcoat and chequered trousers – annoyed her. He was free; he could wear anything, and he *chose* to dress like *that*. No style, no taste. And she disliked his aggressive teasing, his constant jibing and needling. She was expected to laugh and think he was a character but she knew that, had she been free, she wouldn't have spent a minute longer than was necessary in his company.

'Say you can get away,' Markus said. 'It might be that I'm

222

working. By the time I'm off, you'll be gone again, back into durance vile. No, get it done now. Sharp steel edge meets soft flesh – couple of stitches, all done!'

'But what,' said Bob, 'what if – for some reason – Freewoman Perry wants to check up on them between now and – running away day? If she tries to find out where they are, and can't, because you've taken out the tracers?' He spread his hands.

Thorsgift nodded. 'The game will be up.'

'Affie will have to be a very, very good little girl,' Markus said, and leaned over to poke Apollo. 'And you will have to be a very, very good little – monkey!'

Apollo shrieked with laughter at the thought of being a monkey, and Odinstoy laughed. A toddler and a bonder, Affie thought – just the sort of people who *would* find Markus amusing. Then she was aghast at having such a thought about Odinstoy. But it was because Markus irritated her so much.

'Let's stop and *think*,' Thorsgift said. They all looked at him, surprised. He raised his long arms and big hands and made chopping motions on either side of his head. 'We've got to sort things out. Now. Listen. Visas. Before tickets can be issued for travel to Mars, you have to get entry visas.'

'So?' Bob said. 'Apply for them.'

'You have to present yourself at the embassy, with your ID.'

'Once I'm into the database, no problem. I can put in the patch, take it out again. How long before the visas are granted?'

'I phoned to ask. At least a month.'

'Plenty of time,' Bob said. 'Don't worry about it.'

But Thorsgift was still worried. 'When I go to book the tickets, it'll be best if I've already got the visas and the medical forms, all filled out. That'll save time, everything'll go through more smoothly, fewer questions . . .'

'Got the forms,' Markus said. 'Fill 'em out, sign 'em, in two shakes of a – monkey's tail!' Apollo shrieked again, and pranced. 'It's a formality, really,' Markus continued. 'All healthy young subjects – and I know for a fact that Toy's got plenty of wind and stamina.'

'Yes,' said Bob, with distaste. 'OK, we need to think about names. What names are you going to apply for visas in and put on the med forms?'

'The disguises!' Markus cried. 'What name will you have, Affie? Felicia E. Muchlove? Salacia B. Milkythighs?'

Affie looked away from him, refusing to answer. Gods, he was so obvious and boring, and he thought he was so clever and funny.

'Something anonymous,' Bob said heavily. 'Something that won't attract any attention, or be memorable.'

Thorsgift nodded in agreement. Markus just grinned. Affie glared at him, wondering how Odinstoy could have been so foolish as to ask this *idiot* for help. How could they rely on him?

'I thought, maybe, Hera Warren for Affie,' Bob said. 'That's common enough, but not so common that it immediately sounds like a fake name. What do you think?'

'Fine,' Affie said. 'What do I care, so long as it gets me away?'

'You might be stuck with it for the rest of your life,' Bob said.

She shrugged. 'After a while, I'll start to feel like a Hera, I suppose.'

'Good,' Bob said. 'I've had a look at the database, seen how it's done these days. I can mock it up, easy. I'll alter as little as possible of the rest – medical history and school and all that. 'Course, I'll change the bit where you're bonded.'

Affie wished that whole episode in her real life could be as easily erased.

'What about the ID cards?' Thorsgift asked.

'No problem,' Bob said. 'Anybody with a computer and a laminator can make them in no time.'

Thorsgift snorted. 'I couldn't!'

'Well, I can!' Bob said.

'And you can get into the database?' Markus said.

'Yes!' Bob took a deep breath and relaxed. 'I used to work for them, doing all the updating – there's constant updating. And ironing out bugs, and making it run faster – oh, it just goes on all the time. But they only fiddle with it. The basic program's still the same – it'd cost too much and take too long to completely change it. And I know the program inside out and back to front.'

'But security—' Thorsgift said.

Bob laughed. 'Security! When I left, I kept my password – or rather, I changed it for a new one *just before* I left, and stopped access on the old one, so it looked legit. I've got an open door in and out. All the programmers do it.'

'Well, this is cheering news,' Markus said. 'May one ask why?'

'Say I get points on my licence? In I go and wipe 'em off again. I want to get a job, but don't think my qualifications are good enough? In I go and make them good enough.'

There was a silence while Thorsgift, Affie and Markus stared at him. Odinstoy, apparently uninterested, played with Apollo.

'Perhaps it's lucky that not many doctors have these skills,' Markus said.

'Everybody does it! And some doctors do – must do.'

'I'll enquire about their computer capability before I let another quack treat me or mine,' Markus said.

'Anyway!' Bob said. 'We still haven't sorted out the details. How's Apollo going to travel? With Affie, or with Odinstoy?'

'Give me a new name too,' Odinstoy said.

'You're the only one who's free to travel!' Thorsgift said.

'Toy, it just makes more work,' Bob said.

Odinstoy shook her head. 'I'll travel as a man. Call me Thorhall Atkinson.'

'As a *man*?' Bob said.

Markus laughed. 'She's got more sense than the lot of you! She can do it – you've seen her in the temple – she makes a great little chap!'

'It's stupid,' Thorsgift said.

'It'll muddy the trail! If anybody does catch on they'll be looking for two women and a child. But a *man*, a woman and a child – especially if they seem to be travelling separately . . .'

Bob looked thoughtful. 'Then Apollo should travel with Thorsgift. As his son.'

'I don't have a son!'

'Dumbo,' Bob said. 'I change your data, same as—'

'I'm a Martian. I'm going home to Mars. I can't arrive with false papers.' They stared at him. 'Mars isn't like Earth,' he said. 'There aren't millions and millions of people. It's easier to keep track of everybody. I'll probably meet people I know at the spaceport.'

'He's right,' Markus said. 'Toy and Apollo should travel as father and son – or father and daughter! That breaks the link between Affie and App. If everybody bought their own tickets, too . . .'

'I could buy tickets for me and Pollo,' Odinstoy said.

'I can't buy mine,' Affie said. 'How can I? I'm—'

'Got it!' Markus said. 'Toy and Affie travel as man and wife, with their charming little daughter! Toy can buy their tickets – no connection with Thorsgift. Everything's blurred and I'm brilliant!'

Bob's face was very serious; he was thinking deeply. The others watched him, waiting. At last, he lifted his head. 'Yes. I think so.'

'It's ridiculous!' Thorsgift burst out. 'It's play-acting. Pretending to be a man – the boy dressed up as a girl! It won't work!'

'Toy can pull it off,' Markus said.

'For two months? Are you forgetting that the trip will take two months? You're only thinking of the few hours it takes to get on the ship.'

'I can be a man for two months. For two years,' Odinstoy said.

'It won't work! What about when they check for marriage

licences and birth certificates, and find out there is no Freeman and Freewoman Atkinson with a daughter? You can't falsify everything!'

'Don't need to,' Bob said. 'The databases aren't linked. If my patch says Toy's irises belong to Thorhall Atkinson, married to, say – well, say Freya, if she's going to be married to Thorhall – plus one child – well, there's no crosscheck against any other bases. They'll only run the checks if you do something to get yourself noticed – so they already have to be suspicious. And they have to get permission to run the crosschecks.'

'What's the good of that?' Thorsgift demanded. 'Why have ID cards and databases and all that if it's so easy . . .?'

'Personal liberty of the free citizen,' Bob said, as if offended.

'After all,' Markus said, 'Thorhall Atkinson isn't a *bonder*, now, is he?'

'Besides,' Bob said, 'all these security systems are a bloody good source of revenue. Who cares if they don't work?'

'Thank the Gods it doesn't work,' Markus said.

'Anyway,' Bob said, 'once they're on their way to Mars, it won't matter if they are found out. It'll be too late to do anything.'

Thorsgift stared at him. 'Mars isn't the wilderness, you know. If they arouse suspicion, if they're caught out, the authorities will be waiting for them when they put down. They'll be sent back on the next ship. And the Gods alone know what will happen to me!'

'Mars's citizens are free, aren't they?' Bob said. 'They don't check up on everybody, every minute of the day, do they? So long as you're not drawing attention to yourself or doing anything illegal.'

'You're going to have to be good on Mars as well, Affie,' Markus said. Affie ignored him.

'Once you get to Mars,' Bob continued, 'I take the patch out of the database, and Toy becomes Toy again. I can leave Apollo and Affie with their fake IDs, or I can put them back again. Please yourself.'

'It should be easy to alter Apollo's details to make him Toy's daughter,' Markus said. 'You wouldn't have to alter that much.'

'No,' Bob agreed, with an edge to his voice. 'Just everything about his adoption.' He didn't like Markus telling him his job.

'Affie should stay fake. Give her a whole new ID. She can start again.'

Worriedly, Thorsgift said, 'This isn't going to work.'

They broke into protests; Markus jeering, Bob shouting, Affie trying to make herself heard. Odinstoy set Apollo on his feet and stood up herself, with a movement so fierce and sudden that they all fell silent and stared at her.

She made them wait, standing with a muscle-clenched stillness. Even Apollo stared up at her. She said, 'This is what we are going to do. Markus will give us the medical forms, in the names of Thorhall Atkinson, his wife, Freya, and their son, Odinsgift. Thorsgift will buy the tickets for us, in those names. That's what we'll do. That's decided.'

Markus leaned back in his chair and grinned. Bob and Thorsgift hung their heads. They had their doubts, but what was the point of voicing them? The voice of Odin would drown them out.

'When we have the tickets,' Odinstoy said, 'then I'll get word to Affie, and she will bring Apollo—'

'No,' Markus said. 'Affie stays where she is until the day you're to travel. Then, one of us is outside the Perrys' place—'

'In a taxi,' Bob said.

'*Not* in a taxi. It could be traced. In a private car, with the tracker removed. Use my car. Even if I'm not free, use mine.'

'Your car has no tracker?' Bob said.

'I don't want everybody to know where I am all the time. I don't want the car company to know when I bought it, how I use it, and all. That's my business, not theirs,' Markus said. 'I always remove the tracker. I remove them in all my cars.'

'Isn't that illegal? How do you pay your road tax?'

'I pay when the government asks me for it – and I'd rather pay the fines than be spied on. Anyway, I – or whoever – pick up Affie and Apollo. Their tickets and new clothes, everything they need – we'll have to think about that – is in the car, ready for them. I drive them straight to the airport, where they meet up with Toy and our Martian friend. They're well on their way before anybody knows they're gone. Can anybody pick any holes in that?'

There was silence as they all turned the plan over in their minds.

'You'll need to know where Freewoman Perry lives,' Affie said.

'Elementary, my dear Affie. Tell me the address, and I'll look it up on a map. I won't be using a route finder! The signal can be traced. And no communication between us –

no e-mails, children; no phones. We only speak in person. Anything else leaves traces.'

'When Thorsgift gives me the tickets,' Odinstoy said, 'I'll go to Freewoman Perry's and knock on her door—'

'What if she recognises you?' Bob cried, in alarm.

'To the back door, the kitchen door. Freewoman Perry won't even know I was there.'

'I might be working about the house,' Affie said. 'Cook would answer it. She might recognise you.' She remembered how Cook had recognised a photo of Odinstoy. Should she mention that? But it might put them off, and she didn't want anything to upset their plans. It couldn't be important.

'How can we send a message to Affie without phoning her or knocking on the door?' Markus said. 'A fiery cross? A black spot? Brainstorm, gentlemen, ladies! There has to be a way.'

They sat in silence, thinking. Affie felt that her brain was jammed, unable to move in any direction, or produce the faintest glimmer of an idea.

Markus flourished his slender knife again. 'We all work on that. Right now – cut! Blood! Yes!'

Panicked, Affie looked to Odinstoy, who held out her hand to her. 'It has to be done, Affie.'

Affie rose and reached for Odinstoy's hand. She felt she would have been more willing if it had been anyone except Markus. She whispered, 'Does he know how—?'

'I am a doctor, darlin',' Markus said. 'And I know how.'

Affie gripped Odinstoy's hand with both of hers. 'Stay with me.'

Odinstoy said, 'Pollo, go to Thorsgift.' Then she led Affie

by the hand into the bathroom. Markus picked up a case and followed.

Bathroom was an archaic term. In Affie's father's house, there had been real bathrooms, with baths that could be filled with water, and showers that drenched you with water. Odinstoy's small flat was modern and inexpensive. Its bathroom offered only a commode and a sonic shower, saving space and construction costs, besides water.

'Down with the old baggies!' Markus said.

Affie's grip on Odinstoy's hand tightened. It reminded her of how she'd been attacked when she'd first been bonded, forcibly held down while the tag had been inserted. She felt powerless, panicked, felt her control slipping. She was going to sob, to scream. She was ashamed to let them see her fear – especially Markus – but she didn't think she could cover it up.

Odinstoy embraced her, rubbing her back soothingly. 'Ssh, ssh, it's all right. No one's going to hurt you, I'm here, I won't let anyone hurt you . . .' Affie began to sob into Odinstoy's neck, but in a much quieter, calmer way. It was the motherliness of this girl, hardly older than herself, that affected her. 'Never mind, sweetheart, never mind . . .' Odinstoy was soothing her as she soothed Apollo if he fell and bumped his head, and the encircling arms and warmth felt so good.

'What is she carrying on about?' Markus's voice asked from behind Affie.

Affie felt Odinstoy's head move sharply, as she made some silent reply to Markus, but her hands continued to stroke Affie's head and back. No one had cuddled Affie like that for a long, long time . . . Since when? Her father hadn't.

Minerva certainly hadn't. Had her real mother? She had no memory of it. There had been a nanny, dismissed a long time ago. Affie had a dim, but still resentful memory of being soothed after a fall, and then abandoned the instant her tears stopped and were no longer an annoyance. 'Oh, come on! Stop crying! You're a big girl now!' Odinstoy's embrace was like water to one parched. A deep, warm swell of gratitude rose in Affie. She would do anything, anything Odinstoy asked.

So when Odinstoy said, 'Look up, look at me,' she did, blearily, through tears. Odinstoy wiped the tears away with her fingers. 'You want to come to Mars, don't you?'

Affie nodded.

'As my sister?'

Affie nodded harder.

'As my wife?'

Affie surprised herself by giggling, in a slightly manic way. She gasped, gulped, nodded again.

'Then the tag has to be cut out. No other way. You know you can do it.'

Affie reached down and slipped her trousers – they had such a horrible, unstylish elasticated waist – over her hips. 'Good girl,' Odinstoy said warmly, and Affie flushed with pleasure, and never thought how strange it was that she – a freewoman in all but name – should seek praise from a bonder born and bred.

'Lean on the shower, hold onto it, and stick your bottom out,' Markus said, in the most flat, down to earth way she'd heard him speak. Odinstoy let her go and moved aside. Affie did as she was told.

She heard the click as Markus's case was opened, and then a rustling that made her open her eyes in fear. 'He's putting on gloves,' Odinstoy said.

Fingers prodded at her buttock. 'Ah, there it is,' Markus said, and prodded again. 'I can feel it, just under the skin. Toy, open one of those wipes – tear it and pass it – that's it.'

Affie felt something cold swab a spot high on her left buttock. It was followed by a hiss, and an intensely cold touch that made her jump. 'Just a local,' Markus said. 'Not to worry. Won't feel a thing.'

She didn't – except for some more prodding. Then Markus said, 'Got it!'

'He's done it,' Odinstoy said. Affie twisted, trying to see over her shoulder.

'Keep still!' Markus was annoyed. 'Got to put a stitch in.' Another mist of spray, and more prodding. Then he was stretching a dressing over the small wound. 'You can pull your trousers up. Keep it dry, keep it covered, for about ten days. It should heal fine.'

Affie, feeling grateful and lucky that it had been so quick and so painless, pulled up her trousers and turned. She wanted to say that she'd misjudged Markus, to thank him, but before she could speak, he held something out to her in a small pair of tongs. It was a dull, red capsule. 'There it is,' he said. 'That's your ball and chain.'

There were greasy smears on the capsule that Affie didn't want to think about. 'Throw it away!' she said.

'Oh, can't throw it away, m'dear. Not at all. It's still transmitting.'

'Smash it!'

'That *would* give the game away, wouldn't it?' He took a small plastic bag from his case, and inserted the capsule into it, zipped it closed. 'I've got plans for that.'

'What are you going to do?' Affie asked.

'Let that be my secret. Shall we do Apollo now?'

'In the kitchen,' Odinstoy said. 'It's in his arm. He can sit on my lap while you take it out.'

'Freewoman Perry might notice,' Affie said. 'She sometimes baths him, dresses him. She'd want to know what it was.'

All three of them looked at each other.

'We leave it then,' Markus said. 'I shall have to be the one who picks you up on runaway night, no way round it. I'll cut it out of Apollo then.'

'I won't be with him,' Odinstoy said.

'He'll scream murder,' Affie said.

'Gods.' Markus grimaced. 'Isn't there any way you can keep Freewoman Perry from seeing?'

'How?' Affie demanded. 'He only wears little T-shirts most of the time, in the house. How can I hide a big plaster on his arm?'

'Put him in long sleeves!'

'*I* don't choose his clothes!' Affie said.

'It'll *have* to be done on runaway night, then.'

'I still don't know when that is,' Affie said. 'We still haven't decided a signal.'

From her pocket, Odinstoy took a small phone and handed it to Affie. 'Keep it with you. I'll use my other one. Turn the ring off and set it to vibrate. I'll text you on the day.'

Affie took the phone, too full of gratitude, and sadness,

and many other emotions, to speak. It would be hard to keep the phone hidden, but she'd managed before, with the payment card Odinstoy had given her.

'Phone calls can be traced,' Markus said.

'If anyone has a reason to trace them,' Odinstoy said. 'Perry doesn't know where I am now or who I am. She doesn't know Affie knows me. She shouldn't know that Affie has a phone.'

'She won't!' Affie said.

'So why should anyone try to trace the call?'

'Yes, but – still . . .' Markus said.

Odinstoy turned away from him. 'That is what we are going to do.' And that was the end of the discussion.

Visas

The Martian embassy was in a side street, housed in a surprisingly small, three-storeyed building, with steps rising from the pavement to a tall door decorated with Grecian pillars.

A taxi pulled into the kerb, and a young man, dressed smartly in a suit and carrying a leather holdall, got out and ran up the embassy steps.

The revolving doors admitted him into a reception area of white marble, with friezes of fruit and flowers around the walls. A console stood in the middle of the floor, with a notice above it displaying a large white question mark on a black background.

The young man went up to it, holdall on one shoulder, his other hand in his pocket. He spoke to the console: 'Input. Where do I apply for a visa? End input.'

A light lit up on the console. A female voice said, 'Booth 3, please.'

The young man looked round, and saw the numbered booths against the wall. Going over to booth 3, he shut himself inside, where there was a keyboard and a stool. As he sat down, a light lit on the keyboard. A man's voice said, 'Do you wish to apply for a visa to Mars?'

Clearly, the young man replied, 'Input. Yes. End input.'

'Do you wish to make your responses aloud, or by keyboard?'

'Input. Aloud. End input.'

'Please state your name clearly.'

'Input. Thornhall Atkinson. End input.'

'Repeat your name, please.'

It took several repetitions before the computer had the name correctly. Was that being recorded somewhere? Was it being compared to some statistical table of the average number of times people repeated their name before the computer recognised it?

'What is your date of birth? Are you free or bonded?'

Odinstoy answered the questions, drew a long, slow breath, and refused to close her fists. She sat as relaxed, honest men did – knees apart, arms apart and relaxed, resting on her thighs. This computer might or might not be programmed to spot signs of agitation or lying.

I will beat you, she thought, staring into the screen. I will not lick my lips. I will not put my hands to my face. Count my blinks. I am a good actor and a better liar.

'Please insert your ID card into the slot,' said the machine.

Odinstoy took her small wallet from her pocket, took out her card and inserted it. She had checked and rechecked that it was the right card, but even so, there was a tiny doubt that she'd somehow fumbled them, and had inserted her own, genuine card, or the wrong fake.

'Look at the red light, please.'

Odinstoy looked steadily into the red light, while her irises were read, concentrating on breathing slow and keeping her hands relaxed. She was still aware of her heart beating faster.

'That is satisfactory,' said the computer, and slid the card out again. Odinstoy snatched short the long breath of relief that had been about to escape her.

'Are you applying for a short stay visa, to visit Mars, or for a long stay visa?'

'Input. A long stay visa. I intend to make Mars my home.' Thorsgift had taught her that phrase. 'End input.'

'Do you intend to work on Mars?'

'Input. I intend to work. End input.'

'In what capacity?'

The phrase puzzled Odinstoy for a moment; then she grabbed at what it must mean. 'Input. I am a God-speaker. I am going to be the God-speaker for the temple of Odin on Mars. End input.'

The computer absorbed this in silence for a moment. Then it said, 'Are you employed at present?'

'Input. Yes. End input.'

'Please state your employment, and give the address of your place of employment.'

Odinstoy did so.

'Do you have savings? Please state the amount.'

Odinstoy did so.

'Are you travelling to Mars alone, or with others?'

'Input. My wife, Freya, is going with me. And our son, Odinsgift. End input.' It would have been a better disguise for Apollo to travel as a girl, but Odinstoy didn't think they could expect a small child to keep up the pretence.

'Are you applying for visas for these other people, as well

as your own?'

'Input. I am applying for a visa for my son. My wife will apply for her own. End input.'

'Please insert the child's ID card now.'

Odinstoy took the ID card Bob had created for Apollo from her wallet – with a quick glance to check that it was the right one – and pushed it into the slot.

'That is satisfactory,' said the computer, and slid the card out. 'Your application will be evaluated, and you will be contacted in due course. Thank you. Enjoy the rest of your day.'

Odinstoy replaced her cards in her wallet, and left the booth.

Standing in the doorway of the embassy, she used her mobile to summon a cab, and when it pulled up at the kerb, she ran down the steps, opening its door with a signal from her phone. Once inside, she spoke aloud to the cab's computer: 'Command. Delphi Hotel. End command.'

At the hotel, she entered through its gilt and glass doors, and crossed its slate-floored lobby, heading straight for the Ladies. Without hesitating, or looking round, she walked in. There was a woman at the sinks, who gave her a startled glance, but Odinstoy was locked in a cubicle before she could take a second look.

She set her holdall at her feet and unzipped it, before taking off her jacket and shirt and hanging them on the back of the door. She unwrapped the strapping from around her breasts, and dropped it into the holdall. Taking out a padded bra, she put it on.

Sitting on the commode, she took off her man's shoes and socks. Standing, she took off her trousers and the underpants with the stitched in padding. From the holdall, she took a woman's knickers and black tights, and put them on.

Folding the trousers, she packed them away, and took out a black skirt, a cream silk blouse and a black jacket. She took out a pair of high-heeled black boots and set them on the floor while she packed away the man's clothing. Then she pulled on the boots, took out a wig, and ducked her head into it.

Leaving the cubicle, she stood in front of the mirrors, and adjusted the wig. From a side pocket of the holdall, she took a small make-up compact and applied lipstick to her lips and cheeks; then eyeliner. Finally, she made sure that the ID card in the side pocket was the one she wanted.

She gave her appearance a long, final check, and then strolled out into the hotel reception. There she seated herself in an armchair, crossed her legs, and dialled a number on her mobile.

'Yes?' said Bob's voice.

She replied, 'OK,' and waited to hear Bob reply with the same word before ending the call and using the phone to summon a cab.

When the phone signalled that the cab had arrived, she strolled out to it, and returned to the Martian embassy. Going straight to the visa application booth, she said, 'Input. I wish to apply for a visa to enter Mars and work there. End input.'

'Please state your name.'

'Input. Freya Atkinson . . .'

Freewoman Perry was waiting in the kitchen, sitting at the table at which Cook was standing, working. Affie, as she opened the kitchen door, saw only Cook, and didn't under-stand the old woman's slight grimace and sideways nod of the head. 'We're back!' Affie said.

'And *where* have you been?' asked Freewoman Perry's voice. 'You should have been back an hour ago.'

A bolt of sheer fear seemed to rush up through Affie's body and exit through the top of her head. 'Oh, Freewoman, I'm so sorry, I tried, I couldn't help it, Freewoman, please don't be angry.' She heard herself saying these shameful words and couldn't believe it, but she couldn't fall out with Freewoman Perry now: she couldn't risk being sent back to the agency, not now . . .

'I want to take Apollo with me to dinner tonight, and now, thanks to you—'

'Little Mummy gives me chocolate cake,' Apollo chirped up, and fear entered Affie again, sinking down through her this time, chilling her from her scalp to her feet.

'No, you can't have any chocolate, darling,' Freewoman Perry said. 'You'll spoil your dinner. Have you an explana-tion?' she asked Affie. 'Or do I put it down to – what? Arrogance? Impudence? Incompetence?'

'Oh no, Freewoman! I did try to get back, Freewoman, honestly, but it was so busy today, I couldn't get a cab; and when we did find one, the traffic was—'

'All right, all right,' Freewoman Perry said. 'I was going to bathe him and dress him myself, but I won't have time now, so you've spoiled that for us. Bathe him and dress him in clean clothes while I get myself ready.'

'Yes, Freewoman. What clothes shall I dress him in, Freewoman?'

'Oh, paradise! Do I have to tell you every little thing? Something suitable for going out to dinner with me. You know that, surely? You were so famously rich and well brought up, weren't you?' Freewoman Perry turned in the doorway as she left. 'I want him ready for half-seven.'

Affie stood in the kitchen, seething. She wanted to say, 'I *hate* her!' but didn't think it was safe when Apollo and Cook would hear.

'I tried to tell you her was sat here,' Cook said. 'Not that I suppose it would've made any difference. Well? He's gotta be ready by half-seven. I should get on, if I was you.'

Affie nodded, and dragged Apollo from the kitchen.

Upstairs, in the family bathroom, she stripped him, stood him in the bath, soaped him, and hosed him down with the shower attachment. Freewoman Perry preferred him to be washed with water: it was better for the skin. It was, Affie knew, but she didn't care about Apollo's skin. I have to use the sonic all the time, she thought. Why can't he go in it occasionally? Washing him was quite unnecessary, anyway – he'd been washed that morning, and who was going to notice or care if the brat was a bit grubby round the edges? While she performed the chore of drying him with a big towel, pulling him this way and that, she whispered, 'Do you want to see Little Mummy again?'

He stared at her and nodded.

'Then keep her a secret. Understand? Don't tell Big Mummy about her. Don't tell anyone. Big Mummy doesn't like Little Mummy.'

'Why?'

'She just doesn't. She'll stop us going to see Little

243

Mummy if she knows about her. Because she doesn't like her.'

Apollo was still staring. As she turned him round to dry his hair, he said, 'Will she stop us go Mars?'

Affie froze. He understood *that*? She turned him round to face her. '*Yes*.' She whispered. 'Do you want to go to Mars?'

'Little Mummy?'

'With Little Mummy and me, yes.'

'Little Mummy all all time, and Big Mummy never no more?'

Affie nodded.

Apollo nodded back.

Well, they were in agreement on something.

'If you tell *her*, she'll stop us going. Don't think about Mars or Little Mummy while you're here. Don't say anything about them at all, not even to teddy. Understand?'

He nodded, but she didn't know if he really understood.

Oh, Odin, fasten the brat's mouth shut. Keep him quiet. He only has to babble a few words while he's playing with his toys, and Freewoman Perry will guess – if she listens. We could all be arrested. Conspiracy to kidnap. Theft.

'If Big Mummy asks where we've been today, say the park. *Don't* say anything about Little Mummy or Mars. Understand?'

Again, he nodded, his eyes blank. It was so maddening – everything endangered by this nodding poppet. If she were Odinstoy, she'd leave him behind.

She dressed him in clean clothes and delivered him to Freewoman Perry who, without a word of thanks, led him off to her dinner party. But at least she was gone for a while. The house seemed a brighter, more spacious place.

Affie ran up to the narrow attic stairs, where there was no camera. She took the mobile from her pocket and texted Odinstoy. WON'T COME TEMPLE AGAIN. 2 RISKY.

She sent the text, and sat on the stairs, desolate. Giving up the temple meant giving up so much. It was all the life she had: a brief rest from dreary chores, a little friendship and laughter. Odinstoy.

But if she was late returning again, and angered Freewoman Perry – if Apollo babbled something and Freewoman Perry found out where she'd been taking him, found out who Odinstoy was . . .

Much too risky. One visit to the temple could cost her everything: Mars, freedom, Odinstoy, life. If she stayed away, Apollo would forget about the place. He'd be less likely to blurt something out. And he'd been trained not to talk much about Little Mummy.

She, Affie, would have to be so good, just as Markus had said. All the chores done, perfectly, ahead of time, and 'Yes, Freewoman Perry'; 'No, Freewoman Perry'; 'If you please, Freewoman Perry' – so meek and mim and po-faced. The thought of it sent her bolting from the stairs. There were chores to be done. There always were.

Leaving

The phone, vibrating in her pocket, tickled against Affie's leg. Her heart gave a lurch, her breath choked, she instantly felt sick. She froze in the middle of polishing the dining room table, and felt herself turn cold.

It's just another advert, she told herself. Enlarge your breasts! Make ten million before your next birthday! She would finish the table before she looked. Finish the table and sweep the floor. It would only be another disappointment.

The vibrating stopped. Affie polished, rubbing at the table long after it shone, struggling with the conflicting compulsions to look at the message and wait. It probably *was* just an advert. But please, Odin, please, Freya, please, Thor: let it be the message from Odinstoy. If it was, it would bring new terrors, but at least it would end this agony of waiting, this shuffling of the phone from one outfit to another, the frights when she discovered she'd left it in her bedroom, or in the kitchen, where it might be discovered. It would bring the relief of escaping from Freewoman Perry's routine, of speaking to someone other than Freewoman Perry, Apollo and Cook. It would mean seeing Odinstoy again.

It would be an end to the hours of wondering whether Odinstoy would ever text her, whether it was all a big, spiteful joke. And then she would reassure herself that Odinstoy would never leave for Mars without Apollo, and she needed Affie to bring him to her.

That would start off a new fear: perhaps, once she'd risked so much by taking Apollo to her, Odinstoy would dump her, leave her to face Freewoman Perry, and the agency, and the law . . .

The fear made her think that maybe it would be better to stay as she was, a bonder . . . It would be wonderful to be free, but if they failed . . . Her life would be ten times more miserable than it was now. She wasn't clear what would happen, but the not-knowing made it all seem worse. There would be punishment, that was certain, and she dreaded what it might be – imprisonment? Beatings? And no respectable householder would want such an untrustworthy, troublesome bonder – so that would mean being sold, cheap, to the factories Cook had mentioned, where the work was hard, the food bad, the conditions unhealthy, and the bonders died of TB, and scurvy and other horrible things.

Dread settled under her heart in a cold, heavy lump. She couldn't go through with it. When the text came, she would ignore it, stay in bed . . .

And on and on her life would go, like this. Every day of her one and only life, dribbling away in tiresome little chores, not even done for her own benefit. Years and years of keeping her mouth shut, of never being allowed to be angry, no matter how she was humiliated. It was unbearable.

She stopped polishing. Forget the floor. She had to know now. Standing still, she held her breath and listened hard, to be sure that no one was coming.

Then she went to the door, opened it as quietly as she could, and peeped into the corridor. Sometimes, Freewoman Perry would sneak up on her, to check that she was working. The corridor was empty.

Affie arranged herself so that her body hid her right hand from the camera in the corner of the room. She lifted the phone partly from her pocket, so she could see the screen without taking it out completely.

FREE HOLIDAYS IF YOU REPLY

She sagged. She'd *known* it would just be an advert. Tears came to her eyes. Oh, well. Better get on with the floor. And the chore after that. And then the chore after that.

The phone dropped to the bottom of her pocket, and vibrated again.

She held her breath, then lifted the phone.

TONIGHT. 12.30. DELETE.

Affie took a long, long breath. To her surprise, she felt herself trembling; her arms, her legs quivering. She had to lean on the table. This was it. After so long a time of waiting . . . The journey to Mars – all the way to Mars – was starting now, here, in this little dining room, with its smell of polish. She had to look at the phone again, and then again, spelling out every word, making sure it really said what she thought it said – and even then she hardly believed it.

Turning her back to the camera, she pressed 'Delete' – clumsily, because her fingers were barely under her control. There was no chance that she would forget the message.

The only questions were: could she trust Odinstoy? And did she dare to keep the appointment?

*

Twenty-four hundred hours, and Affie was seated on the side of her bed, still undecided what to do. Standing on the floor in front of her was her ancestor tree, made of silver, with its dangling photos. How was she supposed to take that with her? It was heavy. But how could she leave it behind?

And what if Apollo made a noise? What about the house cameras? What if Markus wasn't there?

What about spending your whole life as a bonder?

I can't go on like this, she thought – backwards and forwards, backwards and forwards. It was agony; like rubbing her heart backwards and forwards on sandpaper.

Make up your mind and stick to it!

Mars, then!

But what if she was caught? Prison. A TB factory.

Stay safe then. Safe inside a cage.

What do you *want*? she asked herself fiercely. What do you really want?

The answer came like splashes of cool water. Freedom. Wealth. To be in charge of her own life again. To be with Odinstoy.

She thought: I have to try for it.

There was no camera in Affie's bedroom, or on the narrow stairs that led down to the landing below. But there was a camera on the landing itself. The house computer, looking at her through the camera, would recognise her, and so wouldn't set off the alarm. Nor was it sophisticated enough to pick up her state of agitation, but she would be filmed as she made her way along the landing to Apollo's room. And as she left with him. If she was caught, there would be no difficulty in proving her guilty of kidnapping.

But she was moving now, acting: and it felt easier than the hours of indecision. Don't think – do!

She had wrapped the ancestor tree in a sheet, to try and stop it jingling; and she hugged it close to her as she crept down her attic stair. Reaching the bottom, she cringed, afraid to step onto the landing, which was dimly lit by a plug-in night-light. She could see the little camera, scanning the landing. Probably, it could see her.

Freeman and Freewoman Perry were in bed – but were they asleep? There was no way of telling. Even if she made no noise, either one of them might suddenly come out of their room, on the way to the bathroom, or to fetch a drink.

But the landing had to be crossed. She set out, her pulse beating thickly in her throat, and in her head. If she was caught she would say – she would say that she was desperately hungry and on her way to the kitchen. Yes, while carrying her ancestor tree, wrapped in a sheet. Oh, who cared? If she was caught, it would all be over, anyway.

Apollo's door. Hugging her ancestors under one arm, she touched the handle and eased it round, holding her breath, conscious of the camera watching her. Apollo's room was dimly lit by a diffused yellow light from a night-light shaped like a nymph. The floor of the large room was a clear expanse of smooth carpet – Affie had picked up and put away all the toys, with more enthusiasm than usual. She hadn't wanted to trip over anything.

Apollo was asleep. Why wake him? She could pick him up and carry him outside.

She drew back the covers. The little boy slept on. Bending over him, she placed the wrapped ancestor tree on top of him and, slowly, carefully, eased her arms under his body. He gave a little grunt, but didn't wake.

The boy's little body was hot against her arms, and his breath made a hot breeze against her cheek, shifting strands of hair. Nuisance! she thought. It'd be much easier if she could leave him behind.

She heaved him up, ancestor tree and all, tried to straighten, but tumbled back onto the bed, on top of him. Apollo, asleep, was much heavier than she'd expected.

Brat! Pest! But even that hadn't woken him. He certainly was good at sleeping.

She lay on him for a moment, drawing a deep breath and gathering herself, then she heaved him up again. Her back muscles twanged, but she succeeded in standing upright and, once she was, Apollo didn't seem so heavy. Not *quite* so heavy, anyway.

The door of the room was still standing open – she couldn't have opened it while carrying Apollo. The cameras watched her carry him out onto the landing – she was aware of them watching her, recording her, every movement, every facial expression. Do I look guilty? she thought, and tried to arrange her face in a happy, carefree smile.

She carried Apollo to the top of the stairs. He became heavier with every step. What if one of the Perrys was wakeful and looked at the CCTV to check on their son? What excuse did she have if she was caught? Would 'sleepwalking' be believed?

She started down the stairs, her hips and back and knees

strained by Apollo's weight. He had heavy bones, this little boy. He didn't look so heavy.

I could still go back to bed, she thought. But Odinstoy was waiting . . .

The cameras watched her, recorded her, as she reached the bottom of the stairs. She was panting from the effort.

There was the front door. She stood looking at it, holding the heavy Apollo, trying to remember if unlocking it and opening it would set off an alarm. Surely it would – or would it be delayed, giving time for the security firm to be warned and send men around to investigate? She didn't know. No one had ever bothered to explain it to her.

She shook herself to attention, realising that she was standing there, wasting time – the longer she stood, at a loss, the more chance there was of being caught.

Get on! Get out!

But I might set off an alarm.

Well, if you do – run! Hope that Markus *is* waiting, and run!

Where could she put Apollo while she opened the door? In the end, she had to crouch down and, gently, lay him and her ancestors on the floor. It was going to be difficult to pick him up again, and, if a klaxon was sounding, she might have to do it in a hurry.

I haven't thought this out properly . . .

Too late now.

To open the door from the outside, you had to have the coded key – but from the inside, it opened simply by turning the knob, provided the computer recognised you. As Affie pulled open the door, she cringed, expecting alarms to shrill—

Nothing. It was a delayed alarm! She wasted seconds – valuable, valuable seconds – by standing there, feeling relieved. Then, realising that she should be moving, she swooped down and, grabbing Apollo by the arms, heaved him up.

He was already stirring, disturbed by the cold floor, and now, pained and startled, he gave a sleepy, grizzling cry.

Affie grabbed her ancestor tree by its trunk, hoisted Apollo high into her arms with a strength that amazed her, and leaped out onto the front steps, running headlong down them to the pavement, looking this way, looking that way.

Headlights flashed. Behind the lights, the dark figure of a man rose from the car and beckoned to her. Markus! It had to be – please, Odin, let it be – Markus. She ran towards him.

Behind her, the house screamed.

Rats

Artemisia Perry's heart gave a great lurching leap, and her head was full of circling, running thoughts about—

About what? As soon as they were thought, they jumbled away.

Grunts, subdued cries and wallowings in the bed beside her proved to be her husband, Delphian. And then she realised what was going on.

'The alarm!' She gripped her husband's arm, while the din whirred and screeched. 'The alarm! Apollo!'

'I know! I know!' He threw her off and, stumbling from the bed to the door, in nothing but his pyjama bottoms, charged out onto the landing.

Artemisia, in her nightie, crawled to the end of the bed, where the small television stood. Picking up the control, she turned on the television, and snapped to the camera view of her son's bedroom. It was watching the door and there was nothing to see until the bulk of her husband lurched past it –

And burst back into their bedroom. 'Gone! He's gone!'

'What?'

'Apollo! Gone! Not in his bed!'

'Where is he?'

'How do I—?'

'Wait! I'll look, I'll look.' Kneeling on the bed, Artemisia switched from one camera to another. Delphian leaned on the bed beside her, watching the screen.

Apollo's room. She made the camera scan round it. The bed was empty, the covers folded back.

'He's wandering, he's – maybe he set the alarm off . . .'

The camera briefly showed them their room and themselves, intently watching the screen; and then the neat and tidy guest bedroom. It showed them the dining room, the sitting room, and then the hall – and the front door, standing open.

Delphian started up from the bed and made for the landing.

'Maybe—' Artemisia struggled to get up from the bed as her nightie wrapped about her legs. 'Maybe he opened the front door and set off—'

'How would he open the front door?' Delphian shouted back. 'He can't reach it!'

'He could have stood on a chair.' They were both hurrying down the stairs.

'So where's the chair?' The front door stood open, but there was no sign of anything Apollo might have stood on.

In through the door, startling them, bulked the dark-blue suits and helmets of two security men. 'Freeman Perry, is it?'

The alarm was shrieking down the street. Markus held the car door open. 'In! In! In!'

Affie's chest, between the effort of running while carrying the little boy, and sheer fear, was in agony. She tried to push Apollo into the car's back seat.

Apollo grabbed the edges of the door. He braced his feet against it. Cold and noise had woken him, and finding himself being lugged along in headlight-glared darkness had terrified him. Affie tried to detach his clinging hands, to dislodge his feet – but he seemed to have more arms and legs than an octopus.

Markus gripped both the child's arms at once, in one hand. With the other hand, he grasped an ankle. '*In!* You too, Affie.' Affie dived in after the boy. Markus slammed the door after her.

She fell onto the back seat with the screaming child. She yelled, 'We're going to see Little Mummy! *We're going to see Little Mummy!* We're going to see –'

The car lurched as Markus got in and slammed his door. The engine started. The car was moving.

'– *Little Mummy!*'

Apollo caught his breath, and was silent.

The car moved so slowly. The siren still shrieked.

'Go faster!'

'No, no, m'dear. Go slow.' And Markus slowed the car. 'We're just driving down the street, minding our own—'

A large security van turned into the street, passing them. Affie ducked. 'Go faster!'

'All this uproar is nothing to do with us. Why should I drive fast?' The car bumped sedately into the next street, and then turned another corner. Markus pulled up. 'Everybody out!'

'What?'

'Out, out, out!' Markus was out, and opened her door. 'Little Mummy?' Apollo asked.

Markus half climbed into the car, and hauled Apollo out, over Affie. 'Yes, I'm taking you to Little Mummy.'

Affie wriggled and pulled herself out of the car, ran after Markus down the dark street. She hardly noticed where they were – only that it was dark and seemed like the backs of premises. 'What are you doing? What—'

'Changing cars,' Markus said. A car was parked by the kerb, three metres or so from the one they'd left. It beeped as its doors unlocked. 'In, in!' Stooping, he bundled Apollo into the car, and went round to the driver's door himself.

Affie scrambled in beside Apollo. She hadn't shut the door before the car was moving. 'Why change—?'

'Oh, *think*, girl! If one of your neighbours saw us leave, or we've been picked up on camera, they'll be looking for *that* car, not *this* one. And *that* one was an old junk bucket I picked up for nothing. And I happen to know that there are no cameras on this street.'

It struck Affie as an odd thing for a doctor to know. 'How do you know?'

'I make it my business to know.' He looked at her over his shoulder. 'Not everything I do is strictly legal, my sweet. Now, in that bag you'll find all the sundries you and Pollo could possibly need. Hurry up!'

There was a bag on the floor behind the front seat: a big holdall. Affie snatched it up, unzipped it, delved. Inside, neatly folded, thoughtfully arranged together, was a complete set of clothes for Apollo – underpants, socks, shoes, little trousers, shirt, jumper, little coat. And clothes for her: bra-vest and pants, tights, ankle boots, a dress, cardigan, coat. Even a wig, shoulder-length and dark, to cover her cropped, jellyfish hair.

'Couldn't have your hair giving us away,' Markus said. 'Glowing blue and green every time somebody looks at you.'

Affie set about changing Apollo, as they rocked and lurched with the movement of the car, pulling off his pyjamas, jerking the T-shirt over his head, threading the trousers over his legs.

'Little Mummy?' he asked again, looking and sounding as if he might cry.

'Soon!' Markus boomed from the driver's seat. 'Soon, you'll be with Little Mummy.'

With Apollo more or less crammed into his clothes, Affie hastily dressed herself, gladly throwing off the ugly bonder clothes. Not that the clothes in the bag were anything she would have chosen. A bit dowdy. But, at least, not bonder.

She stripped off in the back seat, indifferent to the brat's giggles, uncaring if Markus saw. She was just so glad and relieved to be on her way and not waiting any longer. She didn't even feel scared.

The car veered to the kerb, throwing her to one side. Pulling herself up, she looked out onto unlit, deserted darkness. 'Why have we stopped?' Now she felt fear, and she couldn't keep it out of her voice. Was Markus about to demand payment in return for helping her? The flesh shrank on her bones, folding her inwards with repulsion. There was nothing around the car but darkness, no one to help. She neither liked Markus nor fancied him . . . But I'll do it, she thought; I'll do it and smile if it means getting away to Mars with Odinstoy.

'That tag's got to come out of the little 'un's arm,' Markus said. 'Think you can hold him?'

Affie felt cold and shivery with relief. Of course, there

was no saying that after the tag had been removed . . . 'Can't you knock him out?' she asked.

'I don't like giving anaesthetics to children.' Markus had got out of the car, opened the boot. His voice was dry and matter-of-fact again. 'It's tricky, even if you're trained in it.' He climbed into the back seat with his case, and switched on the car's interior light, illuminating them in a little box amidst darkness. 'This is going to be awkward, but – can you hold him on your lap?'

Affie hauled Apollo onto her lap.

'Now, Monkey,' Markus said, as he opened his case on his lap, in the narrow space of the back seat. 'Do you want to go to Mars with your Little Mummy?' Apollo nodded. Markus was rapidly taking things from their places in the case and arranging them in a row: swabs, surgical spirit, a local anaesthetic spray, a scalpel, dressing. 'You've got to be brave, then. Can you be brave?'

Apollo nodded again.

Markus poked at his arm. 'Somewhere in here you've got a tag . . .'

'Here,' Apollo said, reaching up under his T-shirt's sleeve.

Markus felt at the spot. 'Mary, Jesus, Joseph and all the saints! He's got it! Clever boy! Now, I've got to cut that out, or you won't be able to go.'

'Why?' Apollo said.

'Can't you just *do* it?' Affie demanded. 'While we're sitting here—'

'There's an old saying, Affroditey, m'dear – More haste, less speed. It's usually quicker, in the long run, to take one's time in a calm, unflustered way, and get it right first off.'

'Oh, get on with it!'

Markus explained to Apollo exactly what he was going to do, how he was going to spray his arm, so he would feel nothing, how he was going to swab it, 'to keep it nice and clean,' how he was going to cut out the tag 'with this very sharp scalpel, so it will be very quick and not hurt at all,' and how he was going to dress it. 'I cut out Affie's tag, didn't I, Affie?'

'Yes, you did,' Affie said, through gritted teeth. She looked out into the darkness, expecting to see headlights approaching, in pursuit.

'And it didn't hurt, did it?'

'No, didn't hurt at all.'

'So can I take yours out?' Markus asked.

'I brave,' Apollo said.

Markus sprayed his arm. 'Cold!' Apollo said. Markus swabbed his arm, and unwrapped the scalpel. Affie felt the little boy tense when he saw the sharp blade.

'You're brave, aren't you?' Markus asked. 'Affie, hold up his sleeve.'

Markus peered and then – very deftly, considering how bad the conditions were under which he was working – made a quick cut. It occurred to Affie that this cutting out of tags was something he'd done several times before. He caught the blood with a wad of cotton wool. 'Affie, hold that.' While she held the wad in place, Markus unwrapped a pair of sterilised tweezers. Apollo was whimpering a little. 'Nearly over. Brave boy.' With the tweezers, he withdrew the tag, and held it up. Taking the lid from a small plastic tub, he dropped the tag inside.

He ripped open a sachet, and staunched the bleeding with the cloth from inside – not that there was much blood. The wound he'd made was shallow. He dressed it with lint and sticking plaster. 'There!'

'Can we go now?' Affie asked.

'One more small thing to do.'

'*What?*'

'I think you'll like this,' Markus said. He'd put the tub containing the tag in his pocket while he closed his case. He put the case onto the front seats, then opened the door and got out. 'Would you like to see some furry little animals?' he asked Apollo.

'Yes!' Apollo clambered out of the car.

Markus gestured for Affie to follow. She climbed from the car slowly and warily. The place smelled of mud and greenery. She could hear tree branches and leaves shifting in the wind. Was Markus going to force himself on her?

Markus led Apollo round to the boot of the car. He opened it and lifted out a cage. By the light from the car, Affie saw it contained two white rats. Disturbed, they circled their cage, making it buck in Markus's hand as their weight shifted. Apollo was staring at them, captivated.

'Know what their names are?' Markus asked. 'That one, the female, is named Affie. And this one is named Apollo.'

Apollo crowed with delight.

'We've got to get out of here!' Affie said. 'What are you *doing*? Playing with disgusting *rats*!'

Markus had put the cage on the roof of the car and was fiddling with it. There was a flat section of wire mesh on the cage roof, which he up-ended. He prodded the rats, to make them run about and, watching his chance, dropped the section of mesh down through a slot so that it divided the cage, trapping one of the rats against the side. It squealed and struggled, but there was nowhere for it to go. 'These disgusting rats are going to help us.' Diving into the boot, he produced a tool she recognised. It was the sort of gun used to inject the electronic tags. She stepped back, alarmed, even as she realised that it was smaller than the one used on her.

'We tag animals,' he said. 'It's useful. We can include all sorts of info on the tag.'

'Then you could have got a thing for turning our tags off, couldn't you, instead of cutting them out of us. Or do you just like cutting people?'

He took the plastic tub from his pocket, and removed Apollo's tag from it. He loaded it into the gun. 'But we don't want to turn the tags off. Do we?' He inserted the gun through the mesh of the cage, against the rat's haunch, and fired. The rat jumped and squealed, and Apollo laughed.

Markus took the cage from the car roof and set it on the ground. 'Shall we let them go?' he asked Apollo.

'I keep!'

'No. Much better to let them go. You can't take them with you.'

'Keep! Keep!'

'They're *my* rats,' Markus said, 'and I'm setting them free!' He opened the cage and up-ended it, tipping the rats out. 'Run, run, my beauties! Run like the wind!'

Affie jumped back, in case they came near her. They scurried and scuttled in circles. Apollo laughed and tried to chase them. Markus caught him, swinging him into the air.

He stamped his feet, making the rats run away from him, towards the trees. 'Let them be off about their ratty business! We've got a plane to catch!'

They were in the car and moving before Affie said, 'You know the tag you took out of me? And kept. Had you already put it in the other rat?'

'That I had, m'dear.'

'So . . . When they try to track Apollo and me, they'll be tracking the rats.'

'You worked it out at last! I wondered how long it would take you.'

Affie hated him. 'Yes, and when they do, it'll lead them in the way we're going – towards the airport.'

'Not at all, darling. Old Markus had thought of that. We're on the opposite side of the city from the airport. Wherever Ratty and friend go – the dump, the sewers, wherever – it won't be towards the airport. Aren't I clever?'

No, you're hateful, Affie wanted to say but then realised that, thanks to Markus, she was in the clothes of a free-woman, without her tag, and heading towards Odinstoy and Mars.

'Markus,' she said, 'have you done this before?'

'What? Driven a car?'

'Helped somebody like me – a bonder – escape.'

'Of course not! Dearie me, what an idea! Do you think I have nothing better to do?'

'Well,' she said, 'you're very good at it.' She set her teeth. 'Thank you.'

At the Airport

The short, slight young man in the loose, casual trousers and jacket wandered in and out of the airport stalls: the places selling bags and wallets, shirts, socks, underwear, jewellery, tanning lotion; the downloading points for books, newspapers and magazines.

He found a soft seat, sitting down with his feet apart in their large boots. His hair was a dark, shaggy mop, and a shadow of beard was on his cheeks, lip and neck, yet his eyes were heavily ringed in black, with lines extending from their outer corners. A spear badge pinned to the front of his jacket showed him to be a follower of Odin, which explained much. The followers of the more primitive, shamanistic religions were often eccentric dressers.

The young man looked around the airport hall, studying the people as they eddied here and there, as if he was looking for someone. He looked at his watch.

'My little boy has gone, he's gone!'

'Have you searched the house?' the Asian security man asked.

'He's not in his room,' Freeman Perry said. 'We can't see him on the cameras.'

'He might be hiding in a cupboard,' said the security man. 'I've known it.'

'But the alarm!' Freewoman Perry was turning from side to side, each movement cut short and started again. 'Somebody got in, somebody got in!'

'I suggest, Freeman Perry,' said the Asian security guard, 'that you search the house thoroughly with my colleague, while I look at the camera data with your wife.'

'But my son!'

'Freewoman Perry, we shall get to the bottom of things more quickly this way. Can you show me the cameras, please?'

Freewoman Perry watched her husband walk away from her, towards the stairs, with the other security man; and then found herself ushered into the sitting room. 'Let's have the alarm off,' the guard said, picking up the controls from the low table. The alarm cut out, leaving their ears ringing with silence.

'Sit down, Freewoman. Don't worry too much just yet.' She obeyed his first order by dropping down on the sofa. It was impossible not to worry.

The security man switched on the television and, still standing, deftly operated the controls, switching the television to the CCTV circuit, and then scanning back through the cameras' recorded data. Shots of the peaceful house; of the Perrys turning in their bed, shutting off their lamps; of Apollo asleep in his bed. And then—

'That's Kylie!' Freewoman Perry said. 'That's my bonder girl.'

There was Kylie, in her maid's uniform, walking from the foot of the attic stair, carrying a sheet-wrapped bundle. She turned into a bedroom.

Freewoman Perry almost shrieked. 'That's Apollo's room!'

The security man flipped to the camera in Apollo's room. They watched Kylie turn back his covers, try to lift him, and succeed. They watched her carry him to the door.

'She took him! *She* took him! That—' Artemisia couldn't think of anything bad enough to call her. 'Kidnap! It's kidnap!'

The security man said nothing, but continued to flip through the cameras, picking up Kylie on the stairs, opening the front door . . .

'She took him! And after I treated her so well!'

'We get a lot of it,' said the security man. 'Stealing. Attacking their bond holders. Not so much kidnapping, though.'

'Find her! I want her found! Can you find her?'

The security man put down the controls and took out his notebook. He switched it on and spoke, giving the Perrys' address. 'Input. Date,' he instructed the notebook. 'Time. Pause input. What agency did you get her from?'

'The Hera. I've used them a few times. Normally they're very good, and—'

The security man spoke into his notebook. 'Input. The Hera Agency. Pause input. Her name?'

'Name? Oh. I call her Kylie. I forget what her name was – something unsuitable.'

'Doesn't matter,' the security man said. 'She'll be tagged, and the agency will have all her details. We'll catch up with her in an hour or so. They don't usually get far.'

'And my little boy? Will he be all right?'

'Not to worry, Freewoman Perry.' Ravi McKenna knew

of cases where mistreated and resentful bonders had taken the pets, and even children of their bond holders, and harmed them, even killed them: but he saw no reason to mention that. While always a possibility, such cases were rare. 'We'll get a trace put on your bonder girl right away. We'll probably have your little boy back before morning.'

'Oh, thank the Gods! Do you think so? Delphian, that girl took him!'

Freeman Perry and the other security man had returned from searching the house. 'No sign of the kiddie,' said the security man.

'No,' Ravi said. 'We've just watched the bonder girl stroll out of the house with him.' Picking up the controls, he replayed the film.

Delphian Perry said, 'That dirty, blood-sucking little—! When we get her back, I'll have her skin off!'

The two security men studied him, and then glanced at each other. What, they were thinking, did you have off her before?

As he turned the car into the airport, Markus said, 'I'll drop you and leave. Have you flown before?'

'Of course!' Affie said.

'Our Toy hasn't. She'll be waiting for you in the cannabis bar in departures. She'll be dressed as Thorhall Atkinson, so be sure you know her.'

'I'll know her. ID cards, tickets, money?'

'Toy – I should say, *Thorhall* has the money. You should have found a handbag with—'

'Yes.'

'Your ID is in there. And a phone charged up with money.'

'Yes. Er – Markus?'

'Yes?'

'Thank you again.'

'Forget it, m'dear.' Markus said. '"No one is born into this world booted and spurred to ride, nor yet saddled and bridled to be ridden."'

'*What?*'

The lights of the terminals were all round them. 'I misquote, sweetheart. But it's something I believe. If you want to thank me, remember it when you're at the top of fortune's wheel again.'

How pompous, Affie thought, but she said, 'I'll try. Don't really understand it, though. What was it? Boots and spurs . . .?'

Markus laughed. 'Never mind. Out! And may Odin the wanderer have you in His keeping. Give my love to – to Thorhall. Give him my special love.'

Affie opened the door. Her heart was thumping fast. She climbed out into the lamp-lit darkness, her handbag on her shoulder, and turned to haul out a dozy Apollo. 'Markus – thank you. You—'

'Go! Go! Goodbye!'

Her delay endangered them all. She slammed the car door and, carrying Apollo, her arms clamped round his chest, she hurried towards the lights of Departures. Behind her, the car pulled away.

Carrying Apollo was awkward, but she thought it easier than trying to wake him and make him walk by himself. The doors of the terminal opened as she approached, and she walked through into the brightly lit, tiled and echoing hall. Cameras would be watching her now, too, perhaps clever ones, connected to a computer that could analyse her body language for signs of agitation. Was she making herself conspicuous?

She could see the bar, but a Ladies was nearer. She dived in there, lugging Apollo, to get herself sorted.

She dumped Apollo in a sink that seemed fairly dry. He didn't even wake up. She sorted through her handbag, found her fake ID, her money, the air tickets. She studied the details: the flight-number, the time. One way.

One way! All the way to Mars. Goodbye, Earth. I won't be coming back. But the thought made her breath short and her chest tight.

Lifting her head, grinning, she was arrested by the sight of herself in the mirror.

The mirror image didn't look like the self she remembered. She saw an older, plainer, though still attractive woman, without make-up except for tattooed eyeliner, and with dark, straight, shoulder-length hair. She was plainly dressed, this woman, in a dark jacket and skirt, and a cream blouse. No jewellery, and her handbag was a simple, functional black one. She looked adult, businesslike, serious. Dull, but nothing like a bonder.

She stood straighter, and smiled at her reflection, which smiled back. I'm myself again, she thought. I'm not Freewoman Bloody Perry's Kylie any more. Oh, all right, maybe I'm not Affroditey Millington just yet – I look much too serious and frumpy. I'm Freya Atkinson, a God-speaker's wife – but that's *my* choice for now. I'm on my way to Mars! It had been easy, she felt. They were going to get there.

I can be a real help, she thought. I'll have travelled more than Odinstoy. I can take charge, I can get us smoothly onto the plane.

She hung her bag on her shoulder and, with a burst of energy, plucked Apollo from his sink and carried him out into the forecourt again. There was the bar. Feeling excited, dizzy, smiling broadly, she walked towards it, into the cloud of scented smoke that hung round it.

A young man rose from a table and came towards her. Only when he continued straight towards her, and smiled, did she recognise Odinstoy – though indeed, her appearance was not much changed, and she should have known her sooner.

The black hair, a spiky mop, was the same; the dark Japanese eyes were the same; but there was the suggestion of beard, and the walk was altered, the stance different. It was like a magic trick – a little misdirection, and the onlooker was convinced that they had seen what they had not. Now Thorhall Atkinson held out his arms and smiled – not at Affie, but at the child she carried. Freya's husband, Affie thought, is a very handsome young man.

Coming close, Odinstoy said, 'I'll take him.' And, like a loving husband and daddy, he took the sleeping child into his own arms. His – her – smile as she – he – cradled the child almost brought tears to Affie's eyes. That fondness, she felt, belonged to her.

'I have the tickets,' she said, eager to be of help – to be so useful that she couldn't be spared. 'And my ID. Do you have yours?' Odinstoy nodded. Affie wondered if she was correct in thinking her a little scared. 'We're on our way!' she said, and glanced at a nearby screen. 'We should check in.'

'Check in?' Odinstoy said.

'Don't worry. Just come with me.' And Freya Atkinson led the way towards the check-in desk. Her husband, Thorhall, followed, carrying their son.

The queue was not long. 'Tickets and ID, please,' said the man at the desk, not quite looking at Affie.

'I have them here,' Affie said, in the crisp, efficient manner she imagined Freya Atkinson would use. 'Three people: myself, my husband and son. Window seats, please.' She didn't feel scared at all: she felt confident and gleeful, under an assumption of cool poise. I'm fooling you, she thought: I'm getting away with it.

Having scanned the tickets, the man inserted her ID card into his machine and said, indifferently, 'Please look into the scanner.' Her heartbeat quickened. If Bob had failed, if the scanner didn't agree with her ID, then the clerk would soon lose his indifference. But with a calm that surprised her, she leaned forward slightly and looked into the scanner.

The man on the check-in desk, with a flick of his eyes, checked his screen. 'Thank you.' He handed her card back.

Affie snatched a breath, but turned smoothly to Odinstoy. 'Let me take him, darling, while you scan.'

Odinstoy bundled Apollo into her arms, and, after the barest flicker of a glance towards Affie, leaned towards the scanner.

Again the man's eyes moved to his screen, then he removed Odinstoy's card from the machine's slot, and handed it to her. 'Thank you.'

'My little boy is asleep, I'm afraid,' Affie said. 'I don't know if I can wake him sufficiently to do a scan.' She congratulated herself on that 'sufficiently'. It was a word Freya would use.

The check-in man looked at his screen again. 'That's all right, madam. Did you pack your own luggage?'

'Take him, darling, he's heavy.' Affie pushed Apollo back into Odinstoy's arms, and Odinstoy took him, settled his head against her shoulder and stood a little aside, rocking him, the very picture of the useful, silent husband. 'We only have a little hand luggage. We're going to Mars.' People didn't take much luggage to Mars – it only increased the charges. They bought what they needed on arrival.

'Very well, madam. Go through to the lounge when you're ready.'

Affie collected their boarding cards and IDs, efficiently tucking them away in her bag. 'Let's go through now, darling, we'll be more comfortable.'

Obediently, carrying Apollo, Odinstoy followed her into the lift. There, standing side by side, they gave each other the corner of an eye. They couldn't laugh, or cheer, or hug, or break out of character at all – there might be cameras watching them. But they looked at each other and smiled.

'Just fancy, darling!' Affie said. She was enjoying this play-acting. 'In less than an hour, we board the plane, and an hour after that we'll be at the Space-El! Isn't it all just Elysium?' Her stepmother would often say that: anything she liked was just Elysium, or pure Elysium. Who would have thought that Minerva would turn out to be useful?

Thorhall, silent Thorhall, hugged his sleeping son and smiled.

'Odinstoy – at the Temple of Woden'

Ravi McKenna switched off his phone and said, 'They're on to the agency, Freewoman. They'll start running the trace in about five minutes. We'll soon know where she is – but let's see if we can beat the trace. Did your bonder girl have any friends, do you know?'

'Friends?'

'Friends, acquaintances. When she had time off, was there anywhere she liked to go?'

'I don't think so. How would I know?'

'Bear with me, Freewoman. I've seen a lot of cases like this. These young girls – and ones a lot older sometimes – they get bored.' And some of them, he thought, get desperate – desperate to get away from neglect and bad treatment. 'So they run away, thinking they'll find a better life.' Or, sometimes, because the life they have is killing them.

'Kylie had no reason to run away,' she said. 'I always make sure my bonders are comfortable.'

'I'm sure you do, Freewoman, but they think they're going to . . .' He laughed. 'Who knows what gets into their heads? But I know that they sometimes get their friends to help them: hiding them, stealing food for them . . . So, if you could think of any friends she had, we could investigate. It might help us find her quicker.'

Freewoman Perry frowned. 'I do remember—' She turned aside, and seemed embarrassed. 'Kylie wasn't a bonder born. She was – her family – her father was – quite rich, I think. I don't know the details – but I remember her once asking me if she could go and see some of her old friends. Rich friends.'

McKenna's face sharpened. 'Do you remember their names?'

She frowned harder, trying to remember. 'No . . . but I know they lived in St Paul's Square.'

He switched on his phone. 'Thank you. That should get us somewhere.'

Thorsgift was on the plane, though he didn't acknowledge them. They stowed their luggage and took their seats.

'I've never flown before,' Odinstoy said. Apollo, awake now, sat in the seat beside her, playing with a small plastic puzzle the stewardess had given him.

Affie took Odinstoy's hand. 'Don't worry. It's all right.'

'Odin has me in His hand. He wants me on Mars.'

Affie took both of Odinstoy's hands – and suddenly thought: this is why I'm here. This is why Odin arranged for me to be here. Because Odinstoy needs me.

'Affroditey Millington?' Berowne said. 'You got me out of bed to talk about *her*?'

'You are friends,' Ravi said.

'Don't you know who she is? Don't you know who I am?'

'When was the last time you saw her?'

'*I* can't remember! Aeons ago. Her father killed himself, you know.'

'I know.' The details from the Hera Agency had been relayed to his phone. 'Have you seen her since then?'

Berowne leaned forward, as if telling a secret. 'She's not one of us any more.'

'Isn't she?' Ravi asked. 'What is she now?'

'A bonder.'

Ravi nodded. He was about to open his mouth to ask something else when his phone buzzed. 'Excuse me.' Turning aside, he flipped open his phone. Its little screen filled with the grey, wrinkled face of Andy Petsas. 'Rav? Problem with that trace.'

'Yeah? What?'

'Well, the two have separated, for one thing. One gone one way, one gone the other.'

'The little boy's got away from the girl?' Ravi said.

'Humph.' Andy looked unhappy. 'Maybe. But—'

'She's abandoned him?'

'If you ask me, there's something wrong with this. They're moving too fast, too erratic.'

Ravi waited for an explanation and, when none came, said, 'So what are you thinking?'

Andy grimaced. 'I've seen something like this before. If you ask me, Rav, I'd say what we've got here ain't them kids at all.'

'But the tags—'

'They've taken the tags out, Rav.'

'But then they wouldn't be moving at all.'

'They inject the tags into summat else. Cats, stray dogs. Rats. Squirrels.'

Ravi took that in. It wasn't good news, but it made sense. 'You say you've come across this before?'

'Now and again. You ain't going to find 'em by trace, Rav. Looks like you're going to have to work.'

Rav grinned. 'Thanks.' He was still thinking. 'Andy – is this Secret Taxi work?'

'It's like them. Putting the tracers into animals is one of their tricks.'

'Bastards,' Ravi said. Poor bonder kids, mistreated, lonely, unhappy – he could sympathise with them when they ran away. Poor little sods – they always got caught, anyway. But the Secret Taxi bastards – free people, even rich people, who helped other people's bonders to run away – they were just thieves. 'OK, Andy. Thanks. G'bye.' He switched off his phone and turned back to Berowne. 'I'm sorry about that, Freechild. Now, you say you haven't seen your friend since her father died?' His tone was harder, even aggressive, and Berowne was shocked.

Freewoman Perry answered the door herself. 'Oh, you've found him!'

'I'm very, very sorry, Freewoman, but we haven't. I—'

Freeman Perry appeared behind his wife. 'You said it was a simple matter of following the trace.'

'May we come in?' Ravi said. 'I'd like to explain.'

'Come through, come through.' Freewoman Perry led them through, into a pale green and gold sitting room. 'Sit down, sit down.'

Ravi sat in a pale green and gold armchair. 'I'm afraid we've hit problems.' He explained the oddities of the trace readings. 'Have you heard of the Secret Taxi Service?'

'Secret—?' Freewoman Perry put her hand to her throat and looked at her husband. 'No. I—'

'People who help bonders escape,' Freeman Perry said.

'That's right. And we have reason to think that they may have helped your bonder. The technique of injecting the tags into—'

'They've kidnapped our son as well!' Freeman Perry said.

Ravi nodded. 'What we'd like to do, with the permission of the two of you, is to search your bonder's room, and question your other staff.'

Freewoman Perry rose immediately. 'I'll phone Cook. Delphian – will you take the other freeman up to Kylie's room, please?'

'I don't know nothing about her,' Cook said, her arms tightly folded. She'd come into work very early, in order to answer these questions, and even though she was being rewarded with a big breakfast, she wasn't in a good mood. 'Stuck-up little piece, I thought her. We never had much to say to each other.'

'But did she never mention where she went if she got the odd hour off?' Ravi asked.

Cook shrugged. 'Why would her tell me? I weren't interested.' She poured herself another cup of tea.

'Did she ever talk about her friends? Did she mention anyone in particular?'

Cook gave a heavy sigh and shifted irritably, just as

Freeman Perry came into the kitchen with the other security man. 'I've told you. I come here to work, not to yatter. These bonders, they'm in and out, they come, they goo. I doe bother to get to know 'em, know what I'm saying? What's the point? They woe be theer next wik.'

The security guard said, 'Er, boss . . .?' Ravi looked round. 'I might have something here.' He handed Ravi a sheet of paper.

Ravi looked at it. A striking photograph of a young girl's face, a Japanese girl, he guessed. Her stare was somehow both dreamy and intense. The lettering said, 'Odinstoy'.

'There's a whole pile of these in her room,' the security man said. 'I took this one, left the others.'

Ravi turned the picture so Freewoman Perry could see it. 'Did you know your bonder had these?'

'No.'

'Mean anything to you?'

'No, nothing at all.'

Ravi turned it to Cook. 'How about you?'

'How would I know what rubbish her had in her bedroom? I've never been up theer, have I?'

'But do you know who the picture's of? Any idea why Kylie had a pile of them in her room?'

'Look, I've told you. I know nowt. I don't care. I got out of a comfortable bed for this, y'know.'

'Oh, there'll be a little extra in your envelope, Cook,' Freewoman Perry said quickly. 'And don't even think of starting work until your proper time. Put your feet up. Have some more tea.'

Ravi was studying the poster. 'The temple of Odin. Why

has a bonder girl got a pile of posters for some God-speaker? I think we'll cut along to the temple of Odin.'

Cook got up slowly from her chair, and picked up the teapot.

'Why?' Delphian Perry demanded. 'It's these Secret Taxi people you should be after. They've kidnapped our son! Probably sold him! Or they want a ransom!'

Ravi stood up. 'Why would people dedicated to freeing slaves sell your son? And to be blunt, Freeman Perry, you ain't rich enough for it to be worth holding him to ransom.'

'Shall we go into another part of the house?' Freewoman Perry said, casting a quick, embarrassed look towards Cook. The old woman seemed intent on making tea and raiding the biscuits but was probably listening. She shooed her husband and the security guards into the corridor outside the kitchen.

'My colleagues are looking into the possibility of Secret Taxi being involved,' Ravi said. 'I think I'll try and find out who Kylie's friends were – who helped her.'

'We are so worried,' Freewoman Perry said. 'You understand.'

'Of course, Freewoman,' Ravi said. 'And we'll keep you up to date.'

'Freemen and Freewomen,' said the pilot, 'if you look to your right, you will be able to see an interesting sight – especially interesting to those of you travelling on to Mars. It's the lights on the famous Space-El.'

Odinstoy immediately leaned over and peered out of the window. Affie pretended to go on reading her magazine, without being interested. She felt that, as a seasoned traveller who strolled through situations that caused anxiety to a streetwise God-speaker, she should be coolly indifferent.

'Look – can you see?' Odinstoy said to Apollo, who was on her lap.

Affie switched off her magazine and leaned over to put her head against theirs. After all, it wasn't every day even seasoned travellers went to Mars. And this was the second step on their way. It was worth a look.

It wasn't easy to see. Peering past Apollo and Odinstoy, squinting through the small window, she could make out, beyond the wing, a greyish bar against the greyish light, twinkling with red warning lights.

Odinstoy said, 'Yggdrasil.'

'What?'

'Yggdrasil. The World Tree. That grows between the worlds. With its roots in the Underworld and its branches in the world of the Gods.'

'Oh,' Affie said.

'See?' Odinstoy said, putting her head against Apollo's. 'We shall climb Yggdrasil, like the squirrel running up and down between the worlds. Up and down, up and down, like squirrels!'

Apollo rocked on her lap, and laughed.

The pilot announced the landing procedure, and the stewards came jostling through the cabin, checking baggage and lockers. The smallness of the cabin, and the cramped seats, had been a surprise to Affie. She hadn't travelled in this part of a plane before. At least you're free, she reminded herself.

Apollo had to be strapped into his seat again, and he

grizzled in a tiresome way, despite Odinstoy's attempts to distract him. Affie shared his anxiety, because she knew that landing was the most dangerous part of the flight. Odinstoy, having grown calm during their time in the air, was quite cool, and Affie let her stay in happy ignorance.

They put down with the usual thump, and sped along the runway. When they finally came to a halt, Odinstoy thought they could get off straight away. 'We have to wait for that light to go off,' Affie said, pointing. But, even when the safety light had gone off, the cabin was so crammed that it was a long time before they were able to get out of their seats. Affie pretended that this was quite as she'd expected.

When they finally did emerge from the plane, it was into great heat, and a brilliant light that reflected from the concrete and made them squint. But a shaded, air-conditioned bus was waiting and, though they were crammed into it with many others, it took them quickly to a building, where an escalator carried them up to a long, long, carpeted corridor, which they hurried along with all the other people from the plane, Odinstoy carrying Apollo.

The corridor disgorged them into a vast, high-roofed hall, echoing despite the carpets on the floor. It was full of people: people standing in groups, people hurrying by, people pushing trolleys, people queuing, people lying or sitting on benches. Odinstoy, hugging Apollo, stared around in despair.

Affie touched her arm. 'Come on. This way.'

Odinstoy hung back, looking bewildered. Was a camera picking up that lost expression? Affie pointed to the lettered signs hanging from the roof, which Odinstoy couldn't read. 'It says, "Mars, this way". So come on.'

Affie set off, in her smart suit. Glancing back, she saw Odinstoy following, carrying Apollo. Affie smiled. It was a good feeling, to be the one in charge, who knew all the answers.

They walked through glass doors, into another hall, and then through doors into the open air – once more into blinding light and dry, baking, oven-like heat.

'This way,' Affie said, and towed the dazzled, squinting Odinstoy by the arm to another bus. This bus too, blessedly, had shaded windows and air-conditioning.

After a short wait, the bus slid away from its stop, cruised through packed streets, where horns blared and voices shouted, and then pulled into another kerb. 'We get off here,' Affie said, standing. Before Odinstoy could ask, she pointed to an illuminated sign at the front of the bus. 'It says so up there.'

Into the heat and brilliance again, and then into the shade and cool of another building. Odinstoy, following Affie as a balloon follows the child that holds its string, was amused. Had Affie not been there, she would have managed. Where the signs were in letters, not pictograms, she would have pretended to have difficulty seeing, and would have asked the way. But with Affie, it was all so easy. She looked about her busily, she read the signs at a glance, and off she strutted, with the crowds parting before her determined march. It was pleasant to have to do nothing more than carry Apollo. Dangerous, though, if she allowed herself to depend on Affie.

They joined a queue. 'This is where we check in for the Mars flight,' Affie said, and then grinned. 'We're going to *Mars!*'

A woman in front of her overheard and half turned to look, smiling.

Odinstoy kicked Affie's foot warningly. Being noticed, for whatever reason, was not good.

Affie carried on grinning. I'm free, she thought. I'm half a world away from the Perrys'. They'll never catch me now.

They reached the desk, and Affie presented their ID cards and tickets. The black man behind the desk checked through them, and then printed out more tickets, which he handed over. 'You're in the Hotel Ares. This will pay the cab to get you there, this voucher is for—'

'A hotel?' Affie said. 'We're going to Mars.'

'Your flight is cancelled,' the man said. 'It's on the notice-boards. Here are your boarding cards for tomorrow, ten o'clock.'

'Tomorrow!'

'I'm sorry, but the Hotel Ares is very nice. As I said, this voucher . . .'

Artemisia Perry wandered from sitting room to bedroom, to kitchen, to garden, to nursery, and back to sitting room again. She could not rest.

Delphian said she should accept a sedative, and lie down, but she refused. 'Ravi says they'll find them soon. When they do, I want to be awake.'

Where was Apollo and what was happening to him? Was that girl hurting him or frightening him, out of spite? Oh, that wicked girl, after they'd been so kind to her! She might not have been born a bonder, but – maybe her father had been a bonder, but had made himself rich and bought his freedom. You heard of such things happening, and it would explain a lot: the girl's cross-grainedness, her ingratitude, her envy and spite, her sheer *vulgarity*.

But she would be caught. She was only a bonder: she would be caught. Apollo would be rescued.

Unless she'd – hurt him. Or sold him. Or abandoned him. That set her roaming the house again. Up to Apollo's bedroom, and his teddy and ragdoll; and then, in a fury, up to the bonder's bedroom, where she threw the bedclothes on the floor, and threw the girl's kit bag against the wall.

Where were those photos? Those photos the girl had been hoarding, photos of some cheap oracle or another. She'd rip them into pieces. Where were they? She couldn't find them.

In the kitchen, Ravi had been showing them to Cook. She ran down the steep attic stairs to the landing and then down to the hall.

Delphian came out of the sitting room. 'Artemisia—'

'Out of my way.' She hurried on to the kitchen.

There was the photo lying on the table. Ravi had left it, in case it jogged someone's memory. Freewoman Perry stared at it, and the face staring back from the poster certainly did something to her memory.

Great Japanese eyes stared through wisps of dark hair. 'Odinstoy – at the temple of Odin.' Artemisia had never heard of the name, nor been to any temple of Odin. Nor would she. That whole 'Native Gods' movement, it was all a bit—

Well, a little hysterical. For people without much taste or style, really. So why was this photograph familiar?

She must have seen it around town . . . But as she looked at it, she could feel memory swelling in her head, tugging and pulling . . .

She had seen that face looking at her like that before . . .

And had reprimanded it for bad temper! Kylie!

She snatched the photo up. Those eyes – they were the same. The photograph flattered, of course, made the face look less round and childish. And Kylie had never worn eye make-up like that while she worked for Freewoman Perry – wouldn't have dared. And the hair wasn't scraped back beneath a cap . . .

But it couldn't be. Kylie – a God-speaker for the temple of Odin? Never.

Delphian came into the kitchen, saying, 'Artemisia, I really think—'

She shoved the photo at him. 'Is that Kylie? What do you think?'

He took the photo, stood looking at it. 'Kylie? Who—?

'Our bonder, she was a bonder for us! Is that her?'

He looked at the picture again. 'I can't remember. I don't—'

She snatched the picture back. 'It is, it is! I've got to tell Ravi. Where's my phone? Have you got your phone?'

Ravi sat hunched on the Perrys' gilded chaise longue, holding the photograph of Odinstoy. 'This is your previous bonder girl. You're sure?'

'The more I look at it, the more certain I am. We're wasting time!'

'My colleagues are already checking with the agencies. It

would help if you could remember what agency you had her from.'

'The Hera! I'm sure it was the Hera! Or maybe the Olympian.'

'We'll track her down. What we have to find out is: how did your bonder fetch up as—' He held up the photo. 'Odinstoy? And what's the connection between her, Kylie, and your son going missing?'

Delphian Perry shifted in his seat, and coughed.

'These – these Odin people,' Freewoman Perry said. 'Don't they have human sacrifices?'

Ravi shook his head. 'No.'

Delphian Perry coughed again.

'I heard they did.'

'I can assure you, Freewoman Perry,' Ravi said, 'that they don't. They're often accused of it, but they don't. I think I would know if they did.'

Delphian Perry said, 'I think you ought to know that – Artemisia, I think we ought to tell him—'

'Tell me what?' Ravi asked, as the couple stared at each other.

'That this girl – this Odinstoy—'

'Delphian, it's not important!'

'Please,' Ravi said. 'What?'

Delphian Perry pointed to the picture in Ravi's hand. 'She's Apollo's – how do you say? – biological mother.'

Ravi raised the picture and looked at it.

'Does that really matter?' Artemisia asked.

Ravi lifted his eyes from the photo to her face. 'Does it really matter that she's the missing child's natural mother?

That we find a pile of photos of the child's biological mother in the room of the bonder who abducted him from your house? Yes, I think that matters.'

'But we adopted him as soon as he was born!' Freewoman Perry said. 'Well, almost.'

'Did Odinstoy have the care of the child?' Ravi asked.

'What?' It really seemed that Freewoman Perry didn't understand the question.

'Was one of Odinstoy's jobs – when she was your bonder – did she ever look after the little boy?'

'Sometimes she did,' Freewoman Perry said, as if surprised. 'Sometimes she'd bathe him, or put him to bed. Or take him for walks sometimes. It depended on how busy I was.'

'Hmm,' Ravi said. 'I think I'm beginning to see a motive.'

'But Kylie took Apollo!' Artemisia said.

Ravi and Delphian looked at her.

Departure Hall

The walls of the tiny hotel room were painted a sickly, depressing pale green, mottled with pale yellow. Two single beds, covered with pale yellow throws, had been shoved together to make room for a small cot beside them. Crammed against the wall at the end of the beds was a dressing table. In one corner was a tiny sonic shower. Affie, looking round, thought that everything in the room – the over-bed lamps, the carpet, the mirror frame, everything – was just out of date enough to be painful. But I'm free now, she thought. I'm free again. I don't have to put up with cheap, nasty, last season things. When I get to Mars . . .

But they weren't on their way to Mars any more. They were stuck in this hotel room, waiting. 'Do you think they're after us yet?'

Odinstoy had thrown herself on one of the beds, and Apollo had climbed up beside her, giggling. Odinstoy was encouraging him, as usual. They could be tiring travelling companions.

'Do you think they're missing us?' Affie giggled.

"Sure – you weren't there to wipe Perry's arse for her after her morning shit,' Odinstoy said, with the startling crudity that Affie still found hard to accept. When she, Affie, used bad language, it showed how feisty she was, and rebellious and free. But when Odinstoy was so crude, it was just – just crude, and low, and like a bonder. She wished Odinstoy would learn not to do it. Perhaps, when they were on Mars, she could teach her.

Affie sat on the other bed, anxious again. 'But do you think—? Will they have figured out where we are?'

'We are in Odin's hands,' Odinstoy said. 'He's brought us here. We'll reach Mars if He wills it. If He doesn't, we won't.'

Affie stamped her foot. 'That's no help, is it? That's saying nothing.'

'It's no help,' Odinstoy agreed. 'There is no help. Why did you think there'd be help? We're in Odin's hand, that's all.'

'What will we do if they catch us?'

Odinstoy pinched Apollo's nose, laughed, and said, 'Suffer.'

Freewoman Atwood was studying the photograph Ravi had been given by the bonder agency. 'Why, this is Affie! Well, we called her Affie in the temple – but her mistress called her Kylie. Yet another Kylie!' She laughed. 'There are so many of them, aren't there? I wish people would be more imaginative, I do, really. But, yes, she came to the temple often. While we worship, we're all equal.'

'Tell me about her,' Ravi said.

'I don't know what you want to know . . . She was rather a nice girl, I think . . . Fallen on hard times – she wasn't born a bonder. Did you know that?'

Ravi nodded.

'She was owned by a – oh, now what was her name? She used to own Odinstoy too.'

'She used to own Odinstoy,' Ravi commented. He gazed calmly at Freewoman Atwood.

'Oh, yes! Odinstoy was a bonder born, you know. I suppose that's what gives her that breadth of vision – well, partly. What was I saying? Oh yes, well, the little boy that Odinstoy used to look after when she was a bonder was the same little boy that Affie – or Kylie – used to bring with her to the temple.'

'Apollo Perry,' Ravi said, still hiding his excitement under heavy calm.

'That's it! Perry, that was the name. Artemisia Perry. And Apollo was her little boy. Odinstoy was always very fond of him.'

'I hear she was quite fond of Kylie, too.'

'Oh yes! It was sweet! They had a lot in common, I suppose, what with Kylie being a bonder and Odinstoy having been one; and both having had the same mistress, and being fond of the little boy – I mean, Odinstoy is a God-speaker, one of the best I've ever known. Touched by the God. Quite frightening, sometimes. But, you know, she's still the same young girl she always was as well. That's why she liked Kylie's company so much, I think. They could be girls together, bless them.'

Ravi smiled slightly. 'I'd like to speak to Odinstoy. She could help me.'

'Oh no! She's not here! Our Odinstoy has gone to Mars!'

'Mars!' Despite himself, Ravi's calm was cracked with surprise.

'Oh yes, it was so wonderful! Our Odinstoy was poached from us. A young man came from Mars, you see – it seems that there's a strong following of Odin on Mars, and they wanted a God-speaker. They'd heard of our Odinstoy on Mars – imagine! So he came here, the young man – he visited other temples too, and – well – he chose Odinstoy. And she – well, being young and looking for a bit of adventure, I suppose – she said she'd go. So off she's gone, to Mars!'

Ravi nodded. 'That's very interesting, Freewoman. Thank you.'

'I hope I've been of help.'

'You've been of great help. Thank you again. Have a good day.' Even as he turned away, Ravi was reaching into his pocket for his phone.

The Departure Hall of the Space-El was huge and echoing; all glass, tiles, and flickering, changing notices. Affie, her arm linked through Odinstoy's, felt Odinstoy stiffen. 'There's nothing to worry about,' she said. 'It's just the same as catching a plane.' She felt a hollow open up under her breastbone. It wasn't the same as catching a plane at all.

'I know what to do,' she said. 'I've got the boarding cards and IDs. We'll go up to the lounge and have a cup of coffee.'

'Biscuits,' Apollo said.

'And Free – *Apollo* can have some biscuits,' Affie agreed. Anything to keep the brat quiet.

*

'Freewoman Perry? Hello. Ravi McKenna here. I'm sorry to call instead of coming to see you—'

'You've found him!'

'Ah, no—'

'You've caught her, you know something—'

'Freewoman Perry, please. Listen. I've been interviewing people at the temple of Odin. Very interesting. It seems clear that your former bonder girl – Odinstoy – befriended Kylie and—'

'Oh, what are you talking about? Where's my son?'

Ravi sighed. 'I'm sorry, Freewoman – this will be a shock. I think he's on his way to Mars.'

'*Where?*'

'Mars.'

'*Mars?* Where's that?'

'The planet Mars, Freewoman. Outer space.'

There was a silence, and then Perry said, bemusedly, 'The planet? *Mars?*'

'There's a colony on Mars, Freewoman.'

'I *know!* I know there's a colony on Mars. Why on Earth are they going there?'

Ravi caught back another sigh. 'Well, it's a long way away, Freewoman. That's probably one attraction. And Odinstoy has a job there, as God-speaker.'

'She can't go *there!*'

Ravi stopped himself answering that she had – besides, with any luck, she hadn't, not yet. 'What I wanted to tell you, Freewoman, is that we've already contacted the authorities at the Space-El. We've sent photos – and, of course, there's the iris and ID checks.'

'Do you think . . .?'

'I can't promise anything,' Ravi said. 'For one thing,

we've run checks on Odinstoy and your Kylie, and they've vanished.'

'What do you mean? How can they vanish?'

'I mean, there's no entry in the database that corresponds to them.'

'That's—'

'Don't worry too much, Freewoman. If they are trying for Mars, I'm confident we can pick them up before they even board the ship.'

'Really?'

'I'm confident, Freewoman.'

'Oh, thank all the Gods,' she said, and started to cry.

We must look such a prim little, mim little family, Affie thought. There they sat, on the bench in the Departures lounge. She, with her feet neatly together, in her so neat and tidy business suit, her black handbag on her lap. Apollo between them, in his little short trousers and T-shirt, like twenty thousand other children. And Odinstoy on his other side, sitting feet apart and arm along the back of the bench, the protective young father.

They'd been sitting there almost an hour. Apollo was playing a game that Markus had thought to include among their things. But it wouldn't occupy him for ever. Maybe they should think about going for a walk round the shops, or for another coffee – or would that mean people noticing them?

The voice through the loudspeakers made them jump. 'Freemen and Freewomen, may we have your attention?'

Affie touched Odinstoy's arm. 'They might be calling us to board.'

'Will Affroditey Millington please make herself known to staff?'

It seemed a long, long time before Affie could make sense of the announcement.

'We repeat: will Affroditey Millington—'

On a large screen hanging in her view, she saw a picture of herself appear. Such a jolt of fright went through her that she felt she'd been punched. There was an instant of darkness. She thought she would faint.

Then she saw Odinstoy's face, with its smudges of moustache and beard. She felt Odinstoy's grip on her hand. 'It's fine,' Odinstoy was saying. 'It's fine.'

Affie realised that she had almost jumped to her feet. Odinstoy's grip on her hand had stopped her. Looking up, she saw that the screen now held a picture of Odinstoy – the glamorous picture from the poster. Odinstoy didn't look like that now. Affie didn't look like the picture that had appeared on the screen.

Now there was a picture of Apollo – and it *did* look rather like Apollo.

'May we ask that any member of the Free who sees any of these people, contacts a member of staff? Please do not approach them yourselves. Please contact a member of staff. Thank you.' The screen filled with a pretty picture of waterfalls, advertising hair wash.

Affie looked round. No one nearby was taking any notice of them. They did not look like the screened pictures, she had to remember that. But cameras were also watching them, cameras attached to computers which could analyse body language, and were far more sensitive to signs of fear than even other people. Her heart felt swollen inside her, as if it had too little room in which to beat. A rapid pulse rattled in her throat.

'What shall we do?' she whispered to Odinstoy.

Odinstoy had an arm round Apollo, was leaning over him to share the game he was playing. She looked up. 'Nothing. Go for a walk. Be happy.' And she grinned, apparently at ease.

Affie sat, bag on lap, feet together, looking straight before her, terror stricken. But Odinstoy was in charge again: Odinstoy was right. There was nothing they could do except play out the role of happy little family.

'I'll go for a walk,' she said, and stood. Her legs shook, but taking a walk was doing something, a distraction.

'Give us a kiss,' Odinstoy said.

Stooping, Affie gave Odinstoy a peck on the cheek, and Apollo one on the head – an affectionate mother taking leave of her family for a short while.

Off she strolled, knees wobbling under her. She tossed her head, tried to sashay, as the old Affie would have done, and then felt that the respectable woman she was meant to be wouldn't walk like that. How would she walk?

She was relieved to stand still and look up at the screens giving boarding information. Their flight was given, but had nothing yet shown alongside it.

'Freemen and Freewomen,' said the loudspeakers, 'may we ask Affroditey Millington to make herself—'

Affie darted off towards a bookstore, and stood pretending to view the posters advertising the books and magazines available for downloading. The pictures, the words, were a blur of colours. She stood in front of one of the computer screens, and touched a category – Romance – and flicked through the titles and synopses available, but took none of it in.

Thinking she'd spent enough time there, she turned away. She'd go to the Ladies, and reassure herself that she looked nothing like the Affie being shown on the screens. A greyness blocked her way.

'Excuse me, Freewoman.'

That jolt of fear again, the one that seemed to rock her on her heels and darken her sight. She looked up. A large man stood in front of her, grey-haired, wearing a grey suit.

'Sorry to bother you, Freewoman, but may we see your ID?'

BondTrace

'We should have gone there,' Freewoman Perry said to her husband. 'We should, though, shouldn't we? And not have wasted time.'

'Freewoman,' Ravi said, 'you couldn't get there in time. In here, please. This is the quickest way.'

They followed him into the little room. Two computers sat on a desk, and a young woman looked up with a smile.

'We've got it all set up, ready,' Ravi said. 'Juno?'

'We're linked in to the CCTV at the Space-El,' said the young woman, nodding towards the screens, where figures moved to and fro. 'This is Departures, and there's a flight due for Mars. If you could watch—'

Freewoman Perry eagerly took a seat, and stared at the screens. Her husband took a seat beside her.

'Oh, it's too much, it's too confusing!' she burst out, after a few moments. 'There are too many, I can't—'

'Just take it calmly,' Juno said, touching her arm. 'You'd know your son, wouldn't you? You'd know two girls who worked for you, who you saw every day. Just let your eyes scan over the screens. Relax. Take your time. If they're there, I'm sure you'll spot them.'

Freewoman Perry did relax, sat back, and watched the screens calmly for perhaps ten minutes, occasionally leaning forward to get a better look. 'I don't see them.'

'There's plenty of time. If you see them, we can notify the El straight away.'

'But are you sure they're there?' Delphian Perry asked.

'Not totally, no,' Ravi said. 'They may have gone to ground. And they may be disguised – but then again, they may not. So look, anyway.'

'May we see your ID, please, Freewoman?'

Affie said, 'What?' but it came out as nothing but a breathy little gasp. The two men eyed her coldly, observing every sign of distress. She cleared her throat. 'What?'

'We'd like to see your ID, please, Freewoman,' said the younger, darker man.

'Oh! Hang on a moment!' Affie fumbled at her bag, feeling stifled. Calm! she ordered herself. They can't know anything. Be calm. 'Here – oh, no, that's my husband's. Here's mine.'

The grey man took it, and his eyes flicked from the picture on it to her. 'Just a routine check, Freewoman.'

'I understand,' she said, trying not to gulp. 'I'm glad to co-operate. It makes us all safer, doesn't it?'

'Quite so, Freewoman.' He lifted a reader from his belt and read her card. 'Your name, Freewoman?'

'Freya Atkinson.'

He handed the card back to her, staring at her unblinkingly and without a smile. 'Thank you, Freewoman.'

'Thank you,' she said, putting her card away again, 'for

doing your job.' Was that a little too oily? She smiled, gave them a little wave, and walked away.

Stroll, she said to herself. Sashay. No, don't sashay. Walk. Slowly.

She was looking for Odinstoy and Apollo, and then realised that the reason she couldn't see them was that two big men were standing in front of them, talking to them. Big men, smart suits – oh, Odin, Frey and Thor!

'Here's my wife,' Odinstoy said, looking round one of the big men. 'Sweetheart, these freemen want to see our IDs.'

'Just routine, Freewoman,' said one of the men, turning to face her.

Affie drew a breath. 'Oh, of course.' She was an old hand at this now, and calmly found the three cards from her bag. 'Here you are.' Inside her, beneath the calm exterior, her heart pummelled.

The man took the cards and looked at them, one by one, sending long glances at Odinstoy and Affie. He said, 'What's your wife's name, sir?'

Odinstoy leaned back on the bench she sat on, spreading her arms, and laughed. 'Freya Atkinson! What's up? Are terrorists on the loose?'

The man didn't answer or smile; he simply handed the cards back to Affie.

Then the other man stooped down, hands on knees, and said to Apollo, 'And what's *your* name?'

Affie's heart lurched and skipped; her breath stopped; she thought she would fall to the ground.

But when she could see and hear again, Apollo hadn't

answered. He'd shrunk close to Odinstoy and was hiding his face against her jacket. 'Don't be scared,' Odinstoy said to him, laughing. 'Tell the nice man your name.'

Oh, *don't*, Affie thought. What if he does?

Apollo pressed his face even deeper into Odinstoy's jacket, and shook his head. 'He only wants to know your name!' Odinstoy said.

Apollo peeped out, then hid again.

'He's not used to strangers,' Affie said.

'Thank you,' said the security man. 'Have a good journey.' And both men moved away.

Affie sank down on the bench beside Odinstoy. She wanted to look at her, and pull a face, or somehow express her relief, but dared not. Then she was afraid that staring before her might look unnatural, so she turned to Odinstoy and smiled, glassily.

Odinstoy had lifted Apollo onto her lap. 'What is your name, little boy?'

'Odinsgift!' Apollo cried, and laughed. Odinstoy and Affie, looking at each other, laughed too.

'What d'you think?' Castor asked.

Elvis, the big, grey-haired man, pursed his mouth and almost shook his head.

'The cameras picked them out.'

'The cameras pick out tension,' Elvis said. 'Not guilt. Tension.'

'Yeah, but it picked them out.'

'Son, don't be too quick to arrest people on the say-so of computers. You can get in a lot of trouble that way.'

'Yeah, but—'

'We're tense for all sorts of reasons,' Elvis said. 'She could be scared of going to Mars. Her husband might kick her around. The kid could have something terminal. She might.'

'Cheerful bastard. She *was* nervous, though.'

'Two big men had just come up and asked to see her papers. That makes women nervous. *I* feel nervous if somebody asks to see my papers.'

'Yeah,' Castor said. 'Well, that's 'cos you *are* guilty, you evil old reptile.'

'*That's* Apollo,' Freewoman Perry said. 'That's him. There. It is, isn't it?'

Her husband leaned closer to the screen. 'Looks like him. Yes. You're right.' Looking round at Ravi, he said, 'That's our son.'

Ravi nodded to Juno, who froze the camera picture. All of them gathered round the screen.

'It is Apollo, I'm certain it's Apollo.' Freewoman Perry's hands were tightly clasped, with white knuckles. 'I don't know the man, but—' She leaned close to the screen again. 'I think *that* might be Kylie. What do you think?' she asked her husband.

He stared intently, then shook his head. 'I'm not sure. I didn't see as much of her as you.'

'She had cropped hair, but that could be a wig,' Freewoman Perry said. 'The face shape is the same . . . I think it is her.'

'That's good enough,' Ravi said. 'Juno, get on to the Space-El, will you?' To the Perrys, he said, 'We'll notify them of the camera number, and they'll view the data and pick them up.' He put his hand on Freewoman Perry's shoulder. 'Your little boy could be back with you by tonight.'

'Oh, thank Zeus,' said Freewoman Perry. She folded up, her face in her hands. 'Oh, thank the Gods.'

Castor and Elvis were stooping over a computer, studying the film from Camera seventy-eight.

'It's them,' Castor said. 'Told you.'

'We'll see,' Elvis said.

'They're calling us to board,' Affie said.

'What?' Startled, Odinstoy looked round, as if expecting to see someone waving to them and shouting.

'It's on the screen, up there.' Affie stood. Her chest was tight again, her heart thumping, her breathing hard. This was it, this was it . . . 'Gate Four. Come on.'

Odinstoy stood, calling Apollo away from the plant bed where he was shredding artificial leaves. As he came running, she said, 'Are you sure? Do we—?'

Affie was filled with a sense of assurance and strength. 'It says – up there – that our flight is boarding now. So come on. Just follow me. I've got the boarding cards and everything.'

She'd long ago checked out where the entrance to the boarding gates was and now set off towards it. Odinstoy followed, leading Apollo by the hand. Knots and skeins of other people were heading in the same direction.

Their ID papers were checked yet again, and though it was a perfunctory, bored check, Affie felt that she was getting close to the end of what she could stand.

Once past that check, they shuffled into line with their fellow passengers, to go through the scanner. Affie caught a glimpse of a very tall, bearded man ahead, who she thought was Thorsgift. She looked away.

Behind her, Odinstoy was talking to Apollo. 'We're going in a big ship, all the way to Mars, in the sky.' Odinstoy looked and sounded perfectly calm. Affie hoped that she seemed as carefree.

'We go sky?' Apollo said.

'Yes. On the red planet.'

'Red?'

'Everything will be red. Red houses. Red peas. Red cats.'

'Red cats! Red mice!' Apollo said, and giggled.

'Purple dogs!' Affie said, desperate to seem part of their little family. Apollo shrieked with laughter. See? Affie thought at the officials. We're just a normal little family, on its way to Mars. No need to take any notice of little us.

She set her bag on the conveyor belt that took it through the scanner, and stepped through the frame herself. No alarms screamed, though her heart skipped and thumped with her own alarm. She collected her bag and stood aside, trying to take deep breaths without being obvious about it, and watching as Odinstoy and Apollo came through.

They joined her. We're getting away with it, she thought; we're getting away with it.

They turned to go on towards the ship, and saw the security men waiting, their hands loosely clasped in front of them: the bulky grey-haired one and the younger, darker one.

Affie's steps faltered. She *knew* the men were waiting for

herself and Odinstoy. She caught herself, continued walking, slowly, slowly, while her heart stuttered and thumped. A voice inside her wailed: I can't do this! Then she straightened, and fell into her confident strut, telling herself: don't be ridiculous. They've already checked and passed your ID. They won't be interested in you again. It could be anybody else they're interested in; anyone. Maybe they're not interested in anybody. Maybe they're just standing there. They have to stand somewhere.

The grey-haired man stepped in front of them. 'Freewoman and Freeman Atkinson? May we have a moment of your time, please?'

'Why, hello again!' Affie said, breathlessly and hilariously. 'How can we help you?'

'If you'd come this way, please?'

Affie was seized by an impulse to say, All right, I'm not Freya Atkinson – you know who I am, so let's stop pretending.' Even when she crushed that impulse down, she wanted to turn and run away. She couldn't think of anything to say. Surely her silence was suspicious?

The security man gestured to his left. 'This way, please.'

Affie turned and walked with him. Glancing behind, she saw Odinstoy and Apollo following with the other man.

The silence went on. And on. What should she say? What would her mother say? No, that was no help: her mother would collapse and say this was too much, it was making her ill, she couldn't deal with it . . . For a moment, Affie was tempted, but where would it get her? She had to behave like an entirely innocent, wrongly-accused person. What would her father, her stepmother have said?

'This is very inconvenient and annoying – not to mention embarrassing, being taken away in front of everyone like this. I hope you have a good reason for this – this infringement of my rights?'

'It's merely routine, Freewoman.'

'You keep saying that. It's not routine to me, I assure you. I'm *very* cross.'

'We apologise. It won't take long.' They were approaching a beige wall. The man opened an almost invisible door, painted in the same beige, and ushered them into a small room. On the desk was an iris reader.

'Another identity check!' Affie said, still playing her step-mother. 'What are you thinking of?'

'Please co-operate, Freewoman,' said the grey-haired security man. 'This won't take long.'

'But this is ridiculous.' Affie sat in front of the scanner. They must be able to see her heart pushing her ribs outwards. 'So much *fuss* . . .' She looked into the scanner, deliberately unclenching her fingers as she did so. Give nothing away – but even as she suppressed one sign of tension, another must be betraying her.

The bulk of the security man leaned beside her. She could smell the cloth of his suit, and sweat. Then he straightened. 'Thank you, Freewoman. Freeman?'

Odinstoy, instead of taking the chair herself, lifted Apollo into it. The security men made no protest. Odinstoy pointed out where Apollo was to look.

Affie stood to one side, struggling to breathe steadily, feeling her legs trembling under her. She tried to read the faces of the security men, but they were slab-like, expressionless. What was the scanner telling them? It must, surely, be saying that they were the Atkinsons. Bob had promised.

'Now you, Freeman.'

Odinstoy lifted Apollo from the chair and sat down herself.

'Thank you,' said the security man.

'Well?' Affie demanded. 'Can we go now?' To her own ears, her voice sounded a little too sharp. Had they noticed? Had the computers registered it?

The security man gestured for Odinstoy to remain seated. 'Just a few questions . . .'

'Oh!' Affie stamped her foot. 'We have a flight to catch!'

'Please bear with us,' said the other security man.

Apollo was distressed by the atmosphere in the room, but, because Odinstoy was so near one of the threatening strangers, he pressed to Affie's side instead, and took her hand. Affie, surprised, was still more surprised to feel herself moved.

'What's the purpose of your journey to Mars?' The grey-haired man sat on the corner of the table, his arms folded.

'I have a new job there,' Odinstoy said. 'As God-speaker to the temple of Odin. It's a new life for us.'

'You're not a man, are you, *Freeman* Atkinson?'

After a heartbeat's pause, Odinstoy said, 'No. But I live as one.'

Grey-hair nodded.

'As he has every right to do,' Affie said. 'What right have *you* to ask us these questions?'

The younger man spoke from beside her, giving her a

slight shock. 'We have reason to believe that one or both of you are runaway bonders, and the child is Apollo Perry, whom you abducted.'

A long, frozen javelin jarred through Affie: that was what it felt like. She had to hold onto her bladder. Her breath stopped. They know, they know, they know . . . She couldn't speak. If she could have done, she would have confessed.

'I am Thorhall Atkinson,' Odinstoy said. 'Freeman. I am God-speaker to the temple of Odin on Mars. Contact them if you don't believe me. This is my wife, Freya, a freewoman; and our son, Odinsgift.'

'Perhaps,' said Grey-hair, 'you'll bear with us while we check you out with another database?'

'What?' Affie gasped.

'We mostly check against Universal, Freewoman. They're the largest database, hold millions of IDs. But there are smaller databases, more specialist ones. We'd like to check you against one of them. Say, BondTrace. It keeps the IDs of bonders. Would you object to being checked against that?'

Affie had no voice. She stood and watched, unable to speak, unable to move, as Odinstoy gave a little wave of her hand. 'Of course not.'

The security man leaned in and touched the screen. The computer beeped as it opened the new program. 'Please look into the scanner.'

Odinstoy leaned forward slightly. Affie closed her eyes. Here it comes, here it comes, she thought. The next hours were going to be so hard. And then – oh, Gods, they would charge her with abducting Apollo. She'd be put in prison with all sorts of horrible, dirty, cruel people. Life would be torture and misery.

Why did I do this? Why did I ever think we could get away with this?

She heard the security man say, 'Result!'

Crash

The other security man moved across the room. 'You've found a match?'

A voice in Affie's head was saying: No, oh no, no, no, oh no—

'Yes, got a – hang on.' The security man studied the screen, while Odinstoy sat at ease in her chair, and Affie didn't breathe.

'Freed,' the security man said. He looked at Odinstoy. 'You were freed.'

'Yes,' Odinstoy said. 'And became a God-speaker.'

'You changed your name?'

'Yes. Why would I want to keep the name I was given as a slave?'

'What was your slave name?'

'Which one? The agency called me Dorcas. They had a list of names and that was the next one. My last owner called me Kylie.'

The men looked at the screen. The younger one said, 'It checks out.'

The elder looked up, looked straight at Affie, who flinched. 'Now you, Freewoman.'

Odinstoy stood and moved away from the chair. They waited for Affie to move.

'Freewoman?'

Affie wanted to shrink back into the corner behind her and curl up. Odinstoy said, 'Don't be angry, sweetheart. They're only doing their job.'

Affie drew a deep breath and shuddered. Odinstoy was trying to help. She had to move. Dragging leaden feet, she tottered over to the table and chair. If this program had Odinstoy in it, then it would have her iris pattern too.

She sat in the chair, facing the scanner. Why am I doing this? she wondered. Why go along with it? Push the scanner off the table and scream. Run round the room, screaming. Run out of the room, lock yourself in the Ladies and scream. Screaming seemed to be urgent.

'Look into the scanner, please.'

Affie looked away.

'Look into the scanner, please, Freewoman.'

I'm only giving myself away, Affie thought. And once I look into the damned thing, I shall be given away. Tears gathered in her eyes. With a fierce jerk of the head, she turned and looked into the scanner.

The security man stooped to look at the screen, swore, and said, 'Command. Exit. Exit.' He stabbed at the little keyboard and swore again.

The younger man said, 'It crashed?'

The older man replied with a string of curses.

'Let me have a go.' The younger man moved over to the table. Affie was in the way, and got up. The two men moved closer together, intent on the scanner. Affie drew back to the wall, where Apollo was standing with Odinstoy.

Odinstoy put her hand on Affie's shoulder. Affie looked at her, and she smiled. Ducking her head close to Affie's, she whispered, 'Odin is with us.'

The men were still huddled over the scanner. Affie looked over at the door. It wasn't so far away. She looked at Odinstoy, and looked at the door again. Could they get out of the door while the men were absorbed? How far would they get?

Odinstoy considered the door. She looked at Affie.

The door opened, making them jump. A woman looked in. She glanced at Odinstoy and Affie. The men looked up and she turned her attention to them. 'A word?'

'Now?' said the older man.

'*Now*,' said the woman and went out again.

The elder man looked round, embarrassed, and then followed the woman from the room. The younger man stared after him, and it seemed that he might follow; but then he turned back to the computer.

Miriam Goldman folded her arms and said, 'You're holding up the Mars launch again. Why?'

'We're questioning suspects who were boarding,' Elvis said.

'Suspected of what?'

'Abduction of a child. Theft of a bonder.'

'You've ID'd them?'

'Ah.' Elvis folded his arms. 'We're trying to get an ID—'

'What's the problem?'

'That piece of junk program's crashed again. Can't get it back.'

'I hope you're not planning to hold the Mars launch until you've got it back. The schedule's already loused up with the cancellation yesterday – if it doesn't get off on time today, it's my head.'

'It could take minutes,' Elvis said.

'And it could take days. Tell me you're not planning on holding the flight.'

Elvis shifted uneasily. 'No.'

'So? Are you going to pull your suspects?'

Elvis shifted again. If he held these people and the Mars ship left without them, *and* they turned out to be innocent – he didn't think they were, but *if* they were – then he was up to his chin in it. So was Castor.

And if he delayed the Mars ship for no good cause, he was in it equally deep.

Behind him, the door opened and Castor looked out. Elvis turned eagerly. 'You got it back?'

'No chance. It's well and truly ballsed up. Can't even get back into Universal now.'

'You were using Universal?' Miriam demanded.

Elvis looked away and didn't answer. Castor looked from him to Miriam.

'You checked these "suspects" on Universal, is that right?'

Elvis still stared into the distance. Castor said, 'Yes.'

'And what was the result? Elvis? What was the result?'

'Negative. They checked out.'

'In other words, they are who they say they are.'

Elvis set his teeth and kept silent. Castor said, 'Yeah, Universal says they're OK, but—'

'If Universal says they're OK, they're OK! For the love of

the Gods! I've got a ship waiting to go to Mars and you're playing games?'

'Freewoman Goldman, there's a child—'

Elvis spun to face Castor, and declared, 'If Freewoman Goldman says they're OK, they're OK. It's not our problem.'

'You bet it's not our problem,' Miriam said. 'Let them go!'

Elvis spun on his heel. 'Let them go!' He opened the door of the little room, and said, 'You can go!'

Affie straightened from the wall, staring.

'You can go!' the man repeated.

Affie looked at Odinstoy, who picked up Apollo and, holding him against her shoulder, smiled.

Affie still didn't dare to move, but Odinstoy walked to the door and through it, and then Affie scuttled after her as if tugged on a string.

Out in the hall, a woman was standing, her arms folded, her feet astride – the same woman who'd looked into the interview room earlier. Odinstoy turned and held out her hand to Affie, who took it.

'I'm terribly sorry for this misunderstanding,' the woman said. 'Let me escort you to the ship. This way.'

The older, grey-haired man, standing with folded arms, said without smiling, 'Have a good trip.'

And then they followed the woman to the ship, and Mars.

As they walked, arm in arm, Apollo carried against Odinstoy's shoulder, Affie said, 'Odin *is* with us.'

ODIN'S QUEEN BY SUSAN PRICE

Affie has finally escaped to Mars in the company of Odinstoy, and her young son, Apollo. Odinstoy has been employed by the Martian Temple of Odin as their God-speaker and Affie goes undercover as her 'wife'.

Affie hopes their new life will enable her to claw back the status and respect she had before she became a bonder - and is frustrated by Odinstoy's disdain for the fame her new role brings. But Affie's craving for attention leads her to fall under the spell of a follower of the rival temple of Zeus, and before she knows it she is revealing more of her past to him than she ever intended. And in doing so, she finds herself betraying Odinstoy; putting all their lives at risk...

ISBN 1-416-90443-3